DIRTY MONEY

A J.J. GRAVES MYSTERY (BOOK 7)

LILIANA HART

To Scott-

This was a tough one. Thank you for always being there, for listening, and for giving me a shoulder to cry on. You're my real life hero. I love you more every day.

ACKNOWLEDGMENTS

A book is never a solo venture! It really does take a village.

Thank you to the developmental team- Lyndsey Lewellen (cover design), Imogen Howson (editorial), Beth Puls (editorial), and Anne Welch (editorial). You guys are amazing and so appreciated!

A huge thanks to my husband, Scott Silverii, for answering so many questions about law enforcement. Your expertise and skill saves me hours of research, and I know how blessed I am to have you. I promise I'll figure out a fun way to pay you back ;-)

And last, I want to thank our kids—Ava, Ellie, Max, Jamie, and Graham—because you know and understand what it means when mom is on deadline, and you order takeout beautifully.

A J.J. GRAVES MYSTERY

A DIRTY JOB

NEW YORK TIMES BESTSELLING AUTHOR

LILIANA HART

1001 Dark Nights: Sweet Surrender
1001 Dark Nights: Dawn of Surrender

The MacKenzie World (read in any order)
Trouble Maker
Bullet Proof
Deep Trouble
Delta Rescue
Desire and Ice
Rush
Spies and Stilettos
Wicked Hot
Hot Witness
Avenged
Never Surrender

Addison Holmes Mystery Series
Whiskey Rebellion
Whiskey Sour
Whiskey For Breakfast
Whiskey, You're The Devil
Whiskey on the Rocks
Whiskey Tango Foxtrot
Whiskey and Gunpowder

The Gravediggers
The Darkest Corner
Gone to Dust
Say No More

Stand Alone Titles
Breath of Fire
Kill Shot

Catch Me If You Can
All About Eve
Paradise Disguised
Island Home
The Witching Hour

Books by Liliana Hart and Scott Silverii
The Harley and Davidson Mystery Series
The Farmer's Slaughter
A Tisket a Casket
I Saw Mommy Killing Santa Claus
Get Your Murder Running
Deceased and Desist
Malice In Wonderland
Tequila Mockingbird
Gone With the Sin

PROLOGUE

Nina Walsh's head was killing her.

Her body jerked as the air conditioner kicked on, and the white Priscillas swayed in the kitchen window. The gray light of dawn was just peaking over the windowsill and bathing the kitchen in a soft glow. She hadn't realized she'd been sitting in the dark.

The white tile was cold against her legs, and she looked around, trying to make sense of how she'd gotten on the floor.

"Stupid," she said, wiping hot tears from her cheeks with trembling hands. Crying only made things worse. If she wasn't so selfish, she would just do what Roy asked the first time, and then he wouldn't get so angry.

He was under so much pressure, and she needed to do a better job of understanding how important his work was to the community. He was a hero, and all he wanted was a neat and orderly home and a wife who didn't nag. It wasn't too much to ask.

It was her fault. She never should have asked him about the woman in Nottingham. But when the woman—she'd said her name was Gina—called and demanded money for a baby she said was Roy's, what else was she supposed to do but ask him about it? Where was the money going to come from? He'd already spent what she'd gotten from her husband's life insurance policy.

Nina gingerly touched the raised, heated skin on her cheek. He'd been so angry, calling her a busybody and Gina a lying slut. Nina knew the woman wasn't lying, and for a brief moment, she'd felt hope that maybe Roy would leave her for his mistress.

Hatred had blazed in his eyes when he'd struck her, and she thought surely this time he'd kill her. But he'd drawn up some self-control from somewhere and slammed out of the kitchen, giving her a reprieve. At least for the next twenty-four hours. Ten days a month she had twenty-four hours all to herself. It had been her saving grace.

She had a feeling his mistress wouldn't fare quite as well as Nina had that morning. The woman hadn't given her name or address, and she'd been on the verge of hysteria, otherwise Nina would've called the police and given an anonymous tip. But there was nothing she could do, and if he killed that woman…it would be her fault.

But she couldn't call the police. Roy had always told her the police would never believe her. Even if they had proof, they wouldn't arrest him. Not that Roy ever left proof. He was good about not leaving bruises. He knew where and how to hit, pinch, or squeeze.

The breakfast dishes lay broken in front of her. A half-eaten bowl of oatmeal, a plate of toast, and the butter crock. The earthenware had been her grandmother's. It was good and strong—made to last—but it hadn't been made to withstand Roy Walsh's temper.

She gathered up the pieces, and a pang of remorse went through her as shards of happy memories went into the trash. Her mother and grandmother were no longer alive, and the pieces were no longer replaceable.

Her thoughts drifted to her first husband as she finished cleaning up the kitchen. Daryl had been a good man. A hard worker, a good husband and father. But Roy would've seen his kindness as weakness. Men were supposed to be tough. To provide for and lead their wives however they saw fit.

Roy had once told her that Daryl chose not to fight against the cancer that had invaded his body. He'd said it was because death was a better alternative than having her as a wife. But she knew that wasn't true. She and Daryl had been happy. They'd had a good marriage, and she missed him terribly. She wasn't trying hard enough with Roy. He was different, and she just had to accept that.

"Stupid," she said again.

At least her daughter had been grown and out of the house before she'd married Roy. Of course, Hailey and Roy never got along. Roy said she and Daryl had been too soft on Hailey. He said she was a disrespectful and willful child.

But Nina had seen the sorrow and condemnation in Hailey's eyes the first time she'd noticed a bruise on her cheek. There'd been so many harsh words between them, and Nina had defended her husband. Hailey just didn't understand how marriage worked. Nina's marriage to Daryl hadn't been all roses. They'd had their share of ups and downs. But you stick it out. No matter what.

But Hailey had called her a fool and told her she wouldn't stick around to watch her die a slow death. She'd already had to do that once. That had been three years ago. They hadn't seen each other face to face since then, only a few brief phone calls that Nina had instigated. As far as she knew, Hailey was still living in Richmond. At least that's where her packages were postmarked from.

She wiped down the counters with a sponge, and then placed it precisely at the back of the sink. The kitchen was spotless. The floors gleamed and the stainless-steel appliances were so polished she could see her reflection in the refrigerator door.

She grimaced at the sight of herself. Daryl had called her beautiful, even though she knew she was nothing special to look at. Her eyes were too big and her top lip was fuller than her bottom one. She was too thin and too short, and her nose was slightly crooked from when she'd broken it ice-skating as a teenager. Daryl had made her *feel* beautiful. But Roy...Roy made her feel old and tired. She was only forty-four, but she might as well have been twice that.

Maybe if she'd bothered to put on makeup and fix up her hair. Or if she hadn't let herself get so thin or could do something about the dark circles under her eyes. Maybe then he wouldn't have gone to that woman in Nottingham. If she was honest, she didn't mind him taking his attentions elsewhere. It had been months since Roy had come to her bed, and she'd been glad of it. There was nothing pleasurable in her marriage bed.

Nina lifted a piece of her mousy brown hair and then dropped it so it fell limp against her shoulders. It had always been too fine and thin to hold a curl. Her dark brown eyes hadn't shown signs of life in so long she no longer recognized the woman in the reflection. His handprint was still visible on her cheek.

This one wouldn't leave a bruise. He'd gotten better at using an open hand instead of a fist or the back of his hand. The swelling would go down after a cold pack and a hot shower.

She opened the bottom freezer. Sandwiched neatly between the lined rows of steaks for Roy and her frozen meals were several ice packs. It barely even registered anymore why she'd need so many. Some days were worse than others.

The dull throbbing in her temples and at the base of her neck would eventually go away, but the headache was worse than usual. She'd have to take something for the pain if she wanted to get anything done today. Lying down would be the fastest way to deal with it, but it would throw her completely off schedule.

Nina left the kitchen and wandered through the house like a ghost, trailing her fingers lightly along the banister as she went up to the bedroom. The room was bright and sunny—cheerful—and the bed had already been made with military precision. The linen sheets had been freshly pressed the day before and she could smell the faint scent of lemons from when she'd polished the furniture earlier in the week.

Everything was exactly in its place. It had to be. She had laundry and ironing to do, so she couldn't dawdle the day away, but she knew if she didn't take care of the headache now, she'd end up in bed for a day or two, and that would really make Roy angry.

Tears leaked from the corners of her eyes, and she chalked it up to exhaustion and the headache. She missed her daughter, and right at that moment, she would've given anything in the world to hold her in her arms. She longed to feel the touch of anyone who could comfort her, or not cause pain.

Her cell phone was plugged in and sitting on the nightstand by her side of the bed, and she went to it quickly, before she could talk herself out of it. Maybe hearing Hailey's voice would be just the cure she was looking for. But the ringing eventually went to voicemail, so she hung up without leaving a message.

"Sorry, baby," she whispered, but there was no one to hear her.

She decided to take the pills and run a bath instead of giving in to sleep. Maybe twenty minutes in the tub would set her to rights. It was habit to check each room she entered to make sure it was perfect, and the bathroom was no different. Thick white towels hung on the towel bar with even precision, and the mirrors sparkled. The white rugs on the floor were straight and the one in front of the shower was still damp from when Roy had gotten out. He provided a good living for them, and it was important she show him how grateful she was by keeping things as perfect as they could be.

But she always seemed to fall short of perfection.

She turned on the hot water in the tub and went to the linen closet to dig out the box Hailey had sent her for Christmas.

She'd only peeked inside to see what was in it, and then she'd immediately hidden it at the top of the closet so Roy wouldn't throw it away. She'd learned that lesson the hard way.

A small stool sat at the bottom of the closet, and she used it to climb up and get the box.

There was a light coating of dust across the top, making her frown. She opened it and saw the cellophane-wrapped basket with the label from the little apothecary in town on top. This made her frown even harder, because Hailey would've had to drive from Richmond to Bloody Mary to purchase it. And she'd still chosen to send it in the mail instead of dropping it by in person.

Nina pulled the basket from the box and unwrapped it, revealing the homemade bath salts, lotions, and scented oils. The pounding in her head was almost unbearable, so she turned on the hot water and poured in a good amount of the bath salts. The sweet scent of vanilla billowed up and permeated the bathroom.

Her bathrobe hung on the hook and her towel sat folded on the stool within easy reach, so she disrobed and immediately put her clothes in the hamper.

She put one foot in the tub.

"Dammit."

And then she looked up to make sure no one had overheard her. She stepped back out of the tub and moved to the mirrored medicine cabinet. Inside was a tiny tin of pain relievers. It was a new box, still wrapped in the plastic seal and stamped with the same label from the apothecary as the basket her daughter had given her.

The tin was wrapped tight, and her hands trembled as she struggled to open it. When she finally managed to get the seal off and the lid open, several of the pills spilled out, bouncing off the vanity. She didn't bother chasing them down. Not yet. Though seeing the red and white capsules littered like candy across the floor made her anxious.

She ignored them and took two of the capsules left in the tin, tossing the pills into her mouth. Then she turned on the sink and leaned over to drink from the faucet.

There were times death seemed like an eternity, but in Nina's case, death came in an instant.

1

DEATH WAS AN OLD FRIEND.

There were those who feared death, who tried to defy it with diets and the newest exercise trends. Or by using creams and serums that erased lines, so the skin-deep lies that faced them in the mirror each morning were more palatable to look at.

I had a different view of death. There was no escaping it, no denying it, and no running from it. In a world more and more divided by race, religion, and politics, it was the one thing everyone could agree upon. Eventually, through no choice of our own, we'd exhale our last breath and that would be that.

I've spent my whole life around death. Even as a child I had a morbid curiosity of the process. Which my therapist says is perfectly normal given that I come from a long line of morticians. I'm thinking the other three thousand residents in Bloody Mary might have a different opinion.

When I was a child, most people stared at me with stricken

horror as if I were the Grim Reaper himself. I was...different. Small for my age and gaunt with it. Sunken cheeks, eyes too large for my face, and my head was usually stuck in a book so I wouldn't have to talk to anyone.

But Bloody Mary's cautious fascination with me might have had more to do with the fact that I'd told old Mr. Miller that my parents would see him laid out on their slab when he'd wrongly accused me of stealing a pack of gum from his grocery store. How was I supposed to know he'd drop dead from a heart attack less than a week later? Nevertheless, the incident gave me something of a reputation.

My name is J.J. Graves, and death is my living.

I sat in a hard plastic chair in a small, curtained-off cubicle in the ICU at Augusta General. The beeps from machines were a familiar sound, and the smells of antiseptic overpowered the less pleasant odors of urine, blood, and vomit.

I hunkered down in my chair and crossed my arms under my breasts, wishing I'd thought to bring something more substantial than the thin T-shirt and jeans I'd put on that morning. I didn't miss the numbing cold of the hospital. It was easy to ignore the bone-numbing chill when you were running from patient to patient on a twenty-four-hour shift. Adrenaline and coffee made great internal heaters.

I'd spent several years during my residency going up and down these halls or crashing on a gurney in a dark room when things slowed down. I didn't miss it. I much preferred the dead to the living, but in this case, I was relieved that death had been cheated for another day.

I stood up and stretched, and then checked all of the drip feeds hooked up to Ben Carver's body.

"Your wife is going to be pissed you interrupted her spa weekend," I said in a soft voice. I'd stopped cursing a while back, but pissed was on the list of words I wasn't sure qualified as cursing. I brushed the hair off his forehead. "If you wanted attention there are better ways of going about it. Posting the pictures of you at Jack's bachelor party on social media would be a good start."

There were few people I could call close friends. Part of that was because I'd never felt comfortable trusting others with the dark parts of my life, of which there were many. The other part was because I was a genuinely private person, and if I was honest, I just didn't like people all that much.

I wasn't the kind of person who made life happen. Jack was that kind of person. He came into a room and commanded it. People were drawn to him—paid attention to him. I did my best to blend into any wall I came into contact with. I was an expert at hiding. It still amazed me that we were married.

I could never hide when I worked at the hospital. Patients and families had questions and needed reassurances. But in my lab, in the basement of the funeral home, I could hide for hours. For days. The dead needed me. And in a weird way, I needed them.

I twisted the wedding band on my finger and then leaned down to kiss Carver on the forehead. "I'm so sorry," I said. "Don't give up. We need you here."

A tear had escaped, and I wiped it away hastily and then

wiped my hand on my jeans. I went back to my chair and pulled it up closer to the side of the bed.

Carver was a brilliant analyst for the FBI. I wasn't exactly sure what his official title was, but his security clearance was high, he had connections everywhere, and he worked miracles with computers—specifically, his computer Miranda—which had gone missing at the time of his accident.

He'd been staying with us for the weekend, helping us solve the murder of Rosalyn McGowen, a longtime resident of Bloody Mary who had been ousted as Madam Scandal. She'd been publishing the *King George Tattle* for months, spilling all of the salacious gossip the county had to offer. Which turned out to be quite a bit. But her identity had been discovered and her life ended because of it. It seemed like weeks ago, but it had only been less than twenty-four hours since we'd made the arrests and filed all the reports.

But there was no sense of closure. Not really. My father was still out there somewhere, and he'd haunt me until we tracked him down and put him behind bars where he belonged. Our relationship was…complicated.

I'd been under the impression that my parents had both died after my dad had lost control of his car and gone over a cliff in the Poconos. It hadn't been long after that the FBI had raided my home, looking for every scrap of information they could find on my parents. I'd also had my life put under a microscope and was questioned for days on end. There'd been no time to grieve. It had just been chaos.

Apparently, my parents had been using their funeral home to smuggle all matter of things from overseas. They'd been working under a government contract—though which government was never made clear to me—and soldiers who'd been killed were transported to Bloody Mary, Virginia, for preparation, meaning my parents removed the contraband from inside them, and then shipped them on their way.

Jack and I had found proof of my parents' extracurricular activities in an underground bunker in my backyard. The FBI had missed it in their many searches of the property, and I wish every day that I had too. Inside had been a gold-mine. There'd been boxes of cash and passports, files and flash drives, including a box that had my name on it. Nothing like finding out your parents stole you as a newborn from your biological parents. A couple who were probably fairly normal and didn't kill people. And let's not forget about the remains of the man who had a bullet-sized hole in his forehead. Finding that bunker had not been a good day for me.

And then my dad showed up, back from the dead, and expected me to greet him with...well, to be honest, I don't know how he expected me to greet him. It's not like we'd ever been close. But needless to say, we didn't hug it out.

Unfortunately for my dad, he didn't return from the dead before I'd discovered the bunker and removed the body and files. Unfortunately for me, he's had a lot more practice at being a horrible person, so he was able to steal everything from Jack's safe where it had all been locked up. Our only saving grace had been the handful of flash drives Jack had given to Carver.

Carver had been keeping the information from his superiors. No one could know what we had until we could find out who else was dirty—and that included the FBI. The whole operation was too big for my parents to be the only ones involved.

If I wasn't his daughter, we'd probably all be dead by now. Believe me, I've asked myself more than once why being his daughter kept me alive. Not for some misguided familial connection, that was for sure. But there had to be a reason, and I had a feeling that his patience was running thin. He needed those flash drives, and he needed them now.

I knew it was Malachi who'd been driving the black SUV that had run Carver off the road. My dad wouldn't think or care about the fact that Carver had a wife, three small daughters, and one more on the way. Malachi only cared about himself, his survival, and whom he could manipulate to make things go his way.

The truth was, Carver's chance of survival wasn't all that great. When Jack and I arrived at the scene, Carver was already on a gurney and being precariously lifted up the steep ravine where the car had run off the road. The paramedics said he'd flat lined twice on the way to the hospital.

Carver's skin was as white as the sterile sheets he was lying on, and there was a large white bandage on the side of his sandy blond head. The only thing that had stopped the SUV from going into the Potomac was a tree. Unfortunately, the tree hadn't been very yielding.

Ben's nose was broken from the airbag, and someone had sewn a straight row of stitches into his forehead, closing the jagged gash there. The smooth, somewhat childlike face was going to be scarred forever.

I'd stolen a look at his chart once he'd come out of surgery and been brought into ICU. Other than obvious contusions and abrasions, he'd had some internal bleeding, and a broken rib had punctured his lung, causing it to collapse. His collarbone and leg had been broken in multiple places, and his pelvis had been crushed. The surgeons had gotten Carver stabilized and stopped the bleeding, but he had a lot of surgeries ahead of him. It was going to be a long and painful road to recovery.

My phone buzzed and I dug in my bag until I found it. Jack's face was on the screen, and I didn't hesitate to answer. It had been hours since I'd heard from him.

"Any luck finding the computer?" I asked by way of greeting.

"None," he answered. "But I didn't have much hope. I don't know how, but Malachi knows we gave those flash drives to Ben. He knows the computer was the key to deciphering his encryptions."

"But he didn't know I'd asked for the flash drives back."

"I'm thinking he's got surveillance on the house. He might have listening devices set up as well. I would if I were him."

"Or maybe Carver's accident is the perfect distraction to get us out of the house so he can do another search," I said.

"He won't find them," Jack said. "And the house is being watched while we're gone. Inside and out."

"Where are you?" I asked.

"Down in the parking lot. I just talked to Michelle again

and she was able to catch an earlier flight. She should land around two, and I've got a couple of guys going to pick her up and deliver her to the hospital safely. See you in a few."

Jack hung up, and I took a relieved breath. There was something about being a cop's wife that was vastly different from being the best friend or lover of a cop. I'd been all three, and the moment I'd said, "I do," I'd felt the weight of what that meant. I paid extra attention when he dressed in the mornings and strapped on his weapon and badge. I noticed the slightest changes in expression or the way he carried himself if he had a rough day.

And I worried. Worried like I never had in my life. Maybe that was because I'd never had anyone to worry about on such a deep level. Jack had always been my friend, and we'd been through a lot together—including him being shot three times while on a SWAT raid in DC—but we were connected on a level now that I didn't realize was possible for two people to achieve. I'd never known true intimacy or what it meant to become *one* with another person until Jack. But there was a price to pay for that kind of love, and I realized every day that one of us might be taken away from the other. It left a hole inside me I couldn't bear to think about.

Jack had been sheriff of King George County for a handful of years, but just because he was in charge didn't mean he had it easy. The budget and resources were small for a county our size, and his cops didn't get a lot of chances to investigate or see the kinds of things cops in the city did. Not that he was complaining. There were worse problems to have than teenagers partying in the fields, breaking up the occasional barroom brawl, or getting livestock out of the road.

But things had changed in our small, sleepy county over the last year. I used to worry about keeping the funeral home in the black, but I'd had more business than I wanted recently. People had lost their minds. Maybe it was the economy, or politics, or toxins floating in the air. Who knows? But people were shorter of temper, shorter of tolerance, and the vast ways of killing their neighbors seemed to be endless. The increase in violent crime was just one of the many things that bothered Jack, though crime was still low compared to other counties our size.

The truth was, there would always be evil in the world. Just like there would always be good. The battle between the two went back to Adam and Eve, and to think we'd somehow change it thousands of years later was naïve. So it was best to suit up, fight, and protect.

2

I HEARD THE ELECTRONIC DOORS OPEN FROM DOWN THE corridor, and the sound of steady footsteps followed, along with a few murmurs from the nurses' station. I glanced at my watch and saw it was well after midnight. I'd lost track of the time.

The curtain slid open and there was Jack. He looked tired, but I was glad to see him. I stood and he immediately came to me and pulled me into his arms. Before Jack, I didn't like to be touched or held. I'd put every distance I could think of between me and anyone who wanted to get close. But I couldn't imagine going without his touch now.

"Mmm," he said, rubbing my back in slow circles. "That's nice."

"Very nice," I said into his neck. "You think Carver would know if we made out a little?"

"Once upon a time, I would've said no," Jack said. "But after I witnessed him at the bachelor party I can't say for sure. Let's just assume that he always knows."

But even as he said it, he leaned down and kissed me softly. It wasn't a kiss of fire and passion, but one of contentment, where the heat could flame into something hotter.

When he released me, I took a step back and really looked at him. "You need to get some sleep."

Jack was tall and broad through the shoulders and chest. Men nowadays seemed smaller, scrawnier, with their thin builds and baby-smooth skin. But when you looked at Jack there was no doubt that he was all man. His beard was well past a five o'clock shadow, his jeans and T-shirt were rumpled, and the scar through his eyebrow was stark white like it got when he was tired, irritated, or under stress. His badge was clipped to the front of his jeans, and his weapon was at his side. I knew he was wearing an ankle holster as well. He never left home without either of them.

"I was about to tell you the same thing," he said. "I've got to wait for Michelle to get here, and there's no reason for both of us to go without sleep. You go ahead home, and I'll come as soon as I see her settled."

"I'll wait with you for a little while," I said, moving back to my chair.

"How is he?" Jack asked.

"Lucky to be alive. He's going in for another surgery in a few hours. His chances of survival still aren't great, but every hour he's with us is a good sign."

"Carver's tougher than he looks. But he's going to be mighty pissed that pretty face of his got messed up. He was always happy it was the one place on his body that didn't have any scars. Plus, he said it was his boyish good looks that attracted his wife."

I'd only recently found out why Jack and Carver were so close. Why they trusted each other unconditionally. Carver had shown me the thatchwork scars across his chest and arms from when he'd been tortured. Jack was right. Carver was tough. And he'd get through this. I had to believe that.

"He showed me his scars," I said.

Jack blew out a breath and took the chair on the other side of the bed, and then he stretched out his legs and laced his fingers so they rested on top of his stomach. "Yeah, he told me. He wanted you to know he trusts you too. Carver is a good friend to have."

"Maybe he shouldn't trust me," I said. "He's here because of me. If there hadn't been a witness to the crash, we'd be standing over his body in my lab right now. He could've been in that ravine for hours without anyone knowing."

"You think it was coincidence there was a witness?" he asked. "I don't believe in those. What I do believe is that God can outmaneuver Malachi Graves any day of the week, and He's on the side of the good guys."

I didn't say anything in response.

"It's not your fault, Jaye."

I flinched when he said the words, especially since I'd been thinking the opposite for the last several hours.

"Really?" I asked. "If we hadn't taken those flash drives, Malachi wouldn't still be hanging around, popping up every time I turn a corner. What could possibly be on them that's so terrible that it's worth all this? How has this become our problem?"

"I could think of a lot of things that could be on them," Jack said grimly. "Your father isn't just a petty criminal."

"If I had to do it again…" I said, shaking my head. "I would've just set fire to that bunker and been done with all of it. I wouldn't know about my real parents. I wouldn't know about any of this. I just want him out of our lives. This shouldn't be our fight."

"Sometimes we don't get to pick our fights," he said. "And I think you underestimate your father. You're still his daughter, whether you share blood or not. You grew up under the same roof. There was a reason the FBI questioned you for so long after he and your mother went over that cliff. For a man who's committed treason, murder, and God knows what else, it's hard to believe anyone around him on a daily basis wouldn't have some knowledge of his activities."

Something cold slithered through me and I stared intently at the monitor, avoiding Jack's gaze. Is that what he thought? What everyone thought? That I'd known all along what my parents had been up to and chosen to look the other direction? Or worse, taken part in it?

"Don't get that look on your face," he said. "I'm not saying I don't believe you. I know you had no clue what your parents were up to. I know what your childhood was like and your relationship with them. But that doesn't mean I can't understand how others might think differently.

"If I was FBI or any other organization who had an interest in your dad, you would be the first person I'd talk to. And

I'd keep talking to you until I was satisfied. Your dad is thinking the same way. He wants those flash drives. But he also wants to see how much you know. He's been watching you, catching you alone so he can have long conversations and bring up the past. It's not because of nostalgia."

"I think I know that better than anyone," I said coldly. None of this was Jack's fault, but I couldn't help the hurt that had been building over the last three decades. "It's time to end this. We've got the flash drives. Carver wasn't able to get through the encryptions to see what was on them. We need to find someone who can. And if we can't, we need to destroy them so Malachi can't get his hands on them."

"That's easier said than done," Jack said. "Carver's the best."

I pressed my fingers into my eyes hard, my frustration at a boiling point, and then I looked back at Jack. "We have to catch him," I said, not bothering to hide the desperation in my voice. "I can't keep living like this. I just can't, Jack. I thought I'd put my childhood behind me. I thought I'd put my parents' deaths behind me. And then his resurrection, only to find out they'd stolen me and smuggled me into the United States along with the dead soldiers they'd betrayed. Who even knows if my mother is dead like he claims? How much more am I supposed to take?"

It felt like the words were coming out of someone else's mouth. I was detached from reality, living in this parallel universe where I watched someone else's life implode with every piece of information collected.

"How am I supposed to hide from him? He pops up like a damned daisy every time I turn around. You think we're safe? He hit Carver today. Who's next? You? Me? You think he cares?"

A ghost of a smile appeared on Jack's lips. "I guess he's not exactly in the running for father of the year."

I knew Jack was trying to lighten the tension, but I was long past that. "We can't live like this, Jack." I didn't have anything left inside of me but a burning rage to see my father taken down. "We can't even enjoy our marriage or the life we're supposed to be building together. Things like this don't happen to ordinary people."

Jack's expression tightened. "I've been enjoying our marriage. Quite a bit, actually."

"That's not what I mean, and you know it."

"Look, Jaye. This whole thing sucks. No one will argue with you on that. And you're right. Things like this don't happen to ordinary people. But you're not ordinary. You're an extraordinary woman caught in the middle of extraordinary circumstances. You have to play the hand you're dealt. There's no other option."

I hadn't admitted to anyone—had barely admitted it to myself—that there was part of me that was angry with Jack too. Jack was a good man. An honorable man. He liked to play by the rules and follow the law to a *T*. And because he was good and honorable, he was right. We had no choice but to play the hand we were dealt. Maybe I just wasn't as good and honorable as Jack.

All I wanted was Malachi Graves out of my life forever, and for him to go back to hauling coal in hell where I'd originally thought he was. I didn't care how it was achieved. I would've been fine burning the flash drives, or I would've been fine with someone putting a bullet in his brain. I wasn't picky at this point. He was too good to be caught. He'd proven that time and again. So Malachi had the ball, and we were stuck playing his game.

But I couldn't admit that to Jack. It would upset him and cause him to worry about me more than he already was. And taking my anger out on him wouldn't be productive anyway. There was too much work to do for us to be at odds with each other, though I felt like we were miles apart from where we'd been even twenty-four hours ago.

"The witness didn't get a good look at the driver," Jack said, "but he was able to describe the vehicle in detail and part of the plate. After Carver went off the road, the SUV sped west on 218. We're going to find him. Cops in three states are looking for him."

"So what?" I asked, not able to hold my frustration inside. "They don't know who they're looking for. Even if you gave them the description from the last time I saw him do you think he looks the same? He'll walk right underneath all our noses and laugh about it the whole way."

"I'm aware of Malachi's talents," Jack said, his voice soft and even. That was never a good sign. "But it's what we've got to work with. People make mistakes. And sometimes you just get lucky."

My laugh wasn't nice. Jack, Carver, and I were the only people who knew my father had returned. I bit my tongue to keep from saying anything I would regret later. But I wasn't encouraged. Our lives were in danger. And all we could depend upon was…luck?

I don't know how long we sat in silence, but a nurse came in and checked Carver's vitals, and neither of us said anything while she worked. Jack's face had been buried in his phone, and his scowl was growing darker.

"What is it?" I asked.

"They found a black SUV matching the description of the one that ran Carver into that ravine abandoned off Glebe Road in Stafford County. No signs of Malachi. They found another set of tire tracks and think he had another car there waiting. That's a dead-end road to the middle of nowhere, and it's pitch black, so it probably wasn't hard for him to get in and out."

"I don't think either of us is surprised by that," I said, stretching my neck from side to side. "You can have a thousand agencies looking for him, and they'll never find him."

"We'll find him," he said. "This isn't my first day on the job."

I stared at Jack intently. I'd had a lot of time to think while we'd been sitting there, and there was only one way to catch my father.

"No, but you're only one man. No one else knows how serious this is. No one knows the game he's been playing with us. He's got resources and experiences that you don't have because you've never played in that world."

"So what? So now it takes a crook to catch one?"

It was rare for Jack to get angry, but I could tell I'd pushed a button somewhere. Jack didn't get loud or violent when he was mad. He was ice. Quiet and cold and efficiently deadly.

"All I'm saying is he's been doing this since before either of us were born. We know that the CIA has trained him, at least in some capacity as an agent. We don't have any clue what he's capable of. Not really. You think local cops are going to catch him? What about the FBI? They're as deep into this as Malachi. It's just you and me on this now that Carver is out of the picture."

Jack was already shaking his head. "Jaye…"

But I didn't let him finish. "Like you said, he wants two things—the flash drives and to see how much I know. There's only one way to kill two birds with one stone."

Jack's lips pressed into a thin white line. "So, what's your plan? You want to stand in the middle of a field holding the flash drives up in the air, and pray he doesn't just shoot you in the head and take them from your corpse?"

"It wouldn't be my first choice," I said, feeling more in control now that I'd said what I'd been thinking out loud. "I'm the only way to get this finished. And it would be foolish for you not to use me in any way possible. He's going to come after me anyway. He's getting desperate. Carver's accident proves that. Use me. And let's put this behind us. We can't start living until he's gone."

"That's where you're wrong," he said, coming to his feet. "You've chosen to dwell on your past instead of living for your future, and it's crippled you. You haven't flourished. Not because you can't, but because you've chosen not to. You've let your past define you, control your choices so you're living half the life you were meant to live. But that's not the life I want to live. We were meant for a hell of a lot more than this, Jaye. And I'm disappointed you don't see that."

White-hot fury consumed me, and I stood, so we were eye to eye. He was wrong. I'd done everything I could to move on to a future I never thought I'd have. I wouldn't have married him or started a new life if I'd been living in the past.

The scar that slashed through his eyebrow was even whiter than it had been before, and his words were clipped and even. "And what? Now you want to become a sacrifice? What's the real reason, Jaye? Is it so you can catch your father, or is it because you think death would be an easy way out of your own personal misery?"

I gasped and gripped the railing on the side of the hospital bed. I was surprised the metal didn't melt under the heat of my hand. The prick of tears stung my eyes, and my spine straightened. I'd never felt anger like this. It spread like liquid heat beneath my skin. And inside...inside I felt the soul-crushing disappointment in the only person in the world I'd ever cared about.

"Things got too good, huh?" he pressed on. "You can't allow yourself even one iota of happiness without trying to sabotage it."

There were a lot of words I wanted to say, but I would've had to have put my whole salary in my swear jar.

"Gosh," I said, sarcasm dripping from my voice. "I've just been wracking my brain trying to figure out what's wrong with me. But you clearly know me better than I know myself, and you're always right about everything, so it must be true. Must be nice."

My face felt like marble—immovable. I reached for my bag, slung it across my torso.

"Jaye…" he said.

"It looks like you've got things taken care of with Carver," I interrupted. "I'm going to get some sleep. Let me know if anything changes."

"Jaye," he said again.

But I'd already pushed the curtain aside, my back stiff with pride. I had to deal with my father first. Then I could deal with my marriage.

3

I WOKE THE NEXT MORNING TO THE GLARE OF SUNLIGHT streaming directly onto my face, and my phone buzzing loudly.

My neck was stiff and twisted in an unusual position, and I held a hand over my eyes, blocking the sun, as I creaked them open. It took me a few seconds to orient myself. I wasn't the sharpest knife in the drawer first thing in the morning, especially before coffee.

It didn't take long for me to remember Jack's words, and I felt the gaping wound in my chest, as if my heart had been ripped out. I'd replayed the conversation in my head over and over again, thinking of different ways I should've responded. I'd let my anger fester until I'd been ready to get in the car and hunt him down to give him a piece of my mind.

Common sense told me to have a glass of wine and get control so we didn't end up on *Judge Judy*. And thank God the *King George Tattler* was now defunct because there was no doubt we would've been on the front page.

I'd finally found sleep sometime around dawn, though it was fitful. I wasn't even sure if Jack had come home like he'd said he was going to. I hadn't made up my mind whether I cared.

My phone stopped buzzing, and I stared at it confusedly on the hardwood floor, wondering how it had gotten there. I looked around my seldom-used office and tried to work out the crick in my neck. It was a wasted room, really. But Jack had wanted me to have my own space when I'd moved in, and he'd turned what had initially been the smallest extra bedroom into a cozy workspace. There was a long oak table instead of a desk, built-in bookshelves, a couch, and a single overstuffed chair next to a corner fireplace.

It had seemed like the place to sleep at the time, though I'd briefly considered staying at the funeral home. But I wasn't an idiot. Malachi could get in and out of that funeral home with his eyes closed. Using me as bait wouldn't work if I made it too easy for him.

Jack had said the house was being watched inside and out, and sure enough, when I'd gotten home, Officer Cheek had been stretched out on our couch watching the big screen TV. He had a walkie-talkie next to him on the table, and I assumed he and the two officers in the patrol car outside were trading off every couple of hours.

I'd done no more than say hello before I headed upstairs to the office. I wasn't in the mood to converse. The office was also a good choice because it faced the front of the house so

I could see if Jack's unit was parked in the driveway. I was an expert at passive-aggressive fighting and avoiding.

I was still in my jeans and T-shirt, and a plush throw was twisted around my ankles. I removed the blanket and sat up slowly, squeezing my head in my hands. I had a tension headache that radiated up the back of my skull.

There were no blinds on the windows, and the sun was brutal in a cloudless sky. I glanced at the door and saw it was still locked, and then I got up and moved around the perimeter of the room until I was standing next to the window. I peeked down at the driveway, but the only cars out front were my black Suburban and the patrol unit that had been parked there the night before. Jack had either left very early, or he'd never come home.

My phone started buzzing again, and I went over to pick it up, half afraid it was Jack calling. It wasn't. The screen on my phone said *Sheriff's Office*, but Jack wouldn't have used that line to get in touch with me.

"Dr. Graves," I said, after I'd put it on speakerphone. I unlocked the office door and headed downstairs toward the kitchen. I needed coffee.

"Hey, Doc," a deep voice said. "It's Nash."

I liked Nash. He was a good cop, though I couldn't imagine why he'd be calling me. Especially before I'd had my coffee.

"What's going on?" I asked. It was obvious I'd just woken up, but I didn't even try to disguise it. I glanced at the kitchen clock and saw it was past nine. That wasn't too terrible for a Sunday morning.

The coffeepot was half full, and I assumed Officer Cheek and the others had helped themselves through the night. It was long since cold, so I poured it in the sink and started to make another pot.

"We've got a body," Nash said.

An image of Malachi flashed through my mind, and I wondered who else he'd gotten to. Jack had the flash drives. He'd taken them back from Carver to keep them safe. Maybe there was a reason Jack hadn't made it home. My heart stopped as fear grabbed me with icy fingers.

"Who?" I demanded.

I heard papers shuffling in the background before Nash said, "Nina Walsh. Got the call about an hour ago and we're at the scene. She was found by her husband. He's a fireman and was working his twenty-four, so she's been dead awhile. No rigor left in the body. It looks like she passed out or something and hit her head. But the tub was running and there's about an inch or so of water covering the floor."

I didn't recognize the name and figured she wasn't a Bloody Mary resident. "What's the address?" I asked, grabbing the pen and notepad that was lying on the counter next to the coffeepot.

My brows rose as he rattled off a street in Bloody Mary, and I copied it down. Nina Walsh didn't live too far away at all.

"I can be there in half an hour," I said. "I need to shower and change. I had a late night."

"No hurry," he said. "Looks like an extreme case of bad

luck from what I can tell. Husband's real broken up about it and his alibi is tight."

Bad luck indeed. It didn't take much water for someone to drown. But no one would know for sure until I got her on my table and opened her up.

I was about to hang up when Nash said, "Hey, any word on your friend?"

The phone was sitting on the counter and I scanned my texts, but there was nothing from Jack about Carver. Or about where he'd spent the night.

"No," I said. "Nothing yet. He's still critical."

"He'll pull through. Gotta keep the faith, Doc."

"Yeah," I said, softly, but Nash had already hung up.

I made a cup of coffee and put extra creamer and sugar in it. I normally had my first cup black, but only when Jack made it. I didn't have the same culinary skills he did and needed the extra enhancements to make my brew palatable.

The TV was off in the den, and I didn't see Cheek or any of the other officers, but I figured they were around some-where. I headed upstairs to the shower, ignoring the sight of our unmade bed or the lack of a wet towel hanging over the rod in the bathroom.

Jack hadn't been home at all.

I stripped out of day-old clothes and took my coffee into the shower with me to kill two birds with one stone. The water was as hot as the coffee, and I stood under the harsh spray so it pounded at the knots in my neck and shoulders.

I wasn't a high-maintenance kind of person, so it didn't take me long to get out and dry off, blow-dry my hair, and get dressed. I briefly looked at myself in the mirror. My skin was paler than normal, amplifying the dark purplish bags under my eyes, and I slathered on tinted moisturizer so I didn't look worse than my victim.

I put on a pair of old jeans and a black T-shirt, thinking about the conditions of the scene. There wasn't a point wearing anything nice if I was going to be kneeling in water. My coveralls were water resistant, but you never knew what surprises a scene might hold.

My black hair was long enough to pull back, so I clipped it at the nape of my neck, grabbed my empty coffee cup, and headed back downstairs.

"What's up, Doc?" Officer Cheek said, his grin letting me know he thought the saying was hilarious.

"Same old," I called out, detouring to the kitchen one more time.

Cheek was a rookie, though he'd had a lot of that rookie polish shined right off when he'd seen what Rosalyn McGowen's cats had done to her body. Animals and death didn't go particularly well together.

Cheek was short, and still a little doughy with youth. His cheeks were round and his face smooth. His blond hair was mussed, and his off-duty clothes rumpled. There was a crease in his cheek that told me he hadn't spent his entire shift keeping a watch on things. I could only hope the officers in the car had better stamina.

"Man, this is crazy," Cheek said. "Can't believe you have a

stalker. You'd think he'd be smart enough to know his days are numbered since you're married to the sheriff. But people are nuts. You never know what they're thinking."

I'd wondered what story Jack had given his cops for why they were on a protective detail. I guess Jack hadn't exactly told a lie. Malachi had been watching me for months. Cornering me when I least expected it.

I had a pretty strong constitution, and nothing much rattled me. Doctors who worked in the ER didn't have that luxury. But Malachi's visits were starting to frazzle my nerves, and I could feel I was right on the edge of the breaking point.

"Yeah," I said. "It's pretty crazy."

"You have any idea who it could be?" he asked.

"Wish I did," I lied. "I guess we've had some pretty high-profile cases lately. It might just be someone who's fascinated by what I do."

"That makes sense," he said. "Well, don't worry. We've been rotating and checking the perimeter every hour, and the sheriff says you're our top priority. We'll catch the bastard."

"Thanks," I said, pouring my to-go cup half full and adding a generous amount of cream and sugar before securing the lid.

"I heard about the body on the radio," Cheek said. "Sounds like the whole squad is over there. You get the call?"

"On my way now," I said. "Nash said she's a firefighter's wife. Fell in the bathroom."

"It's a damn shame. Roy's a good guy. He plays in the

Guns and Hoses charity basketball tournament. Got a wicked three-point shot. I heard he was the one that found her."

"That's what Nash said," I confirmed. "Why don't you tell the others to come in and help themselves to the coffee? Things should be quiet here today."

"They just left," he said. "I've got my personal vehicle in the garage, so I'll head out for some shut-eye as soon as the sheriff gets home."

"No one is staying while he's here?" I asked, my brow furrowed.

"He said you were the priority. He figures you'll be okay on the scene and back at the funeral home. There will be cops everywhere. Why? You think the sheriff could be in danger?"

"Yeah," I said. "Actually, I do. I know he doesn't want to split all of his resources right now, but this guy would know hurting Jack would hurt me."

"Don't worry, Doc. Me and the guys will figure out something. We won't let anything happen to him."

"Thanks, Cheek," I said, feeling more relief than I wanted to let show. I didn't even know where Jack had put the flash drives. And I was guessing the reason Jack hadn't told me was to keep them safe in case I was tempted to cut a deal with Malachi. That thought only refueled my anger at Jack. And now I had his safety to worry about on top of everything else.

I was hoping Malachi wouldn't be stupid enough to tangle with Jack one on one. I believed in Jack's abilities one hundred percent, but I knew he was handicapped by the fact that he was only one man. True, Malachi was only one man too, but the law or a conscience didn't hamper him, and he'd never been overly concerned about playing fair.

Still, Jack was no one to tangle with up close and personal. Which made me all the more aware of the danger he was in. If Malachi wanted Jack dead, he'd figure out the most efficient way to go about it, and being up close and personal would have nothing to do with it.

I grabbed my bag, said goodbye to Cheek, and then headed out the front door. I didn't see Jack's unit until I'd already gotten in the Suburban and turned on the ignition. He'd parked on the other side of the three-car garage for some reason, and since he hadn't come through the front door, I could only assume he'd gone around to the back.

My jaw ached from grinding my teeth together, and I decided I was still too angry for any kind of confrontation. I looked up at the house, wondering where he was. I guess that was the plan, to avoid each other until we couldn't help it any longer.

"Fine," I mumbled under my breath. "Just fine." I threw the Suburban in reverse and pressed down on the accelerator, my tires squealing, and then I threw it in drive just as abruptly and sped down the long driveway.

It wasn't until I'd gotten to the road that I realized I'd left the directions I'd written down on the kitchen counter. But it would be a cold day in hell before I turned around to get them.

4

JACK AND I LIVED ON THE OUTSKIRTS OF BLOODY MARY ON Heresy Road. It was a two-mile stretch of gravel that ran parallel to the Potomac River and acres of forestland. The few houses that were on the road were secluded and mostly obscured from passersby. We didn't get a lot of trick-or-treaters, and there were some days we didn't get mail if there was too much rain or snow.

The good news was it was easy to spot unfamiliar vehicles on the road. The bad news was there were countless hiking trails and other ways to approach the house. We were fortunate that we had motion detectors, sensors, and cameras around the perimeter where the clearing and the trees met. But Malachi had proven on more than one occasion that security meant nothing to him.

My childhood home was at the opposite end of the road, recently purchased by a couple from Ohio who didn't know the unhappy memories that rested inside those walls. It had been falling down when I'd owned it, due mostly to finances and disinterest. But the new couple had started renovations, and there'd been construction trucks up and down the street since the weather had turned nice.

I took a left out of the driveway, heading toward Cromwell Road. I at least remembered the street name. Cromwell was even farther from civilization than we were, and the only reason I was familiar with the area was because the heavily treed fields had been perfect for high school parties, illicit trysts, and the occasional drug deal for the last fifty years.

A cop would patrol the area from time to time, but it was so far out of the way and took them so long to get there that the kids had plenty of time to be warned by lookouts before the cops arrived, so it was kind of a losing battle.

Gravel crunched beneath my tires, and when I finally turned onto Cromwell the terrain changed to a one-lane dirt road. Someone had taken the time to mow the ditches so it wasn't overgrown with weeds, and it was much easier to see the tire tracks that veered off toward the woods. I drove for a mile or so without seeing a house or any cars.

It was Sunday, which meant I was on my own today. The good thing about a booming business was that I'd been able to afford to hire employees. I had a receptionist who worked regular weekday hours and an assistant who worked with me during the week, and on the weekends only if there was a funeral. I also had two interns, but their schedules were built around their classes. Which meant I was stuck transporting a body by myself, dealing with mounds of paperwork, and an autopsy.

The dirt lane seemed to go on forever, and I was just thinking about calling Nash to ask for directions again when I saw a police cruiser coming toward me. I pulled as far to the side of the road as I could so they could pass, but it was going to be close unless I went into the ditch.

The cruiser pulled to a stop next to me and the window rolled down. Officer Kristi Chen pushed her Ray-Bans on top of her head and smiled, though it was more of a grimace.

"Hey, Doc," she said. "Great way to spend a Sunday, huh? I've got to say that I've had my fill of bodies for the week. And that's something considering I came here from Atlanta."

Now that I thought about it, it had been a pretty eventful week. Rosalyn McGowen and Carl Planter had both been murdered in their own homes. Rosalyn's remains were some of the worst I'd ever seen, and I'd spent some time at the Body Farm studying various levels of decomposition from different elements.

Rosalyn had been eaten by her cats, so she'd been cremated, but Carl was still in my walk-in cooler, waiting for his final burial arrangements to be made.

"Now that you mention it," I said. "It has been a red-letter week." Then I stopped to look at her more closely. I could see she was pale and there were dark circles under her eyes. "You feeling okay? Maybe you need to take a sick day."

"I had a rough night," she said. And then a dimple flashed as she smiled, and she waggled her eyebrows. "But he was worth it."

I coughed out a laugh, completely taken off guard. Chen was one of Jack's newest recruits, and she was sometimes hard to read. She was one of the few who had big city experience, and I couldn't imagine it was easy being an Asian-American woman in King George County, and holding a position of authority at that. This wasn't a part of the country that was exactly progressive in its thinking.

I didn't think she'd been here long enough to feel out the dating pool, as limited as it was, but apparently, I was wrong. But my interest was piqued. I hadn't heard any rumors about Chen being involved with anyone. Either I was way out of the loop, or she was doing a great job keeping her mystery lover a secret. Cops were terrible at keeping secrets, especially if there were two of them involved in anything. I'd find out who it was eventually.

"I'm heading to the scene," I told her. "Where's the turn-in?"

"About half a mile up on your right," Chen said. "It's the only house on that side of the street. Husband's a veteran firefighter, so there's been a lot of traffic in and out."

I sighed. Traffic was never good. "Lovely."

"Pretty much Nash's feelings too. I guess it gave the husband quite a shock to come home from shift and find her like that, but he called his station chief before he called 911. There were firemen here before paramedics or cops could assess the scene."

It wasn't what Chen was saying so much as how she was saying it. Being a first responder was a hard job. There was a lot of day-to-day grief and pain that went along with it. But the elephant in the room was that there was a tension between cops and firefighters that was always simmering under the surface. They worked together when they had to, but for the most part they stuck to their own. And when the two worlds collided it could be explosive. And not in a good way.

"Who's on scene?" I asked.

Chen snorted. "Better question is who isn't on scene."

I blew out a breath, already dreading the headache to come. "Well, I hope to God this is just an accidental death."

"You and me both," she said. "You just missed the sheriff. He came out and talked to Nash a few minutes and then said he was heading home to get some sleep."

"It was a long night at the hospital," I said, trying not to think about Jack. Which was stupid because I'd done nothing but think about Jack and the words he'd said since I walked out of the hospital the night before.

"Oh, right," Chen said. "I heard about Carver. How's he doing?"

"Still critical, and he's still not breathing on his own, but he made it through the first surgery."

"I'm sure he'll pull through," she said, dropping her sunglasses back over her eyes. "I think you might be right about taking a sick day. I don't have the patience to deal with the public today. Good to see you, Doc."

I waved goodbye as she moved on, and then I drove the rest of the way until I came to the first turn-in. The trees became sparse and the area opened into a square plot of land with a long driveway and a simple, two-story white house with black shutters. The flowerbeds were neat and weeded, with a variation of colored blooms, and the hedges had all been evenly manicured. There were no toys or other things scattered in the yard or on the driveway. There was a dark blue sedan and a white pickup truck under the carport.

It looked like the solid, middle-class home of someone who worked hard and took care of what they earned.

There were two police units parked in the driveway along with two other pickup trucks and a Jeep. They were parked so I didn't have a clear path to get the body out of the house, and I sighed in annoyance. I could see the tire tracks in the yard from where cop cars and the rest of the parade had driven in and out.

I pulled in close behind them, not caring that I was blocking the exit. It was going to be a long day, and the sooner I could get back to the funeral home the better.

Lieutenant John Nash was standing on the porch by the time I got out of the Suburban.

"Need any help?" he called out.

"I've got it," I said. "Just let me get my bag. We can mess with the gurney later. I'm without interns today."

"Yeah," he said, sighing. "It's always a pain in the ass when someone dies on a Sunday."

Nash was somewhere in his mid-forties and graying at the temples. He was tall and lanky, broad through the shoulders and narrow through the hips, and he reminded me of a gentleman cowboy in his Wranglers, boots, and button-down shirt. He wore a shoulder holster and his badge was on a lanyard around his neck. All he was missing was a cowboy hat. He was almost as popular with the ladies as Jack had been before he'd taken himself off the market. Nash was twice divorced and hadn't given up on finding the next Mrs. Nash. He was a hopeless tease and a ridiculous flirt.

I opened the back end of the Suburban and dressed quickly in my coveralls and then stuck my feet into a pair of utilitarian black galoshes that came up to my knees. I went ahead and put on my gloves and then slung my camera around my neck and grabbed my medical bag.

It was only the beginning of summer, but the sun was ruthless without cloud cover. I was careful not to step in the flowerbeds since they were so well tended and the flowers in full bloom.

"Nice house," I said, coming up to shake Nash's hand.

"Gives me the creeps," he said. "Like one of those Stepford houses. No one is this clean."

"Maybe you're just a slob."

"I don't think so," he said. "My mama taught me better than that. But there's clean and then there's *clean* if you know what I mean. Apparently, Mrs. Walsh was a perfectionist. Liked things around the house and yard just so. The husband said she had a routine. Followed it like clockwork. Certain days for cleaning and weeding and baking. She was a professional homemaker."

"Good for her," I said and meant it.

I was pretty much a disaster in the kitchen, and boiling water exceeded my skill level, so I was always impressed with people who seemed to have a knack for homemaking. Jack had the talent in the kitchen, but we had a housekeeper and someone to take care of the lawn. Otherwise we'd be living under a layer of dust and weeds.

"You've let your hair get long," Nash said out of the blue. "I like it. You should wear it down more often. Shows off those sexy cheekbones."

"I'll remember that when I'm elbows deep in a body and my hair is dragging through entrails," I said dryly.

Nash chuckled and opened the front door for me, and I stepped inside the Walshes' home for the first time. Sterile was the first word that came to mind. In fact, it was so sterile that it was impossible for it to feel homey, despite the fact there were muted rugs and comfortable-looking furniture throughout. And Nash was right. It was creepy.

It was two stories and shotgun in style. The living room was at the front, the dining room in the middle, and I could see the kitchen at the back of the house. I could hear several low voices and figured that's where the husband and friends were gathered.

There were stairs to the right side of the room, and on the wall were framed photographs. Each frame was exactly the same and placed precisely the same distance apart. Everything was so perfect I didn't see how people actually lived here.

"It's creepy, right?" Nash whispered.

"Definitely," I said. "Husband in the kitchen?"

"Yeah, and halfway to being drunk. Chief Edwards and some of the other firefighters are in there too. He started with a shot of whiskey to calm his nerves and then they all started. Lewis and Martinez are watching them, trying to get any extra information about the wife, but at this point they're probably just babysitting to make sure they don't do anything stupid."

Since it was barely ten thirty in the morning, I figured that was probably a good idea.

"Sorry about the mess," Nash said as we made it up to the landing. "It took me a while to convince everyone to get the hell out of the bathroom."

Things weren't quite so perfect upstairs. The hall rugs were bunched and someone had left boot prints on the floor, and several of the pictures on the wall hung askew. There was a dent in the sheetrock next to the master bedroom.

"Things got a little heated up here when I told everyone to clear the area. Roy didn't want to leave her, and then he just flew off the handle at one of the guys who tracked dirt on the floor. I thought he was going to throw the guy out the window. Things kind of escalated from there, but Jack showed up in time and talked some sense into everyone."

"Yeah, he's good at that," I said.

Nash snorted. "Maybe effective is more of the right word. Threatening to lock people up for the night tends to get the point across."

"Da…" I started to say but remembered my swear jar and that there was already a healthy amount of money in it. I'd made the decision to clean up my vocabulary a few weeks back. It was a personal choice, and not one any of the cops I worked with understood, but I was doing it for me and not them, so I didn't really care.

I peeked over at Nash to see if he'd heard me and saw his lips twitch. "It doesn't count if you don't say the whole thing," he said. "All I can say is I don't know what side of the bed the sheriff woke up on this morning, but it wasn't the good one. I've never seen him so mad."

"We had a rough night at the hospital. We're both working on little sleep and a lot of coffee."

"He mentioned that. I saw the crash scene yesterday. Your friend is lucky to be alive."

"Yeah," I said, but I was distracted by the room.

The master bedroom hadn't fared much better in the scuffle, but I could see the same underlying tidiness that the rest of the house had, even amid the sopping wet carpet and boot prints everywhere. Even the curtains had been pressed and the lace doilies that sat on the furniture had been starched. A cell phone sat plugged in on the nightstand table.

"Hey, Doc," Riley said. He and Walters were standing guard outside the bathroom door. They were both in their early twenties and in uniform.

"Long time no see," I said.

Riley snorted out a laugh, but Walters was clearly not amused. Everyone had put in a lot of hours the past week.

"Man, you missed a good one," Riley said. "The sheriff was pissed. Told everyone if they didn't get themselves under control and clear the scene, they could answer questions behind bars. I thought Chief Edwards was going to have an aneurism, but he got his guys under control and got them out."

"I always miss the good stuff," I said, moving past Riley and Walters so I could enter the bathroom.

"Not true," Riley said. "I saw you punch Floyd Parker the other day. You've got a mean right hook. It was probably best you weren't here."

"You're probably right."

My boots squeaked as I stepped onto the wet tile. Most of the water had seeped into the carpet and walls, but there was still a fair amount standing on the floor with no place to go. I saw Mrs. Walsh crumpled next to the tub, but I didn't immediately go to her. I liked to get a mental picture before I looked at the body.

It felt odd being without Jack. We'd developed an easy rhythm working scenes together, and I felt out of my element with Nash. Cops were nosy, and I didn't want to feed the gossip machine if even a hint went out about our disagreement. All I could assume was Nash was the primary working the case, and Jack had no plans of becoming involved. Fine with me.

The bathroom was simple in design. Beige tile and walls, his and hers sinks with white marble counters and a built-in vanity. The bathroom was perfectly square with a shower in one corner and a big tub with jets in the other.

"Huh," I said.

"What?" Nash asked.

"The tub seems out of place. Big and fancy with all those jets. Seems like a splurge. Everything else in the house is in good shape and in perfect order, but there's nothing expensive. The furniture, appliances and electronics…everything is within their means. Except for that tub."

"I can see it though," Nash said. "Guy's got a job that can put strain on the body. Maybe he likes to come home and soak his muscles after a rough shift."

"Could be," I said, moving toward the body and looking down into the empty gaze of Nina Walsh.

"Who moved her?" I asked.

Nina was lying face up and she was marble pale, her skin almost translucent so the blue of her veins could be seen beneath the skin. But the reddish marks told their own story. When a person died, the blood settled to the parts of the body that were touching the ground, and her skin was a dark red at her breasts and left arm and hip. The palm of her right hand and the left side of her face was also red.

I frowned at the color of her lividity. Normally the blood settled and turned a dark purple, but for whatever reason, Nina's was still red. But you couldn't say that something always happened the same way with the same results. There were too many factors in science and the human body, and the mixture of any outside element, like lying in water, could alter the results.

"The husband moved her when he came home from shift," Nash said. "Saw her in here and freaked out. Thought she'd just passed out or something. Said he turned her over and started administering CPR."

"Anything in her medical history that would explain this? Fainting spells or heart issues?"

"He said she was healthy as a horse. Never been sick at all

that he knows of. How long do you think she's been like this?"

I put my bag on the stool in front of the vanity to keep it from getting wet. "She can't weigh a hundred pounds."

I focused on the body. The body always told its own story. I took a complete set of pictures of her front side and then dug into my bag to grab the thermometer to take her temperature. Though I had a pretty good inclination as to what I'd find.

"She's room temperature," I said. I'd been able to move her easily. "Like you said, all signs of rigor are gone from the body. I'm assuming the water was running hot and that there would have been quite a bit of steam and condensation. Full rigor occurs about eight hours after death, but her size could have sped up the process by an hour or two. It usually stays in the body at least eighteen hours, but same goes. With her size and weight factored in, the heat from the water, and the steam, I can give you a range for time of death sometime between twenty and thirty hours. What time did the husband leave for shift?"

"Six thirty," he said, raising his brows. "But I've got to tell you, Doc. I'm just not feeling it. It's hard for a guy to fake that level of grief. When I got here, he was still holding on to her and sobbing like a baby. It was heartbreaking to watch. She's got no visible marks other than the bump on her head, and he's got no defensive wounds."

"Maybe his time is wrong," I said. "Maybe he left earlier."

Nash snorted. "I don't mean to judge…"

"That's just what Gladys Pip says right before she's about to lay into someone," I said.

"But the Walshes would make Mussolini's train schedule look like it was drawn by a kindergartner with a crayon. It took Roy Walsh about twenty minutes to run down his schedule, with precise times for everything from when he eats his oatmeal to when he takes a dump."

"Fascinating," I said, fluttering my eyelashes. "You're such a charmer."

"Takes one to know one, sugar. You're the one dragging your hair through entrails to up your sex appeal."

I snorted out a laugh. The nervousness I had for working with someone besides Jack began to ease. Those who weren't around death like we were wouldn't understand, but inappropriate jokes and gallows humor were pretty much SOP at any fatality. We had to process too, and laughter was usually the best way to keep from crying.

"Run down the schedule for me," I said. "Maybe I can make a tighter estimation after I get her on the table."

Nash flipped open the little spiral notebook he had in his shirt pocket and flipped it open, but I knew he didn't need to look at it. Nash was sharp. Sharper than he let on most of the time, which was why he was so good getting information out of criminals. He remembered everything, and people who remembered everything were great at catching people who were lying.

"The vic is forty-four and has been married to Roy for almost four years. Before their marriage she worked as a paralegal for the county, but Roy said her passion was being a homemaker, so he told her to do what made her happy and stay at home. He works his twenty-four and then he and a couple of his shift mates own a moving company to fill the rest of their time.

"He said she lived and breathed this house, and sometimes he had to make her get out for dinner and be around other people. I guess she's something of a recluse."

"Well, who'd want to make that drive to town all the time? It's got to take a good half hour. I'd be a recluse too."

"You live ten minutes from here," Nash said. "And you were kind of a recluse before you and Jack got married."

"That's because I didn't have much business and I could only afford to eat at home."

"Fair enough," he said, shrugging. "Anyway, apparently living and breathing this house meant she got up at four thirty every morning, seven days a week."

"Yikes," I said.

"She'd make sure Roy's uniform was crisply pressed and starched, and then she'd start his breakfast. Roy gets up a half hour later, showers, and then he comes down for breakfast before he dresses for the day. He likes to have oatmeal and wheat toast by the way."

"I'm sure he's very regular."

"Indeed.

"The victim's breakfast consisted of half a grapefruit with sugar. They both drink their coffee black."

My knees were killing me, so I sat on the vanity stool.

"After breakfast, they brush their teeth and then he gets dressed and she makes the bed. He leaves for the station like clockwork at six thirty. It's a twenty-six-minute drive. He gives himself an extra fifteen minutes if the weather is bad. You still with me, Doc?"

"No, I think I fell asleep. Do you know the husband?"

"Roy?" he asked, putting his notebook back in his shirt pocket. "I've seen him around the station a time or two, but I don't know him on a personal level. Didn't even know his name until the call came in and I recognized his face."

"Rumor has it he called his chief after he realized she was dead instead of 911."

"Rumor would be correct," Nash said. "Roy said he was in shock and it was just habit to call the station. It's not really a big deal. He was on duty and able to send the EMTs out immediately, and then he notified police.

"Edwards told me he kept Roy on the line because he was afraid Roy might do something rash. Apparently, he was just screaming incoherently. Edwards said Nina was Roy's whole world, and he treated her like a queen. Kept her picture in his locker at the station and clipped to the visor in the fire truck."

"They didn't text or talk on the phone during his shift?"

"He said it was a busy one, so there wasn't time."

"Yeah, I guess it would have been," I said, remembering the fire trucks and personnel who'd worked for hours to clear the scene after Carver's accident. "Even so, twenty-four hours is a long time. And if she was his whole world, you'd think she'd at least warrant a 'Hey, how's it going?'"

Nash frowned. "Do you always look for the bad in people?" he asked.

I was taken a little off guard by the question but said, "You're a cop. How can you not? In my experience, the only people who tell the truth are the ones laid out on my table. Everyone's got secrets. No one's life is perfect, even if it looks like it. Besides, we work it as a homicide until we prove it's not."

"Pretty cynical, Doc. I think you need to have more fun in your life. When was the last time you went to a movie or did something that has nothing to do with work?"

"I went on my honeymoon last month."

"Yes, and ended up solving an eighty-year-old murder. What do you do for fun?"

"My work is fun," I said primly.

Nash chuckled. "Doc, I just found my new mission in life. We're going to find you a hobby."

"Uh-huh," I said. "That sounds like loads of fun. Maybe check with Emmy Lu to see if I have any openings in my calendar."

I squatted back beside the victim and moved her head to the side, so the knot on her temple was visible, and then I took a quick photo.

"There's nothing to indicate she was struck with anything. No debris in the wound. Just a tiny puncture mark with a little blood where she made impact."

I looked closely at the faucet and then took a swab kit from my bag. The Q-tip was dipped in Phenolphthalein, and I swabbed the edges of the faucet. When I held the Q-tip up to the light there was the tiniest sliver of pink showing.

"That's settles that," I said, showing Nash the Q-tip. "For whatever reason, she lost consciousness and hit her head on the faucet when she fell. Livor mortis suggests she fell in a kind of crumpled position, and once she was down, she stayed down until she died."

I tried to demonstrate by rolling onto my left side and pulling my left knee up slightly. I put my weight on my left side and made sure my chest was pressed down, and then placed my right hand palm down. All the points where lividity had set in.

"The discoloration on the left side of her face is consistent with the rest of her body," I said, and then got back up to my knees. "Man, I'm not as young as I used to be."

"You're not going to use old age as an excuse. There are plenty of hobbies for women your age."

I narrowed my eyes at him. "What do you mean women my age?"

"You're only as old as you feel," he said. "How old are you feeling?"

"Yesterday I was feeling my age," I said. "Today, I feel about ninety."

"Yeah, those bags under your eyes remind me of my grandma."

"You know, Nash, I've got a whole lot more room in my freezer."

He held up his hands in surrender, but he was grinning.

Nash had the kind of charm that was impossible to get too irritated with.

"Okay, okay. Back to business," he said, and squatted down next to me. "If she was lying on the left side of her face as lividity shows, do you think it's possible she drowned? The water would have to come up at least a couple of inches to reach her mouth and nose."

"It's possible," I said. "It doesn't take much. She could've just as easily died from cardiac arrest or some other undiagnosed medical issue. I'll be able to say for sure once I open her up to see if there's water in the lungs."

I looked down at the familiar scar on her abdomen and traced it with my finger. "They have children?"

"Roy said she has a daughter from a previous marriage. First husband died of cancer, so the daughter's her only other kin. Name's Hailey Hartford. She's a third-year law student at the University of Richmond. But Roy said they haven't spoken in several years. Said the girl was rebellious, liked to party and drink. He said she resented it when her mother remarried, and as far as he knew there's been no contact between them. He said he'd contact her and let her know."

"Okay," I said. "I've done everything I can do here. Let's get her loaded up and back to my lab. I'll have some answers for you by the end of the day."

"No rush. I don't plan on doing any paperwork until tomorrow. I'm supposed to be off today."

"How'd you draw the short straw?"

"I heard about the problem with the stalker," he said.

"Seemed like a no-brainer. Besides, a little overtime never hurt anyone."

I winced in sympathy. Malachi was stretching already stretched resources to the max. "Sorry about that," I said.

"Not your fault," he said, shrugging. "Like I always say, better to be safe than sorry. We're all on rotation until the SOB can be caught. We'll make it work. But I'm still not doing any paperwork until tomorrow. This seems like a case of bad luck all around to me."

I called out to Riley and Walters in the bedroom. "Do you guys mind getting the gurney from the back of the Suburban?"

"You got it, Doc," Riley said back.

I unfolded the body bag and unzipped it, and then Nash and I lifted Nina Walsh gently and placed her inside.

"Looks like I get to be your intern for the day," Nash said.

"If you really wanted to be my intern you'd come help with the autopsy."

"Been there, done that. Why don't you put off the autopsy until tomorrow and we'll go bowling? Maybe that can be your new hobby."

"Jack and I each stole a pair of bowling shoes when we were teenagers. Mr. Hertz banned us for life."

"You know I'm going to check out your story. I'm a detective."

"It's the truth, I swear," I said, holding up two fingers. "I promise the autopsy will be fun. There's nothing else to do today. I'll let you make the Y-cut."

"I'd rather do almost anything else."

"Funny," I said. "I can't think of anything I'd rather do more."

Nash laughed. "That's messed up, Doc."

He had no idea.

5

KING GEORGE COUNTY ONLY HAD A POPULATION OF A little over twenty thousand, but what it lacked in people it made up for in square miles. It was a farming community—mostly tobacco, though there were fewer tobacco farms now than there had been ten years ago. Some say it's progress, but I'd wager the people who lost their farms don't agree.

Our slice of the country was tucked away on the northeast side of Virginia between the Potomac and Rappahannock Rivers. The scenery was beautiful if you stopped to look at it long enough, but I think most of us took it for granted. I know I did. Most of the residents were busy going about their jobs and lives, griping about the increase of taxes and the decrease of wages. Nothing much had changed in the last several decades.

I'd grown up in Bloody Mary, one of the four towns that made up King George County. There'd been numerous attempts and petitions over the years to change the name of the town to something more appealing and friendlier, but people around here were as excited for change as they were for higher taxes, so the name had stuck.

The three thousand residents—give or take a few—were set in their ways and ornery with it. They were people who worked hard for a living and liked the idea of the American dream. The buildings downtown were a snapshot of the fifties, with painted glass windows and mismatched awnings, and people still flew the American flag from their porches and pulled their cars to the side of the road during a funeral procession.

The citizens of Bloody Mary lived on gossip, but they didn't have too much interest in what was happening in the rest of the world. They lived in their own insular bubbles, and they didn't really care what their elected officials were doing across the river because they thought they were mostly a waste of everyone's time and money anyway.

I'd been glad to get out of the Walsh house. I'd been even more glad to pass the entrance to my driveway and see Riley and Walters turn in to check on Jack. Nash was in his unit behind me, and it took almost twenty minutes before I turned onto Catherine of Aragon and the funeral home came into view.

Graves Funeral Home had been in my family for four generations. Since I'd found out I wasn't a Graves by blood, I didn't feel near the attachment to it that I once had. I'm not even sure that attachment was the right word. More like a noose around my neck. It had been an obligation that I'd resented and a choice that I hadn't been given, but had been forced to take, after my parents had died and I'd resigned from the hospital. I was more at peace with it now, and serving the dead was my calling, just like serving the living was Jack's.

I figured Nash would have turned off to head into the station, but he was still behind me when I turned into the carport at the funeral home. Traffic was nonexistent on a Sunday, but there were a couple of cars parked in front of the laundromat in the strip mall across the street.

"I thought you were going home," I said to Nash when I got out of the Suburban.

"Nah," he said. "I figured I might as well wait and see what you find. Besides, I can watch baseball on the big screen you've got in the lounge while you're doing your thing."

It was then I realized Nash was doing double duty as my babysitter for the day.

"You know I'll be fine," I said. "I can lock myself in the lab, and I'll turn all the cameras on so I can see if anyone is skulking about."

"A fat lot of good being locked in the lab is going to do if he decides to set fire to the funeral home."

"Well, that's comforting," I said.

"The sheriff said this guy was dangerous. He said he's been inside your home and even whacked you over the back of the head. Why didn't you report that? We could've been out combing the area for this guy."

"I reported it to Jack," I said, shrugging it off. This was the exact reason I hadn't wanted to tell anyone. There were too many questions to ask, and just because Jack gave them some made-up version of what was really going on didn't mean his men wouldn't keep asking.

"Besides, everyone has enough to do, and things got a little busy with the murders last week. I thought we could handle it on our own."

"That's what we're all trying to tell you. You're one of our own, and we always take care of our own. It's not hardship for me to sit on your couch and watch the game and order a pizza."

"I've got beer in the fridge," I told him as consolation.

"Don't tell the guys, but I'm not much of a drinker," he admitted. "But I'll take coffee if you have it."

I snorted out a laugh. "Of course I have it. I'd go without food and sex before I'd go without coffee. It makes the world go round. Or at least more tolerable."

Nash laughed and said, "Sugar, I knew there was a reason I liked you."

We lifted the gurney out of the Suburban and made sure everything was stable before we started rolling Nina Walsh up the ramp.

The funeral home was a three-story, red brick Colonial that had been modernized with each generation. My parents had added the state-of-the-art kitchen and a lab in the basement with the kind of equipment that made most scientists drool with envy. Of course, there was a reason for everything.

All of the entrances worked on a keypad system instead of a key, so I typed in the code and waited for the click before pushing the door open. There was a mudroom that served as a transition space before the kitchen, but it was bare except for hooks on the walls that held extra gurney straps and other things I needed for transport. The floors were concrete and there was a drain in the middle since rain, snow, and gurneys didn't go well together.

The door locked automatically behind us, and I keyed in the code to the basement. I hadn't found it odd at the time, but it probably should have set off alarms that my parents had invested in a stainless-steel door and security that rivaled Fort Knox to protect the bodies they were interring. Or looking back, maybe I just hadn't wanted to ask too many questions. There was a reason I'd moved away and gone to med school.

There was a quiet *pfft* as the door unsealed, and I pulled it open. Cold air blasted us as we wheeled her onto the lift, and my skin pebbled from the chill.

"Good grief," Nash said. "It's an icebox."

"Bodies and heat don't really go well together. Besides, it helps with the smell."

He closed his eyes and shook his head. "We're really going to work on getting you that hobby."

"I'm married," I said. "I don't need a hobby. I like being at home."

"That's because you've been married all of fifteen minutes. In fifteen years, you're going to wish you had a hobby. Take it from someone who's been married a couple of times."

I arched a brow. "Maybe the reason you've been married a

couple of times is because you had too many hobbies and weren't at home enough."

He opened his mouth to say something, and then his lips twitched. "Maybe you're right, Doc. You sounded an awful lot like my ex-wife just now."

"I like both your ex-wives," I said with a cheeky grin. "So I appreciate the compliment."

He choked out a laugh and then took a step back into the kitchen. "Whew, you've got a sassy mouth. I bet you keep Jack on his toes."

"It's mutual, I think."

"You got things from here?" Nash asked. "Not that I'm afraid of going down there or anything, but the game starts in a few minutes."

"Uh-huh," I said. "Maybe you should check all the viewing rooms to make sure I didn't forget and left someone lying out."

He visibly shivered. "That's just mean, Doc. And to think I was going to make you a cup of coffee and figure out a way to lower it down to you."

I full out laughed and felt lighter than I had in days. "Go watch your game," I told Nash. "I'll call you when I'm done."

I pushed the lift button and Nina Walsh and I started our descent into the lab. Nash closed the big metal door, and it locked automatically. The basement was the safest place I could be. Unless my dad had put in a secret exit that I hadn't found or, like Nash said, burned the funeral home to the ground. Then I was pretty much screwed.

The lift came to a stop, and I rolled the gurney past my embalming table and the refrigeration unit to the opposite side of the lab. The room was white and sterile. There were drains in the floor and the ventilation system was top notch. Even so, I always kept the air-conditioning on high.

The space was almost two thousand square feet, and the walk-in cooler took up most of the space on the east wall. I had a stainless-steel embalming table on one side of the room with the appropriate drains for body fluids, and I had an autopsy table on the other. Metal shelves lined the wall and held various equipment and my microscope.

Behind my autopsy table was a drying cabinet where I hung blood-soaked evidence, an x-ray illuminator, and a limited testing area for basic tox results. My desk was stacked with autopsy forms, a box of latex gloves, and my tape recorder.

Nina Walsh was a tiny woman, and moving her from the gurney to the autopsy table was like moving a bag of bones. Even for her height, I was estimating she was well under weight. I unzipped the bag and skidded it from beneath her with little problem, and then I tossed it on top of the gurney and pushed it all aside, so I'd have plenty of room to work.

The routine was second nature, and I only needed to find cause of death. All I knew was there was no good reason for a seemingly healthy woman to be on my table unless what Nash had said was true. It was just an unfortunate case of bad luck.

I did a quick set of x-rays, focusing on the lungs, and then I put them up on the light screen. I looked closely, but there was no sign of any cloudiness or water. In fact, other than having suffered from a broken finger at some point, she looked pretty darned good.

"Well, that makes things interesting," I said under my breath.

I went to examine the hematoma on her temple, but it didn't seem like a serious injury. She had a nice lump that had turned an interesting shade of black, purple, and green, but it would've settled down after about a week. Head wounds always looked worse than they were because of the amount of blood in the head. She also had slight swelling to her left cheek, and the skin was discolored there from where she'd lain so long after death, but the swelling was on the same side as the lump on her head so it made sense it happened in the fall.

I put on my gown and surgical gloves, and then I turned on my recorder and documented the day and time on the autopsy sheet on my clipboard.

"Caucasian female listed as Nina Evans Walsh," I said, checking over the notes Nash had given me. "Age forty-four." The table had a built-in scale and I documented her weight in my chart. "Ninety-eight pounds. Five feet, zero inches tall. Blonde and blue. No discernable birthmarks or tattoos. Abdominal scar consistent with caesarian section."

I put down my clipboard and picked up my scalpel. I made my Y-incision and frowned at the sight of the cherry-red blood that sprung up as the blade passed through. I used my scalpel to peel back the skin and soft tissues, and as soon as I pulled back the chest flap, I could smell it.

I pulled down my surgical mask and leaned closer to the

open cavity. The scent of bitter almonds. I hadn't imagined it.

"Note for the record the signs of cyanide poisoning are present in the victim, most notably the smell of bitter almonds and the cherry-red color of her blood."

I started working a little more quickly. This case had just taken an interesting and unexpected turn. I made cuts along the rib cage, disconnected the tissue, and then pulled the rib cage from the skeleton, setting it aside on a sterile tray. The organs were exposed, and I detached arteries and ligaments, and then I severed the attachments to the spine, bladder, and rectum.

Once everything was detached, I was able to pull all of the organs out in one piece and lay them on a smaller table to my right. The human body really was amazing. It didn't take me long to detach and weigh the organs, and then notate everything on my chart.

"Contents in the stomach include grapefruit and coffee, consistent with the husband's story of what she had for breakfast the morning of her death. The heart does show signs of cardiac arrest. This result is consistent with the effects of cyanide poisoning. Tests will confirm conclusively."

I took blood and tissue samples to send off to the toxicology lab in Richmond. I could do basic tests for alcohol or drugs in the system, but I knew cyanide wouldn't show up in the standard test. Poisons never did. And while I needed the lab in Richmond to back up my findings, I happened to have a cyanide test kit. It wasn't one that I'd ordered, but my parents had obviously had cause to use the

ChemSee test indicators in the past because the box was open and several of the test strips were gone.

I put two of the tests on the table, and I used three drops of blood on one and three drops of urine on the other. I'd never actually had to use the tests before, on the living or the dead, and I had no idea how long it would take to get results, so I pulled my mask back up and went back to the body.

I put a block under Nina's neck so I had room to work with my skull saw, and then went about the task of removing her brain. I didn't expect to see any damage from the fall she took, other than the exterior hematoma, but I examined everything methodically and then weighed the organ.

I made sure to take extra samples of blood, tissue, and other fluids because I knew the tox lab would want to do several tests to make sure, but the signs were all there. I put Nina's organs back where they belonged and then held my breath as I walked over to look at the two test strips.

Despite the frigid room, I used the sleeve of my gown to blot at the sweat on my brow. And then I carefully picked up the first test and held it under the light. The strip had turned bluish green. Positive. I held up the second test and saw the same result.

I turned on my recorder and said, "Homicide. Cause of death is suspected cyanide poisoning, pending formal results from the tox screen.

I peeled off my gloves and tossed them in the trash and then called Nash. "You're going to want to get down here," I said when he answered. "I'll buzz you in."

I hit the lock release on the door and Nash was already waiting to come inside. He closed the door behind him and took the stairs two at a time. His gaze briefly rested on Nina before they returned to me.

"Whadda ya got?" he asked.

"It's probably a good thing you didn't start your paperwork today," I said. "I'm calling homicide."

"No shit," he said, clearly surprised.

"Cyanide poisoning."

His brows lifted so high I thought they'd disappear into his hairline. "Well, that's a first for me."

"I thought the color of her lividity was off when I saw her on the bathroom floor," I explained. "I figured it might have been a result of her lying in hot water for so long. But when I made my first incision her blood was the wrong color, and then I smelled the burned almonds."

"I've always heard cyanide gives off that smell."

"I was able to do a localized test with blood and urine and they both came back positive. We've got to get these samples to the lab in Richmond for a definite positive, but for now I'm comfortable calling it."

"We're going to have to get a warrant," Nash said, pulling out his phone. "Let me call the sheriff and he'll know which judge is on call."

I cleaned things up and pretended not to try to hear Jack's voice through the line. Nash relayed what I'd told him, and at that moment I wished it were Jack standing in my lab. I wanted to hear his thoughts and impressions. I wanted to work with my husband. But he was so damned stubborn. And so was I.

"We'll wait here until the warrant comes through," I heard Nash tell Jack. "I have a feeling we'll need to move fast, and we'll need all hands on deck. We don't want another showdown with the fire department and have potential evidence destroyed. Roy Walsh is going to have to narrow down his alibi a little better."

I couldn't hear what Jack said next, but Nash agreed and disconnected. I checked my own phone to see if I had any texts over the last few hours I'd been busy with Nina Walsh, but there was nothing there.

"We need to get in that house," Nash said. "If I was him, I'd have scrubbed every inch of that bathroom and thrown away anything that would leave a residue. You have any idea what we could be looking for?"

"Cyanide is an interesting poison. It could've been administered any number of ways. In her grapefruit, coffee, or even topically if she put on lotion. I saw some in the bathroom."

I looked up at the clock and saw I'd been working on Nina a little over four hours. My neck and shoulders were stiff, and I walked over to the little fridge in the corner and grabbed a water and then tossed one to Nash.

"The warrant should take an hour or two. I've got my laptop in the car. I'm going to run out and get it so I can fill out the affidavit and get it turned in. I'll call whoever's free and have them keep watch on the house."

He headed back up the stairs, a spring of excitement in his

step. Cops were weird. They could be on their last leg of exhaustion and if a new case came up, they were fresh as a daisy.

"I made another pot of coffee," he said. "Want some?"

"More than I want life," I said. "Let me clean up here and get her in the cooler, and I'll be right up."

I checked my text messages one last time and then stuck my phone in my back pocket. Not one word from Jack. Not about Carver or the case. Of course, he hadn't gotten one word from me either.

6

IT TOOK ALMOST TWO HOURS BEFORE THE SIGNED WARRANT was sent back to Nash electronically. I had time for a cold piece of pizza, two cups of coffee, and a shower and change of clean clothes. Despite the ventilation system, I was never quite sure what I smelled like when I came out of an autopsy or an embalming.

I kept extra clothes in the office closet just off the kitchen. It was my personal space, and I never brought clients there to talk. I used the front parlor for that. It also had a private bathroom and shower. I scrubbed and washed my hair twice and then changed into black slacks and a sleeveless blouse in the same color. I blow-dried my hair, left it down, and put on a touch of makeup. I found men tended to respond better when I questioned them if I put on some lipstick. Go figure.

When I came out of the bathroom and walked past my desk, I paused and backed up a step. My desk was stacked with files in the neat piles I'd left them in. But right in the center of the desk was a silver ring. It was a heavy band

and intricately carved. It had belonged to my mother, and she wore it always.

"Hey, Doc," Nash called through the door. I jumped and then started looking around to see if my father was still in the room. "Can I use your printer?"

"Be my guest," I said.

The room was empty. It was possible he could've left the ring on the desk anytime over the last couple of days. I hadn't been in the office to check. It was just as possible he'd waltzed in right under Nash's nose and put it there over the last few hours.

The last time I'd seen it was when my father had come back from the dead. He'd slipped it into my hand after I'd blacked out from shock. The silver band had felt like a lead weight, and I'd tossed it into a drawer so I didn't have the constant reminder.

It hadn't been the first time Malachi had breached our personal space. I was sure it wouldn't be the last. I picked up the ring and turned it between my fingers. Whatever was in those remaining flash drives, Malachi had said that his freedom relied on them. I didn't much care about his freedom, and I couldn't trust him as far as I could throw him.

But he had said something that resonated as truth, and that was that all governments were the same, and all the players were following the same bureaucratic rules. Labels meant everything. Patriots and traitors were often one and the same, depending on which side of the line they were standing at the time. And patriotism wasn't always synonymous with doing the right thing. Loyalty only existed as long as you were coloring inside the lines of whatever agenda was most pressing. And agendas changed as frequently as the people who created them.

Maybe there were others involved. Maybe Malachi really thought he was doing the right thing and working for the right people. It wasn't my place to make those decisions. But I knew he wasn't completely innocent, and he'd left a body count behind him that he needed to pay for. Maybe even my mother. And the only way to get the answers was to get into those flash drives.

"Checkmate, Dad," I said, shoving the ring into my pocket. "Let's see who comes out on top."

When I came back into the kitchen Nash was closing his computer and holding up his phone. "Got the warrant," he said. "Let's roll."

I grabbed my bag and slung it across my body. I didn't think I was going to need it, but I'd found out the hard way that the times when I didn't have it were the times I *always* needed it. I just assumed we were taking Nash's unit. It seemed pointless to take two cars, and he could always drop me by the house on the way back since it was on the way.

George Strait blasted through the speakers as soon as he turned the ignition, and he backed out of the driveway with practiced ease before speeding down Catherine of Aragon and toward the Walshes' house.

When we finally turned onto Cromwell, I saw a line of police cars pulled off on the shoulder, waiting for us to get there. And a little farther down the road was Jack's black Tahoe. I watched in the side mirror as they all pulled into a processional line behind us, no lights, but the anticipation in the air was heavy.

When we pulled into the Walshes' driveway I was glad to see the only cars left in the driveway were the car and truck under the carport.

I didn't know anything about Roy Walsh, so I was waiting to meet him face to face before I gave Nash my initial impression. I might work with the dead all day, but I was extremely gifted in reading people, and my first impressions were usually correct.

There were no outside lights on and the trees surrounding the house gave it an ominous feel, but every room inside the house glowed with a soft yellow light.

"I'm surprised he's still here," Nash said as we got out of the car. "There's no way I'd be able to stay in the house if something like that happened."

I didn't say anything, but followed him. He had the warrants he'd printed out in hand, and we stood together on the dark porch. I couldn't really see who else had come along, but I heard Martinez's voice, so I could assume Lewis was with him since they were pretty much inseparable.

A couple of the guys split off and went around to the back of the house, and a couple more headed to the carport so they could get started searching the vehicles. I felt Jack come up behind me, his presence recognizable even in the dark. I couldn't help myself. I turned and looked at him. His gaze met mine, and I wanted to move closer. I'd gotten used to his touch and going without it seemed like torture now.

He moved a little closer, and I had to keep myself from leaning into him. I was brought back to reality by Nash's quick raps on the front door. It didn't take long for the front porch light to come on and the sound of locks opening.

"What's going on?" Roy Walsh asked when he opened the door.

He was a big guy, well over six feet, and he was in the kind of shape you'd expect a firefighter to be in. He was dominating and had that immediate presence of someone who was used to intimidating others. I thought about how tiny Nina was and wondered how often she'd been bulldozed or bullied during their marriage.

He had a rather angular face and was clean-shaven. In fact, it looked like he'd come fresh from the shower. His dark blond hair was slightly damp and combed back off his face, and he was wearing a pair of cargo shorts and a T-shirt advertising a local brewery. He had a pair of brown Birkenstocks on.

Nash must have noticed too because he said, "Going somewhere?"

"I was about to head out," Roy said. "I don't really want to stay here tonight. I can't after...after finding Nina that way."

"I understand. We'll try not to take too long," Nash said politely. He handed over copies of the warrants, and Roy took them automatically, but it was clear he didn't know what he was holding.

"What's this?"

"They're search warrants for your home, vehicles, and your

locker at the fire station. Nina's death has been ruled a homicide."

"That's crazy," Roy said, looking directly at me. "No one was here. It was just an accident."

"I'm sorry, Mr. Walsh," I said. "But your wife was poisoned. It was no accident."

He squared off in front of the door, blocking the entrance. "Bullshit. What does some hick town coroner know about poisons? This is bullshit. You can't do this based on some hack's whim."

I was assuming I was the hack he was referring to, but I'd been called worse things.

"Look, Roy. The best thing you can do is cooperate and let us do our jobs. The sooner we get the facts, the sooner we can clear all this up. Don't you want to find who did this to your wife?"

A red flush worked its way up Roy's cheeks, either from anger or embarrassment, I wasn't sure.

"Don't give me that," he said with barely restrained anger. "You think I'm stupid? You wouldn't be here if you didn't think I killed her. I wasn't even here! You've already asked me all these questions, and I have an alibi."

"Then it won't hurt to ask you a few more questions just to be sure. Then we can start looking for whoever did this to your wife."

I was impressed with Nash's professionalism. It was the first time I'd really gotten the chance of watching him work up close and personal. Jack was there to back him up if he needed assistance, but Nash seemed to be doing fine on his own.

"Look, why don't we go into the kitchen and let the guys do what they need to do. We can just have a casual conversation."

"I'd rather have my attorney present," Roy said.

"That's fine," Nash said. His voice was friendly. "You're more than welcome to do that, but we'll need to go down to the station, and you're probably going to be there a lot longer than if we just had a nice and comfortable conversation in your own home."

"Fine," he said, taking a step back. "But when y'all are through I'm calling my lawyer and suing every one of you."

I looked at Jack and rolled my eyes. If I put a quarter in a jar every time someone threatened a lawsuit it would be fuller than my swear jar. Jack's lips twitched and I felt some of the tension go out of my shoulders. Maybe we both just needed some space to cool off. Maybe everything was going to be okay between us.

Having an actual relationship where you wanted to put your spouse's needs above your own and learn about compromise was still a very new concept for me. I'd spent my whole life having to rely only on myself. I'd told Jack I wasn't the best bet for a relationship, but he hadn't seemed to care. Now he was stuck with me, because we were in it for better or for worse.

We followed Roy back to the kitchen, and I noticed he had a couple of duffle bags and a backpack sitting in the hallway. Wherever he was going, he was planning on being there awhile.

I didn't look back as I heard the team make their way up the stairs toward the bathroom. I'd told Nash everything I could about how the cyanide could've been administered. There really wasn't much to do except test everything that could've been the culprit.

Roy grabbed a beer from the fridge, but didn't bother to offer anyone else anything to drink. Not that any of us would've taken a drink from someone we suspected of poisoning his wife. He slammed himself down into the chair at the breakfast table and it skidded back a couple of inches.

The kitchen wasn't any warmer than the rest of the house. Just white, gray, and stainless steel. There was a bowl of grapefruits sitting on the counter and I knew the team would bag them all up when they made their way in.

I took the seat to Roy's left, and Jack took the chair next to mine. He still hadn't uttered a word, but there hadn't been a need to. Not unless we wanted marriage advice from a twice-divorced cop who thought bowling should be my new hobby. Nash took the seat across from me and scooted his chair a little closer to Roy.

"Like you said, Roy. You're not a stupid man," Nash said. "You know the first person we've got to look at is you. You know the statistics."

"I didn't kill my wife," he said through gritted teeth.

"Then let's figure out who did. But first you've got to

answer all these questions and let us eliminate you. Walk us through yesterday morning."

"I've already told you," he said. "It was just another morning. We have a very regimented schedule. Nina likes…" He stopped and swallowed. "She *liked* order. Shift work is hard on everyone. It's not like we work Monday through Friday normal jobs."

"That schedule can be hard on a family," Nash said. "Nina got up first?"

A ghost of a smile touched his lips. "She was an old soul. Went to bed around eight o'clock every night and got up at four thirty, rain or shine. I wake up at five and shower, and then we have breakfast together. I get dressed and then leave for the station at six thirty. There's nothing complicated about it."

"You left at six thirty?" Nash asked. "Do you punch a time card at the station?"

"Sure," Roy said. A red flush was working its way up his neck and his finger was tapping on the table.

Nash noticed too because he asked, "What time will your punch card say you arrived at work?"

Roy looked down at the table and his finger stopped tapping. He tightened his fist into a ball, and he remained silent.

Nash looked at me and Jack and raised his eyebrows.

"You really need to help us out here, Roy, and give us a great alibi. Anyone who saw you driving on the street or anyone you talked to at the station. We can't pin down Nina's time of death to the minute, but what I did pin down doesn't look great for you if you're not completely honest with us."

"What kind of window?" Roy asked, finally meeting my gaze.

"Anywhere from two hours before you last say you saw her to two hours after. A whole lot can be done in four hours. And you know we're going to check your punch card anyway. Might as well come straight with us now."

Rage flashed in his eyes, and I watched his fists clinch tighter, so the veins in his arms stood out. He had a rigid control of an impressive temper, and I couldn't help but wonder what happened when he let it loose.

"We had a fight that morning," he said. "Before I left. A woman called and told Nina that she and I were having an affair. Nina confronted me about it."

"Was is true?" I asked.

"Look," Roy said, sitting forward in his chair. "Nina and I had our problems like any couple. But I loved her. I would never kill her. I have needs that she wasn't able to meet." He shrugged like that was the only explanation needed. "Nina could be cold. And I honestly didn't think she'd care all that much. She was never exactly excited to burn up the sheets."

I'd never been a good poker player, and I knew there was no way I could mask my dislike for Roy Walsh, so I examined my fingernails until I thought I had my expression under control.

"What happened when Nina confronted you?" Nash asked.

Roy blew out a breath. "We had a big fight. Gina had told her that she was pregnant, and Nina was more angry about the thought of paying child support than she was about Gina. I don't really remember what I told her. I was angry. I broke some of the breakfast dishes and stormed out of the house. Gina hadn't told me about the baby, so I drove out to Nottingham to see her and hear the news face to face. I never wanted kids. She told me she was on the pill."

Roy sat back in his chair and crossed his arms over his chest like a petulant child. Roy had a dead wife and a pregnant mistress he was probably going to leave high and dry, but somehow, he was the victim.

"Can Gina verify this?" Nash asked.

"She sure as hell better," Roy said. "I was there about forty-five minutes or an hour. She showed me the pregnancy test, so I guess she wasn't lying. After I left her apartment I drove straight to work. I punched in a little before eight thirty."

"Did you call in and tell anyone you'd be late?" Nash asked.

"I called my captain as soon as I left the house. Told him I had to take care of an emergency personal matter."

"What's Gina's full name and address?" Nash asked.

He hesitated again, and it was obvious he didn't want to give up the information. "Gina Garcia. She lives in Sherbrook Heights in Nottingham. I don't remember the address."

"That's fine," Nash said. "We'll find her."

Nash looked at me again to see if I had anything to add.

"Did Nina have products or medications that she used regularly?" I asked.

"I don't know," he said, shrugging. "She didn't take prescriptions regularly that I know of. She kept little tubes of hand lotion in her purse that she'd use. Lip balm. Things like that. She wasn't much on makeup. She rarely wore any."

"Where were you planning to stay tonight?" Nash asked.

"The Holiday Inn in King George. Gina told me I couldn't stay with her. She's pretty pissed."

"Has Gina ever been in this home?" I asked him.

"No way," Roy said. "I'm not stupid. I'd never take the chance of bringing Gina here. Nina would've known if another woman was in her house. Besides, Nina barely left the house. She was married to this house more than she was to me. I mostly met up with Gina at her place, or at Firehouse Movers. That's my moving company. We've got an office in King George."

"Yeah, I've seen it," Nash said. "Who are your partners?"

"Gabe Roland and Chance Walker. We've got a good business. Lots of good reviews."

"Did they know about Gina?" I asked.

"Sure," he said. "It's not like it was a secret or anything. Just from Nina. The guys know not to blab about stuff like that. It's part of the brotherhood. We do it all the time. You know how it is."

He nodded at Jack and Nash, and I had a feeling they knew exactly what he was talking about. I'd been around cops long enough to know that some of them put their law enforcement brothers above their own wives and children, especially when their behavior was less than stellar.

"Do you think it's possible Gina was jealous of Nina? That she wanted to do her harm?"

"Nah, Gina's been around the block. And the firehouse. Smokin' hot, so it's not like anyone would turn her down, you know? It is what it is. Nothing long term. She'll move on to someone else when she gets tired of me. Badge bunnies are a dime a dozen."

"What about anyone else? Did Nina have a disagreement with anyone? Did she have any close friends?" I asked.

"Nina was a loner for the most part. She sometimes met up with, ah…" He snapped his fingers a couple of times trying to remember. "Marilee Hedge-something. I think they went to school together. They'd have coffee."

Roy rolled his eyes. I didn't think my dislike for him could get any bigger, but he kept proving me wrong.

"Look," he said. "I loved Nina. She was a good woman. Stable. Dependable. She didn't make waves. She wasn't full of drama or flashy. I hate to say it, but in a room of twenty people probably no one would notice if she was standing there. I can't imagine anyone wanting to kill her. And I sure as hell didn't kill her."

"Did Nina have a life insurance policy?" Nash asked.

The flush that had started to dissipate spread back up his neck and chin. "She's got a policy, but it's not a big deal.

Just a hundred thousand dollars. She had it long before we got married."

"Are you the beneficiary?" Nash asked.

"Last time I checked," Roy said. "Are we done here?"

"I'm sure we'll have some follow-ups once we check out your timeline," Nash said. "When do you go on shift next?"

"I don't know," Roy said. "The chief told me to take a couple weeks of leave and take care of whatever I needed to take care of."

Nash passed him a card. "Make sure you stick around. Call me if you think of anything."

7

THE LONG LIGHT OF THE SUMMER DAY HAD FINALLY stretched into darkness, and I looked down to see the time illuminated on my watch. There wasn't much more we could do for the night, and the day was starting to catch up with me. I could feel the knots in my shoulders and the tightness in my back.

Nash had decided to drive the tissue and blood samples to the lab in Richmond in the morning and wait for the results since time was of the essence when you were dealing with cyanide, which meant Jack and I were left to run down any leads.

I hadn't planned on Jack being at the Walsh house when the warrants were served, otherwise I would've driven myself in the Suburban. I couldn't exactly ask Nash to drop me off at the house with Jack standing right there, so I sucked it up and went around to the passenger side of his Tahoe.

I could've sworn I saw his lips twitch as he unlocked the doors and got in. Jack and I handled fights very differently.

I had a tendency to isolate myself and let my anger fester until I exploded. Jack liked to antagonize and draw me back into the fight, but not so we could necessarily resolve anything.

I'll admit that I didn't really want to fight with Jack. I missed him. And I knew the fight came from frustrations on both of our parts—things that were completely out of our control. We'd work it out. Eventually.

"How's Carver?" I asked. I kept my gaze straight ahead. It was easier that way.

Jack started the car and pulled away from the Walsh house before he answered. "He's stable. They took him back into surgery this morning and he did well. His chances are looking better and better. He's got another surgery in the morning and another tomorrow afternoon."

I sighed and felt the knot in my chest release a little. You had to be alive to go to surgery, and as horrific as his injuries were, Carver could still be put back together so he could live a normal life. I felt guilt for getting so caught up in Nina Walsh and the autopsy that I'd momentarily forgotten about Carver.

"Speaking of Carver," Jack said. "I set Michelle up in the guest room and told her to get a good night's sleep. She's exhausted."

I felt bad for being glad that Carver's wife was staying with us. She was just another buffer between me and Jack. Between her and the cops keeping an eye on us, we wouldn't be spending a lot of alone time together and the opportunities to discuss personal things would be scarce.

"What do you think about Roy Walsh?" I asked.

Jack grunted and turned onto Heresy Road. "I think he's a narcissistic jackass who was probably torture to live with. But I'm not sure he killed his wife."

"Really?" I was surprised by that response. "He seems like exactly the kind of person who'd kill her like that and expect to get away with it."

"I don't know," Jack said. "Something just plays wrong about it. It's more of a gut feeling. He's a control freak. A bully. Arrogant. He definitely has a temper. A guy like that doesn't seem like the type of person to poison his wife. I want to talk to the girlfriend and the business partners. Get a better picture of what he's really like."

"That poison could've been in anything," I said. "It's going to be hard to track it down."

"They collected every pill bottle and hand lotion in the house. Nash will get answers. He's like a pit bull with a bone between his teeth when he wants to be."

"So I discovered," I said.

Jack pulled into our driveway, and there was an unfamiliar dark blue Explorer in the driveway with rental car plates. There were no police cars in sight.

"Martinez is inside, and he's staying through the night. His POV is in the garage."

"The overtime has to be costing a fortune," I said.

"We've got the budget in the surplus account now," he said. "Thank God that tax passed in November. It went into effect April 1, and it's already given us the bump we've needed. I've been able to hire new deputies, and we're in desperate need of a weapons upgrade and a new fleet of cars. That's on my list for the end of the year."

"You don't think the council will be upset at the spending?"

"I don't really care," he said. "That's the good thing about being sheriff. The council is not in charge of the department and they can't control what we do with the budget. I'm elected just like they are, and I'll run my department how I see fit."

I raised my brows and snuck a look at Jack from the corner of my eye. He didn't normally let his frustrations show when dealing with the political side of his job. While the council didn't have any control, Jack had always been diplomatic enough to listen to their concerns and see if there were nuggets of wisdom buried somewhere in the conversation.

The council hated that they didn't control the sheriff's department, and if it were up to them, the position of sheriff wouldn't be elected at all. They'd much prefer to appoint one of their old cronies and tell him what to do.

"Wow, where'd that come from?" I asked.

"The council is going to propose a vote next month for each city in the county to have its own police department. It's a nightmare waiting to happen, and it's going to cost a fortune that they don't have."

"The people in King George aren't stupid," I said. "No one is going to vote for that, no matter how much Ernie Rodgers tries to convince them. He's just sore because he couldn't beat you for sheriff when you first got elected.

And even if they do create their own police agencies, maybe that'll take some of the workload off you. Like you said, you're still in control and that tax has already passed, so you've really set the department up to be financially solvent. They're just jealous. And in the end, they still won't be able to control you or the choices you make for the department. No one is going to beat you in the election. No one has even officially put their name on the ballot."

"Ha," he said, shaking his head. "Never say never. There's a lot of time between now and November. And don't think that I haven't noticed that you're avoiding any serious discussion about last night."

"Takes one to know one," I said, feeling very mature.

He got out of the Tahoe and I blew a raspberry at him. And then I grabbed my bag and followed him into the house.

The shutters were all closed at the front of the house so no one could see inside, and though the temperature was still warm, I couldn't help but shiver. Locks and blinds had never stopped Malachi.

I loved our home. I'd loved it even before it had been mine. It felt like home, and Jack had built it for that purpose alone. He'd wanted a place that was a sanctuary. That would make whatever he'd seen or dealt with while on the job disappear the moment he stepped through the door. Now it was our sanctuary, and I hated Malachi for making it feel less like one.

It was a three-story rustic log cabin, built so it looked like it was part of the trees and cliffs around it. The entire back of the house was nothing but windows, and the drop-off down to the Potomac and the trees that seemed to grow sideways out of the cliffs was an awesome sight to see. The view was spectacular from every direction. And I had to wonder what my dad thought about the view from the outside looking in. I could feel his eyes on us.

I hung my bag on the hook in the foyer and ignored the mail someone had put in the bowl on the front table. Jack moved toward the den where I could hear the indistinct rumbles of the TV, and I assumed Martinez was in there.

I headed back to the kitchen to see what I could find to eat. The two pieces of leftover pizza I'd eaten before we'd gone to interview Roy Walsh were no longer cutting it.

The kitchen was the heart of the house, and it was open to the living room and a dining room we only used at Christmas and Thanksgiving. It was a mix of wood, stone, and heavy timbers on the ceiling. It was a kitchen built for someone who knew what they were doing in the kitchen, which was not me, but cooking was Jack's escape and he was good at it. The appliances were state of the art, and he even had fresh herbs growing on the windowsill.

I made my way to the fridge and looked inside. I'd had nothing to drink but coffee all day long, and I figured my body could probably use some water. I got a bottle of water and then bent down to the freezer to grab a frozen dinner, but I put it back. It didn't look appetizing, and I wasn't all that sure I was hungry anyway. My stomach was in knots. It had been a long two days.

It wasn't until I turned around that I noticed the tiny woman sitting in the breakfast nook, staring at me intently. She was wearing baggy gray sweats, and I could see the bump of her stomach beneath the table. She held a steaming cup in her hand with the string from the tea bag hanging over the side.

Her white-blond hair was cut pixie short and her eyes were so dark they were almost black. It was an arresting combination. She had the most beautiful alabaster skin I'd ever seen. She definitely didn't look like the mother of almost four, or someone tough enough to handle what she'd been through the last couple of days.

Her mouth twitched once and then it turned into a smile and she said, "I would've said something when you came in, but you were having a pretty good conversation with yourself. I didn't want to interrupt."

I must've been more tired than I thought. I had a tendency to talk to myself and not realize I was doing it.

"Apparently, I do that sometimes. I hope I didn't say anything too interesting."

"Only something about hardheaded, insensitive men. Other than that, I only caught the occasional swear word."

I lifted my eyebrows in surprise and pinched my lips tight. "Don't tell anyone that part, okay? My jar is almost full, and I've been doing pretty good lately. For the most part." I pointed to the mason jar on the kitchen counter that was three-quarters of the way full of quarters.

"Where does the money go?" she asked.

"It was going to go to the local food bank, but I'm thinking about just putting it in a sock and bashing my husband over the head with it."

She laughed full out at that, and I walked over to the table and scooted onto the bench across from her. "I'm convinced that the reason women are so strong is because they have to deal with men. But killing him probably isn't the answer. You look like you need a glass of wine and a massage."

"Now that's a much better idea," I said. "But I'm too tired to get it, and I'm afraid if I do get it I'll fall asleep at the table and miss this excellent conversation. You must be Michelle."

"And you must be Dr. Graves."

"Jaye," I said.

She nodded. "I feel like I know you. Ben talks about you all the time. Between you and Miranda, I'm never sure who I should be jealous of."

"Definitely Miranda," I said. "Their relationship is not normal."

"That's what I'm talking about," she said, holding both hands up. "I've actually had to tell him she can't sleep with us in the bed. Of course, maybe if I'd let him put her in the bed we wouldn't have had four children in five years," she said with laughter in her eyes,

There were shadows beneath her eyes, and I could see the grief she was trying so desperately to keep hidden.

"Ben's been a good friend to Jack. And to me," I said softly. "I'm so sorry about what happened. I don't know how much Ben or Jack have told you…"

"Enough to know that it's not your fault," she said, reaching out a hand and putting it on mine. I wasn't normally comfortable with outward displays of affection, but I was touched by her sincerity. I should've been the one comforting her. "Ben and I don't keep secrets from each other. I don't know if Ben's ever told you what I do…"

"He mentioned you have a PhD in English," I said.

"Well, that's kind of an understatement." She rolled her eyes.

"If it makes you feel better," I said. "He mostly talks about how hot you are and how lucky he is that you sleep with him. And he seems confused about how you keep ending up pregnant, so you might want to have a talk with him about that."

She laughed again. "That does make me feel better. Thanks." She squeezed my hand and then let it go. "Anyway, I do have a PhD in English, but I got it because I wasn't really sure what I wanted to do with my life. I also have a PhD in finance, and I speak several languages. It turns out a PhD in English doesn't really open up a lot of job prospects, so I work as a financial analyst for the FBI. In other words, I follow the money for domestic terror organizations."

I felt my mouth drop open in surprise. "Yeah, that's a long way from the English professor I assumed you were. He told you about my father?" I asked.

"He did," she said. "But I knew about your father long before he came back from the dead. I want you to know you can trust me. Just like you trust Ben. I know your father wasn't working alone. There was too much money going in and out through his and your mother's operation for them to facilitate everything themselves."

"He told you about the flash drives too?" I asked.

"He told me what your father told you," she said. "That his freedom relied on those flash drives and whatever was on them. And believe me, I'm just as interested to find out what's on them as you are, because I've followed his activities for years and was part of the team wrapping him up in a nice tidy bow before he drove over that cliff. If your father is caught, I can guarantee there's not any freedom in his future."

"No," I said. "I would imagine not. But I don't know what he meant when he said it. If you were part of the team to bring him down, then why have you agreed to keep quiet about his return from the dead?"

"Because there are people over my head involved and they're just as guilty as Malachi. We've got to find out what's on those flash drives. It's our only hope of bringing everyone down. It's time for the FBI to clean house from top to bottom."

I snorted out a laugh. "I'm not sure the FBI can take any more black marks. They've been taking hits for the last couple of years, and the same people are still at the top or they've had untimely deaths."

"They've been autonomous for too long. We all believe in a system of checks and balances, but the people running the FBI and the CIA have forgotten that. They're above the law, and they've been doing it so long they truly believe that. There are a lot of good agents left in the Bureau. In fact, most of us just want to do the right things and what's best for the country. It might make a dirty mark on us all, but it's time to right a lot of wrongs."

"Do you know how the CIA fits into this?" I asked. "From what we've found out so far, Malachi was working in some capacity for the CIA. I'm not sure exactly what he did though."

Michelle smiled and took a sip of tea. "Your dad was working in some capacity for a lot of agencies and a lot of different countries. He sold secrets when it benefitted him. And he smuggled weapons and anything else if the price was right. The only person your dad really worked for was himself. No matter what he tells you, he's not innocent in this. I've studied him, and he's a master manipulator. A professional liar. There was a reason he lasted as long as he did doing the kind of work he was doing."

"And my mom?" I asked.

"Honestly," she said, putting down her cup. "I think she got pulled into something she never planned on. Her background doesn't suggest that she was recruited by any agency. They both grew up in Bloody Mary, though he was several years older. And when she came home for Christmas break in her sophomore year of college, it looks like he pursued her hard and she never went back to school. He'd already taken over the funeral home from his parents at that point, so he was in place. And he had a young, impressionable wife at his side.

"I'm sure he told her they were the good guys. I'm sure she believed him. At least at first. There comes a point when you know too much and you either have to keep going along the path of what's wrong, or you have to cut your losses and hope no one kills you as you try to escape."

"Whelp," I said, blowing out a breath. "That's pretty much

what I needed to know. I don't know much about their past. I barely remember my grandparents, and it's not like anyone was interested in sharing family photos or anything. I found out more about my family when I looked in those boxes in the bunker than I ever did from someone with the last name Graves. Of course, considering they stole me from other people and passed me off as their own, I'm sure they didn't see any point in telling me about a family that wasn't really mine."

"I can help you find them if you want," she said. "Your birth parents."

I froze. It wasn't an option I'd considered. And now that I knew it was an option, I wasn't really sure how I felt about it.

"No pressure," she said, reading the shock on my face. "It's been a lot of years. It's just an option. One that's totally your choice.

"Thanks for the offer," I said, taking a long sip of water to cool my dry throat. "I'm really glad you have that English degree. It's been very helpful."

Michelle snorted out a laugh. "It comes in handy from time to time. Mostly crossword puzzles, or when I want to write a sternly worded email."

"I can very much see why you and Ben are a good match," I said.

She nodded and said, "Look. Ben is tough. He's going to be fine. I know he is. We're all going to be fine. He's got a long recovery ahead of him, and I'm going to look for a house to rent close to the hospital so the girls and I can stay there and be close to Ben. I can work remotely. All I need is my laptop. And my mother will come help me out once the baby comes. It's going to be a logistical nightmare, but at the end of the day it doesn't matter because my husband is alive."

There was an inner strength in her that made me want to cry. I'd noticed women were experts at finding that strength whenever it was most needed.

"You're a lot stronger than you look," I said.

She rolled her eyes. "When you've known Ben Carver as long as I have you learn how to hop from train to train without getting flattened by them. We need to know what's on those flash drives, and there aren't very many people in the world who are as good as Ben on a computer."

"And I'd venture to say most probably aren't very trustworthy," I said.

"With great power comes great responsibility," she said, using the Spider-Man quote. "And it's easy to abuse when you've got that much talent in the tips of your fingers."

"You are definitely Ben's wife," I said.

"Sorry, it's hard for the nerd to not rub off a little. If I start sleeping with my computer then I'll know things have gone too far."

"I'm assuming the ones who are reputable also have a high price tag?" I asked.

"I know someone," she said. "He's actually Ben's nephew. But he's a little unorthodox."

"Unorthodox I can deal with," I said. "Is he expensive?"

"Is who expensive?" Jack asked, coming into the kitchen. He'd changed clothes and wore a pair of athletic shorts and a threadbare Nationals T-shirt. He looked good and he knew it. The jerk.

He moved effortlessly between the fridge and cabinets, getting out a few things and setting them on the counter. I couldn't take my eyes off him. He was so easy to watch, not only because of his looks, but just because of the way he moved. There was a poetic grace to every movement, but he was always alert and watching, waiting for the unexpected.

"Michelle thinks she knows someone who might be able to get into the flash drives," I said.

Jack brought a tray of crackers, cheese, and grapes and set it in the middle of the table. "Eat," he said to Michelle. "Feed that kid. If she's anything like Carver she's probably wanting to eat every half hour."

"It might not be a she," Michelle said. "We're waiting to find out the sex."

"You and I both know it's another girl. It's what Carver deserves."

Michelle grinned a little mischievously. "It's definitely a girl."

I scooted over on the bench so Jack could sit next to me, and the warmth of his leg against mine made me momentarily forget why I was mad at him.

"You didn't tell me what Michelle does for a living," I said, looking at Jack. I took a grape and popped it in my mouth, figuring it was as close to wine as I was going to get.

"That's because I don't really know. Ben never goes into any detail and I don't ask."

Michelle picked up a cracker, but she didn't eat it as she filled Jack in on what she did for the FBI and the history she had with my dad. Then she told him about Ben's nephew.

"His name is Doug," she said. "Like I was telling Jaye, he's a little unorthodox. But he's brilliant."

"As long as he can do the job, I don't care how unorthodox he is," Jack said. "When can he get here? I'm hoping those flash drives will give us a clue as to where Malachi is hiding or how to catch him."

"I'll have to call and check with his mom," Michelle said. "The biggest problem is going to be not setting off any red flags in the system as soon as there's activity about Malachi. We don't want the wrong people to know he's alive. You'll have a swarm of agents on both of you before you can blink."

"Wait a second," I said. "You have to call his mom?"

"He's fifteen," she said. "As long as you have plenty of junk food and soft drinks he'll make himself right at home."

Jack rubbed his eyes with his fingers and I could sense his frustration. "I can't put a fifteen-year-old kid at risk," he said. "Look what happened to Ben."

"You've got security inside the house, and I know you have it outside too, even if I can't see them. I've spent most of my career trying to pin Malachi Graves down. I want him just as much as you do. More now that my husband is lying in the hospital. I knew some of the agents who got caught in the crosshairs of his betrayals. This is personal for everyone."

There was a lot more to Michelle Carver than met the eye. She might look delicate, but I'd hate to cross her.

"Just think about it," she said. "I've got to go to bed. I want to be up early to go to the hospital before Ben's surgery. And from what Martinez told me about the lady who was poisoned, you both have a busy day too."

"Small-town life," Jack said, smiling.

"Sounds like big-town problems," she said. "Thanks for the snack. My stomach is still in knots, even though I know Ben's going to be okay. I just need a decent night's sleep, and I'll be back on track tomorrow."

"You're not alone," Jack told her, reaching out a hand to touch hers. "Ben's family. Which means you're family. Whatever you need, we'll make sure you get it."

She nodded and squeezed his hand, and then hefted her bulk out of the seat.

Jack blew out a breath. "What the hell are we going to do with a fifteen-year-old computer hacker?"

"Feed him snacks and hope he has a little bit of his uncle's charm," I said.

8

I woke up in the right room the next morning, and in the right bed, but things weren't back to normal.

My conversation with Jack had been brief the night before, both of us avoiding the elephant in the room. He'd gone off to talk to Martinez, and I'd put away the food and gone to bed. I didn't remember him coming up, but his side of the bed was messed up, so I assumed it was him who'd slept there.

The space was empty now, and the sheets were cold, but there was a cup of coffee sitting on the nightstand. I narrowed my eyes in suspicion. What was he playing at?

It was still shy of seven, and the sun was shining through the windows of our third-floor bedroom.

"Gah," I said. I squinted and pulled the pillow over my face.

I'd lowered the blackout shades before I'd gone to bed, but I was guessing Jack had raised them when he'd woken.

I didn't have the energy to think too hard about what Jack was playing at, so I rolled out of bed and reached for the coffee. The first sip tasted like ambrosia. It just made me realize how bad my own was. And Nash's hadn't been much better.

My feet hit the floor and I shuffled into the bathroom to shower and get ready for the day. Jack hadn't filled me in on who we'd be interviewing first, but if we had to make the half-hour drive to Nottingham, I was guessing he'd want to start with Gina Garcia and then we'd work our way back toward Bloody Mary. Jack was nothing if not efficient.

I took a quick shower and did my morning routine, and then I went to stand in the large walk-in closet Jack and I shared. My wardrobe wasn't spectacular. It consisted of a lot of jeans and T-shirts on the casual side of things, and a lot of black dress clothes, which was an occupational hazard of owning a funeral home.

Since I had to talk to live people today I pulled out a pair of black leggings, a black-and-white sleeveless pinstripe silk shirt—because it was going to be hotter than Hades—and a lightweight black suit jacket. My black ballet flats finished off the outfit. I'd figured out the art of a messy ponytail from a YouTube video, so I pulled my hair up, slathered on my moisturizer and put on lip-gloss.

It was still shy of eight when I went down to the kitchen. Jack was sitting at the bar with his own cup of coffee and talking on the phone, so I went to the coffeepot to fill my to-go cup. I watched him out of the corner of my eye. He was wearing jeans, a white dress shirt and a gray sports coat. I could see the bulge from his holster beneath his jacket.

"We're heading out now," Jack said into the phone. "I'll keep you posted. Let me know what you find out about the samples." And then he hung up without saying goodbye.

"Was that Nash?" I asked.

"Yeah. He'll be at the lab by the time they open. You ready to roll?"

"Ready as I'll ever be," I said, snapping the lid on my cup.

The conversation was stiff and stilted between us. There was no good-morning kiss or affectionate touch. It felt like we were two strangers living in the same space.

"I figure we'll see if we can run down Gina Garcia," he said. "She's a bartender at Rick's on the River in King George. She works the dinner crowd, so she should be home."

"I'm sure she's an early riser," I said sarcastically. I grabbed my bag from the hook and my sunglasses from the table, and I followed Jack out to the Tahoe.

"Is Martinez still here?" I asked.

"He took Michelle to the hospital to see Carver a couple of hours ago. Cross is inside now, and I've got a unit making pass-byes every hour."

"Who's Cross?" I asked.

"New guy," he said. "John Cross. I've got five new hires from other counties I've been able to bring in with the new budget increase. They're all experienced, and they were all looking to move to an area with less violent crime, so I had them hook up with their field-training officers last week to learn the ropes. They're ready to go solo now. It gives me extra bodies to put in the protection rotation. I'll have about five more fresh from the academy in a few months."

"Make sure you tell the newbies I'm your wife so no one pulls me over."

"I sent out a photo on their first day and told them you're the one in the black Suburban who drives like a bat out of hell. They've all been warned."

"Thank you. What about the kid?" I asked. "Any word on him?"

"Michelle said she'd call her sister-in-law this morning. From what I understand, it's just a formality. Doug might be a minor, but he pretty much does what he wants. His body hasn't caught up with his brain yet."

"That sounds promising," I said.

"Doug is Ben's sister's son. Apparently, the dad walked out when the kid was a couple of years old and hasn't been back since. Joanie, that's Ben's sister, has busted her tail teaching school in the daytime and working part-time at some craft shop in the evenings to make ends meet. That doesn't leave Doug with a lot of supervision."

"I'm getting the feeling from your story that Doug needs a lot of supervision," I said.

"Doug is a certified savant. His IQ is off the charts, and he graduated high school a couple of years ago. He's enrolled at Georgetown in the online program and starts grad school in the fall."

"I feel like an underachiever," I said.

"He needs to stay busy. An idle mind is the devil's handiwork."

I snorted out a laugh.

"No, really," he said. "Doug hacked into the Pentagon when he was nine years old and the U.S. Treasury when he was eleven. He did a little rearranging of some financial accounts, and he got himself put on house arrest for a couple of years and is on every watch list known to man. We're lucky because the kid lives in Williamsburg. If he leaves the state he has to alert the authorities."

"Oh, good," I said. "We've got a teenage felon coming to visit who eats like a Gremlin. This should be fun."

"As long as he can do what we need him to do," Jack said. "I'll feed him whatever he wants."

"You don't think they're going to notice he's disappeared from his home?"

"Between Michelle and Doug, they can make it look like he's there," he said. "I'm guessing Michelle's no slouch on a computer. We'll have a few days with him at least."

It was almost a half-hour drive to Nottingham, and I was finally starting to wake up about fifteen minutes into the drive.

"You still haven't told me where you've put the flash drives you got from Ben," I said.

"No."

"You're not going to?" I asked.

"I figure it's safer this way," he said. "Never put your eggs all in one basket."

I didn't know what to say to that, so I turned the radio on low for the rest of the trip.

Gina Garcia lived in the Sherbrook Heights neighborhood of Nottingham. Nottingham was the second biggest city in the county, and it was a big industrial area with a lot of plants and manufacturing buildings on the south side of the river. There were a lot of restaurants and bars on the north side of the river.

Gina's neighborhood was mostly apartment complexes and manufactured homes. There weren't a lot of trees like in Bloody Mary, and the grass was mostly brown because of the direct sunlight.

Jack turned right next to an outdoor basketball court surrounded by a chain-link fence, but it was empty at this time of the morning. Up ahead of us was a gated complex with four apartment buildings inside it. The gate was open, so Jack drove through.

"She's in building four," he said, finding a visitor's parking spot.

"I can feel about a dozen eyes on us," I said.

"That's because there's at least that many watching us. This neighborhood is no stranger to cops. We get calls out here all the time. Mostly drugs or domestic violence."

I followed him along cracked sidewalks until we reached a cloudy pool surrounded by a white iron fence. The number four was on the outside of the building, and I looked at the zigzag of stairs all the way to the fourth floor.

"She lives at the top, doesn't she?" I asked.

Jack looked over his shoulder and grinned. "Yep."

"It figures we'd be that lucky." It was already warm outside, and I was glad I was in sensible shoes.

I was only huffing a little when we got to the top, a fact I was pretty proud of considering I hated to exercise and I mostly sustained myself on coffee and gluten. Jack wasn't out of breath at all and looked as perfect as he had when we left the house. I felt wilted from the inside out, and hoped my messy ponytail had held up through the ordeal.

Jack knocked three times on the ugly brown door of apartment 408. Then he did it again a couple of minutes later.

Jack looked like a cop. It didn't matter what he wore or what mundane circumstance he found himself in. If I saw him standing at my door, I'd be hesitant to answer too.

"Gina Garcia," Jack said through the door. "This is the police. Open up."

"She's probably sleeping," I said.

"She's standing on the other side of the door," he said. "I saw her look through the peephole."

I heard the locks snick open and a chain unlatch, and Gina cracked the door open.

Jack held up his badge and said, "I'm Sheriff Lawson. We need to ask you some questions."

"Geez," she said. "What do you want? People are going to think I'm trouble with the cops showing up here. The landlord will kick me out."

Gina was what some would call a brick house of a woman. She was Latina with dark bedroom eyes and full lips, and she was all curves and sexy as hell, even though she'd clearly just rolled out of bed. She was wearing a silk floral robe that barely covered the essentials and she was sporting a fairly recent shiner.

"I've got to work tonight," she said. "I need to go back to sleep." She tried to close the door, but Jack's booted foot was in the way.

"We'd really appreciate it if you'd let us come inside," he said. "It'll be a lot easier than having to do it at the station."

She narrowed her eyes, but knew she didn't have any other choice, so she stepped back and opened the door wide so we could come inside.

I was surprised by the inside of the apartment. Gina took care of what she had, and she had a flair for design. Brightly colored pillows littered the couch and purple sheers hung in the corners of the tiny living room. Different sizes of pillar candles covered almost every flat surface.

"We can wait if you want to get dressed," Jack said.

"Hell, no," she said, tossing long black hair over her shoulder. "And give you an excuse to snoop around my place? What's this about?"

"Roy Walsh," Jack said.

Gina froze and her eyes darted over to me. "Who are you?" she asked.

"I'm Dr. Graves," I said. "I'm the coroner for the county."

"Did something happen to Roy?" she asked. Her eyes went wide and she took a step back.

"No, but Roy's wife was murdered. We need to ask you some questions."

She put a hand to her ample chest and breathed out a sigh of relief. "You had me worried. I thought something had happened to Roy."

"It doesn't bother you that someone killed his wife?" Jack asked.

"I didn't know her," she said. "I can't pretend to feel something for someone I never knew." She went over to an emerald-green Papasan chair in the corner and curled up in it like a cat, pulling a turquoise throw over her lap.

Jack and I moved toward the couch and didn't wait for an invitation to sit down.

"I'm surprised Roy didn't tell you about his wife," Jack said.

"I'm not taking his calls at the moment," she said.

"He mentioned that he came out to see you yesterday morning," I said.

"Yeah, that's two mornings in a row I haven't gotten to sleep," she said. "So what if he came to see me? He's here all the time."

"He told us you called his wife and told her about the baby."

Gina shrugged and her robe slipped off her shoulder. "So what? Is that a crime? I know that bastard Roy has money.

Not from firefighting, but from that other business he has. I just wanted to make sure I'd be taken care of. I figured the best way to make sure of that was to tell the wife. From what Roy said about her, she seemed like the real conscientious type."

"Well, now she's the dead type," Jack said. "Roy says his wife was alive when he left her. What time did he get here?"

"I dunno. I had a little trouble seeing the clock," she said, pointing to her eye.

"He gave you that?" I asked.

"He barely waited until I had the door open," she said. "Which is why I'm not taking his calls. He called me a bunch of names and told me I was a liar, but I showed him the pregnancy test. I took three of them. He started to wind down and then I kicked him out. I don't need that in my life. He was starting to get stale anyway. Married men are a pain in the ass."

I raised my brow at that, but I didn't say anything.

"What did you do after he left?" Jack asked.

"I got a bag of ice for my eye and then went back to bed. I turned my phone off. I don't work Sundays, so I didn't have to be anywhere."

"Have you ever been to Roy's house?" Jack asked.

"Never," she said. "I don't even know his address. I usually met him in King George at his office. I didn't spend a lot of time with Roy outside of my bedroom or his office, you know? It's not like we were dating. It was purely physical."

"Is there anyone who can corroborate your whereabouts yesterday?" Jack asked.

"You think I killed Roy's wife?" she asked, and then burst into laughter. We waited while she finished and then she wiped her eyes. "Man, that's a good one. Look, I don't do serious entanglements. Just ask anybody. There's no man worth killing over. Guys like Roy are a dime a dozen. I like my life just how it is, and now I've gotta worry about bringing a kid into it. I don't need any more problems."

"Do you think Roy's capable of killing his wife?" I asked.

"Roy's got a temper," she said. "Sure he's capable. But they had a really weird marriage. He, like, worshipped her or something. It was creepy the way he talked about her."

Jack handed her a card with his number on it. "Let me know if you think of anything else," he said. "And call if you feel like Roy is a threat to you. We'd prefer not to have any more bodies show up."

"I'd prefer that too. Good luck."

We left Gina in her chair and showed ourselves out.

9

FIREHOUSE MOVERS WAS IN KING GEORGE PROPER, AND since Roy and his partners were all shift mates and they didn't go back on shift until Tuesday, the plan was to catch them at the office. We made good time coming from Gina's place, and Jack pulled through a Starbucks drive-thru to replenish our tanks.

"You should drink more water," he said, handing me my cup and then opening his bottled water.

"You should mind your own beeswax," I told him.

He snorted out a laugh and then asked, "Do you need to be back at a certain time?"

"I've still got Carl Planter in the cooler, and I'm still waiting to hear from the city about what day they want to do Mrs. McGowen's memorial service."

Rosalyn McGowen had been an influential member of the community for decades, and she didn't have any remaining family so the city was stepping in to make sure she had a proper send-off and burial. It would be a simple affair since we'd had to cremate her on account of her cats had eaten her.

"Carl's family is from Atlanta, so they're making arrangements to have him transported back home for burial. Sheldon will take care of all of that."

Sheldon was my assistant, and he'd really made my life a lot easier, especially since my job as coroner had ramped up over the past few months.

"I think Gina was right," I said as we took the exit off the highway. "It looks like their side business is doing well."

"Well, Gina strikes me as the kind of person who gets what she wants and sets personal goals of a certain caliber. She's probably twenty-two, twenty-three years old. She won't be in that run-down apartment complex forever."

It was hard to miss the Firehouse Movers building. It was a bright red metal structure with a giant wooden cutout of three men in their fire gear moving a sofa on top of the building. There was a matching billboard at the highway exit. There were moving trucks parked at the back that matched the billboard and I could see the phone number to call all the way from the highway.

There was a truck, a Jeep, and a little compact car out front, and I was pretty sure the truck and the Jeep were the same ones that sat in Roy's driveway the day before.

Jack parked and I got out of the Tahoe and pushed my sunglasses on top of my head. The front door of the building opened before we could get to it, and a man who looked vaguely familiar stood there.

"Hey, Sheriff," he said. "Thought you might be coming by. Come on in."

Jack shook hands with the guy and said, "Thanks, Walker. We won't take up much of your time. This is Dr. Graves."

"Chance Walker," he said. He was a big guy, several inches over six feet, and he was in good shape. His hair was blond and well cut and his smile a blinding white. He had frat boy written all over him, but he was personable and probably good for business.

I held out my hand to shake his. "Nice to meet you."

"Likewise," he said. "I've enjoyed reading about you in the paper. Looks like you've been busy lately."

"I've definitely been busy, but I don't read the paper. The stories have a tendency to be inflated."

Floyd Parker had been a blight on society since birth. Unfortunately, he and I had a past, and he never let me forget it. Unfortunately, Floyd had the *King George Gazette* as his platform.

"Floyd Parker is a horse's ass," Walker said. "But no one takes him too seriously. I notice he didn't write a story about how you punched him in the face."

I grinned at that. "I take interfering with an investigation seriously."

"I'll remember that," he said and ushered us inside.

There was nothing special about the inside of the building. It was a simple structure with utilitarian gray carpet and light gray walls. There was a counter for customers and a woman sitting behind it on a barstool typing on a computer.

There was a door on each side of the counter, and the one on the left was a bathroom, so I assumed the one on the right led to the back of the building.

"We've actually got a couple of trucks out this morning doing a big move," Walker said, "but we've got enough employees now that we don't have to be on every job. This is Shirleen. She keeps us organized."

Shirleen nodded and then went back to her computer. She was somewhere in her mid-forties, wore her makeup heavy, and her hair big. She looked like she didn't take crap from anybody.

"Y'all can come on back to my office," he said, leading us through the door to the right side of the counter. There was a long hallway with a series of doors on the left and a glass door at the very end that led to the truck lot at the back. "Gabe's on a phone call, but he'll be in as soon as he can. Do you want water or anything?"

"We're fine," Jack answered. "Do you mind if we look at Roy's office first?"

"Sure," Walker said, leading us to the third door on the left. "Your guys called us last night to serve the warrant, so they've already been inside. I came out to unlock the doors for them."

"We appreciate it," Jack said.

"Hey, I know how these things go," he said. "Best thing to do is to cooperate. We've got a business to run."

The door wasn't locked and Walker turned the knob and pushed the door open. I felt a chill rise across my skin the second I passed over the threshold. I seriously had my doubts that it was Nina who had a schedule and a place for everything.

The room was cold, just like the house had been. The walls were white and unadorned. Not one picture or personal item could be found. The desktop held a pencil sharpener, and a stapler. Everything was precisely aligned. There was a bookshelf with several three-inch binders, and they'd all been labeled by name and year with a label maker.

"Does it always look like this?" I asked.

"Oh, yeah," Walker said. "Roy hates clutter of any kind. His nickname at the station is Mr. Clean. His locker and everything are always in order. He gets really upset if something is out of place. Back when he was a rookie the older guys used to move his stuff just for the hell of it, but they laid off after a couple of rounds of broken noses and stitches."

"Yikes," I said.

We left Roy's office and followed Walker into the office next door. It was the same size as Roy's, but it couldn't have looked more different. The walls were painted a soft gray, and he had lots of pictures—mostly of him on the golf course or hunting big game. There were knickknacks and old fire trucks set on top of the shelves, and his bookshelf was full of well-read paperbacks with creased spines. I saw one small-framed photograph of him with a pretty woman and small child.

"Y'all have a seat," Walker said, moving behind his desk to sit in the chair there. "We just couldn't believe it when we got the news about Nina. I don't know how Roy's going to get through it. He worshipped her."

"Did Roy tell you it was homicide?" I asked.

"He mentioned that when I talked to him last night," Walker said. "He called and let us know you'd probably be stopping by. He said someone poisoned her. I can tell you right now there's no way Roy did something like that."

"He came into shift late on Saturday?" Jack asked.

Walker blew out a breath. "Yeah, well," he said. "I know that doesn't look good for Roy. But I'm sure he told you the reason. Gina's never been anything but trouble for any guy at the station. I tried to warn him, but..." He shrugged and gave us that "boys will be boys" look. "I'll tell you one thing, I'd bet my whole salary she isn't pregnant."

"You talking about Gina?" a man asked from the doorway.

He was a couple of inches taller than me, maybe five ten, and his head was shaved to cover his natural baldness. He had a short dark beard that was flecked with gray. He was muscular and stocky, and he wore khakis and a red Fire-house Movers polo with the logo over the breast pocket.

"Hey, Sheriff," he said, coming to shake Jack's hand. "Don't get up." And then he turned to me and introduced himself. "Gabe Roland."

"Dr. Graves," I said.

"I recognize your picture from the paper," he said, leaning against the edge of Walker's desk. "Heard all about how you punched Floyd Parker in that smug face of his. He's a horse's ass."

I couldn't help it. I smiled again. I was starting to think

maybe the guys at the firehouse weren't all that bad after all.

"You know Gina?" I asked.

Gabe put both hands over his heart and gave an aggrieved look. "I'm just one of many hearts she's left in the dust."

"I warned you too," Walker said, smiling. "Nobody listens."

"Gina's one of those lessons you have to learn for yourself. Of course, Roy's going to be paying for that lesson a hell of a lot longer than the rest of us."

"Nah," Walker said. "No way she's telling the truth. A kid would ruin her plans."

"Did you know Roy's wife, Nina?" Jack asked, getting the conversation back on track.

"Not really," Walker said. "First time we met her was at the wedding. Surprised the hell out of all of us. We didn't figure Roy would ever get married again."

"He was married before?" I asked.

"Yeah," Walker said. "To Caroline. She and Roy had only been divorced maybe a year before he and Nina married."

"The first wife didn't get part of Roy's share in this business?" Jack asked.

"Nah," Gabe said. "We started this place after his divorce. Actually, it was the money Nina got from her first husband's life insurance that gave us the collateral we needed."

I raised my brows at that, and felt more sorry for Nina than

I already did. Roy might not have abused her physically, or maybe he did since people rarely saw Nina. Maybe that was the reason she stayed in the house all the time. But if he didn't abuse her physically, there was no doubt in my mind he abused her verbally or emotionally. My first impression of Roy was right. He was a bully, and when he wanted something he'd strong-arm anyone he needed to so he could get what he wanted. And it was looking like he'd needed Nina for her money.

"Did Nina ever come here to see Roy?" Jack asked.

"No way," Gabe said. "This is where Roy and Gina typically meet up, so there was too big of a chance that they'd get caught. Roy and Gina weren't exactly subtle. Walker had to tell them to get a room because they were so loud in Roy's office. These walls aren't real thick. But Roy wasn't big on spending money unnecessarily, so they'd usually just go out to Roy's truck or one of the trucks parked in the back."

"He sounds like a real stand-up guy," I said.

"Hey, I trust him to have my back in a fire," Gabe said. "That's all that matters."

I figured that was debatable. I recognized the brotherhood mentality. It was the same one cops had. They'd cover for each other in their personal lives as long as they could trust each other to have their backs on the streets. It always amazed me that brotherhood trumped being a decent person. Jack recognized it for what it was, which was an excuse for getting away with things most people wouldn't get away with. It was why he liked being sheriff. Why he liked setting himself apart from the others. He learned a long time ago the brotherhood wasn't all it was cracked up to be.

"When was the last time you saw Nina?" Jack asked. "Did you notice anything odd between them?"

"The last time I saw her was at the firemen's ball. That was back in January. But we didn't speak or anything. Nina didn't really talk to anyone. She never hung out with any of the wives. Firemen's wives are usually a pretty tight group, but my wife said Nina never came to their gatherings."

"Roy's real..." Gabe couldn't seem to think of the word he was looking for. "Roy is kind of a perfectionist. He likes things how he likes them. And I guess he was kind of that way about Nina too. It was more like she was a trophy he kept up on a shelf for people to look at. He'd bring her out for special occasions, but she wasn't for everyday use. Kind of like china you only bring out for company."

"I think Roy just wanted to make sure he kept his personal life separate," Walker said. "We all have a tendency to drag our personal lives into the job. I'm sure you guys know how that is. It's hard to get a picture of them. It's like their puzzle pieces didn't really fit together. But that could be just because I never really saw them together."

"Do you think that's why Roy hooked up with Gina Garcia?" I asked. "Maybe he figured he made a mistake with Nina and he found someone he had more in common with.

Walker snorted out a laugh. "The only thing Roy and Gina had in common was sex. I guarantee she doesn't even know his last name."

Gabe broke in. "Look, Roy's never been great about monogamy. Not even with his first wife. If it wasn't Gina it would've been someone else. But I don't want to paint Roy in a bad light. He's a great guy. You couldn't ask for a better friend or teammate. He'd give you the shirt off his back."

"What about the poison?" Jack asked. "Y'all have use of all kinds of chemicals around the fire station. Anything ring a bell as far as where the cyanide came from?"

"Beats me," Walker said. "I can't think of any foams or chemicals we use that have cyanide in them. But you'd be better off checking down at the firehouse to be sure."

"Can you think of any reason Roy would kill his wife?" Jack asked. "Maybe financial troubles?"

Walker and Gabe looked at each other, but it was Walker who answered. "I can't imagine they'd be in any financial difficulties. I mean, we don't make much as public servants, but this business is very profitable. My wife and I just bought a vacation home in the Bahamas. And she stays home like Nina did."

"Maybe it was just some freak accident or something," Gabe said. "I just can't imagine Roy killing anyone."

"You should see the shiner he gave Gina when he found out about the baby," I told him. "Has Roy always had a temper?"

Walker's lips went tight at that information, but neither of them seemed surprised.

"The job affects some more than it does others," Gabe said. "It's easy to let things get bottled up and then find the closest outlet to release it all. Sometimes it's the nearest bottle of booze. Sometimes it's the nearest warm body, someone like Gina who's convenient. And sometimes fists get involved. Usually we get off shift, get a solid twelve hours of sleep and then head to the bar to blow off some steam. Drunk is a lot less complicated than the other outlets."

I was getting tired of Gabe making excuses for Roy's behavior. I guess because he kept telling us that Roy was a good guy he thought that we'd eventually believe it."

"We're not going to sit here and lie to you and say that Roy is incapable of killing someone," Walker said. "But I think if he did, there would be violence involved. Poison just seems like too easy of a way out for a guy as angry as Roy."

"What's Roy got to be angry about?" I asked.

"He and Caroline had a daughter. They lost her to leukemia several years ago," Gabe said. "That was pretty much the nail in the coffin for their marriage. And he's been pretty angry at everyone ever since then."

10

It was noon by the time we left Gabe and Walker and headed toward Marilee Hedgepeth's house. As far as we knew, she was Nina's only friend. Or at least someone she spent a regular amount of time with. Roy hadn't known her full name, but she was a Bloody Mary resident, so it hadn't been hard for Jack to track her down. No one had called to tell her about Nina's death, so Jack had been the one to break the news to her.

My mood had only darkened since we'd left Chance Walker and Gabe Roland. This whole case felt wrong. Maybe it was because the shadow of my dad was clouding the whole thing. But I didn't think so.

"What's wrong?" Jack asked. "I kept watching your face while we were in there, and I started to wonder if punching people was going to become your norm."

"No, I'm reserving all my violent tendencies for Floyd. But that doesn't mean I can't imagine it."

"Babe," Jack said. "We've talked about this. When you

imagine things, it shows up right there on your face. It's why I told you for years to stop playing poker."

"Yet you took my money anyway," I said, narrowing my eyes.

"I can't help it that you're stubborn. And it's not like you didn't benefit. I used almost all the money I won off you at poker to pay for our wedding."

"Hilarious," I said. "And just because we're talking doesn't mean I'm not still mad at you."

He sighed and rubbed the back of his neck. "One issue at a time," he said.

"You heard them," I said, feeling myself getting worked up. "Just to recap, Roy has a habit of treating women badly. He's a cheater. He's a liar. He married Nina for her money so he and his friends could open a business. He's got anger issues and punched his girlfriend in the face. He was so controlling he made Nina live like a slave in her own home, and he got upset if anything was ever out of place. But he's a good guy because he's got their backs when they're fighting fire. That's some ridiculous bullshit right there."

He opened his mouth out of habit.

"And if you say swear jar, I'm going to lose my mind," I said. "Not one person gives two craps about Nina Walsh. She was a possession. She was just there to serve Roy. It's textbook abuse. He kept her isolated. Controlled her. Demeaned her. And I bet if we check the florists in town, he buys her flowers pretty regularly. And yet, somehow, everyone is worried about Roy, even though statistics show he's probably the one who killed her."

"You're not wrong," Jack said. "Roy is a class-A asshole. His friends know it, but it's the first responder culture. I wish we could change it. It's part of the reason I went back to graduate school. I wanted to understand why people who wanted to serve the community, and hold others to a certain standard, couldn't seem to live by that standard themselves. The divorce rate is higher. Unwanted pregnancy is higher. Domestic abuse is higher. And alcoholism and drug use are higher.

"It's completely messed up. If first responders spent more time encouraging each other to do the right thing instead of promising to cover up for each other, you'd have a lot tighter, more accountable, and more trustworthy brothers. Those are the people I'd want watching my back. But it's a lot easier to keep things the same than it is to change it. That's just human nature."

"Well, it sucks," I said, sitting back in my seat. "You haven't heard anything from Nash?"

"Nothing," he said. "It'll take time. We'll talk to Marilee Hedgepeth and see if we can put more of the puzzle together. I'd like for Roy to be guilty just as much as you."

"But you don't think he is," I said.

"The truth will come out. It always does," he said. "And we know that Nina wasn't completely alone. After talking with Marilee on the phone last night I can tell you they were close, and she mourns Nina, even if no one else does."

It did make me feel better. "What about the daughter? Do you think Roy called her and told her the news?"

"I don't know, but I called and left a message with my

contact information," Jack said. "Just in case he didn't. I want to get her impression of Roy too. It's probably not coincidental that Nina's relationship with her daughter fizzled after she and Roy married."

Jack's phone rang and we both looked at the caller ID to see if it was Nash. It was a Washington number, but not one I recognized. Jack put the call through Bluetooth, so it came out through the speakers.

"Jack Lawson," he said.

"Hey, Jack. It's Michelle."

"How'd the surgery go?" he asked. "Jaye's in the car with me."

"Hi Michelle," I said.

"Hey," she said. "The surgery went really well. He goes in for another around three o'clock."

"Make sure you get some rest in between," I told her. "Stay hydrated and off your feet when you can."

"I just got the same speech from Ben's surgeon," she said. "They moved a recliner into his room for me, and my feet are up as we speak. I wanted to let you know I spoke to Doug's mother. She's headed this way to see Ben, so it actually makes sense for Doug to come with her and have an excuse to be in the area."

"Oh," Jack said. It had never dawned on either of us. "I guess it does."

"He's glad to help," she said. "He said it had been a while since he had a challenge, so he's looking forward to it."

"Glad we can give him a challenge," Jack said.

"Remember that when he gets to your house. Joanie's going to stay at the hotel by the hospital, and I told her I'd stay with her, so Doug can have the guest room at your place. I figure it'll be safer for him to stay put rather than traveling back and forth."

"Good thinking," Jack said. "What time should he arrive? I want to make sure we're at the house and I've got a couple of officers in place. I don't want to take any chances with him."

"Joanie will appreciate that," Michelle said. "Doug has a tendency to leap first and look later, so she pretty much lives in a constant state of stress. They're about an hour out."

"I'm really looking forward to meeting Doug," I said.

"Joanie would probably let you adopt him without having to persuade her too hard," Michelle said. "Oh, I almost forgot. Someone from the FBI came by while Ben was in surgery. They're wanting to get some information about the crash. He seemed especially interested in where Ben's computer was. I told him last I saw it Miranda was at home."

"You get a name?"

"Clay Hawke," Michelle said. "He's out of Ben's unit, but he's a junior agent. He's sniffing, hoping he can find something that'll make him rise through the ranks. I told him it was just an accident and there was a search for the hit-and-run driver. But he's probably going to track you down. He's not stupid, and he's got a good gut."

"Always a dangerous combination," Jack said, smiling. "Thanks for the heads-up."

"I'll send you Joanie's number so you can give her your address."

"Good," Jack said. "Get some rest."

We were back in Bloody Mary by the time he disconnected, and I noticed he was turning down a familiar road. We'd spent a lot of time driving down Oleander this past week, and I breathed a sigh of relief as we passed by Foxglove Court. The people who lived on Foxglove were probably breathing a sigh of relief too. They'd seen way too much of us lately, considering that's where Rosalyn McGowen had been murdered and eaten by her cats.

He drove to the next street and took a right onto Wolfsbane, and he stopped in front of the first house on the corner. All the houses in this part of town were built in the fifties with the exception of a few.

Marilee Hedgepeth lived in a blue craftsman house with white trim and a screened-in porch. Her flower beds reminded me of Nina's, and I wondered if the two women shared a love of gardening. Now that I thought about it, Nina's flower beds were the only inviting thing about the whole house.

A woman was standing on the front porch holding the screen door open for us before we could get out of the car.

"Sheriff Lawson?" she asked.

"Yes, ma'am," Jack said. "Thank you for seeing us. I know this has to be a difficult time for you."

Marilee was probably a good twenty years older than Nina. She was a handsome woman, with wavy hair that was silver at the roots and turned dark toward the ends just above her shoulders. She wore pearl earrings and an oversized denim shirt and jeans.

"I appreciate you calling me," she said. "The thought of Nina being gone breaks my heart. You'll never meet a sweeter woman. But I can't say I'm surprised she's gone."

"This is Dr. Graves," Jack said. "She's the coroner for the county."

"Nice to meet you," she said. "I recognize you. Y'all got married a couple of months back, didn't you?"

"Yes, ma'am," I said.

"You don't have that newlywed glow," she said, looking me up and down. "Y'all have a fight?"

I couldn't help but smile at her straightforwardness. "Yes, but it'll pass. Hazards of the job."

"I imagine it must be hard, doing what y'all do," she said. "I was married for forty years before my husband passed on a few years back. He worked at the sanitation department all his adult life, so our conversations weren't as exciting as I'm sure the two of yours are. I never had to worry about him bringing his work home with him," she said, chuckling.

Jack and I both laughed, and we followed Marilee into a sunroom. She already had a pitcher of iced tea and some cookies sitting on a platter waiting for us. The room was bright and sunny, and white fans spun lazily from the ceiling.

"Y'all have a seat," she said. "The tea is sweet, and the cookies are snickerdoodle. I made them fresh this morning."

"They smell amazing," I said, taking a seat in a white wicker chair with a yellow and blue striped cushion. Her backyard was a showpiece designed around two big oak trees. There were flowers everywhere, and a pond with a small waterfall in the back corner. It was peaceful to look at and probably the devil to maintain.

"I couldn't stop thinking about Nina last night after you called," she said, taking the seat across from us. "I want to do whatever I can to help. Nina deserves better."

"How long were you and Nina friends?" I asked her.

"Oh, I'm guessing more than ten or so years now," she said. "I kept seeing her at the nursery, buying up all the flowers." Marilee stopped and smiled as she reminisced. "She'd get lost in her own little world. She was always happy around her flowers. Talked to them and everything. She could make anything grow.

"That's what I do, by the way," she said, looking at us expectantly. "I own the nursery over on Elizabeth Street in King George. Been there thirty years, but I've got a manager to run the day-to-day things. I'm enjoying retirement."

"Sure," I said, smiling. "The Secret Garden. You always have those lovely hanging baskets out front. I love the colors."

"Bougainvillea," she said, nodding approvingly.

"I'm always tempted to stop by and get some, but I know I'd kill them. I don't have a green thumb."

"Flowers are meant to bring joy," Marilee said. She poured the iced tea and then pushed the plate of cookies toward us. I happily took one. I was starving. "And if they die, then they die. And you appreciate the joy you had for a short time. You can always buy new ones."

"I'll remember that," I said. "Maybe I'll stop in after all."

"There's a girl," Marilee said approvingly. And then she looked back at Jack. "I suppose you want to know about Nina."

"I'd like to know why you weren't surprised to hear about her death," he said.

"Like I said," she started. "Nina was the sweetest thing. Tiny as a fairy. And she had this naïve innocence about her. She looked like she was barely out of school, but she had a teenager she brought with her some days. Looked just like her. Lord, it broke Nina's heart when Hailey stopped talking to her. She'd already been through so much when she lost her husband, and Hailey was her last connection to him. But Roy Walsh made sure he killed every bit of happiness Nina had."

"Did you meet Roy before they married?" I asked.

"No, Nina never asked me to," she said. "I think she knew deep down that she was making a mistake. I'd pick up on little things she'd say in conversation. I think she was lonely. Hailey was away at college, and Nina was left to ramble around the house she shared with Daryl by herself. She was a loan officer at the bank then. I think that's where she met Roy. He came in with his buddies wanting to get a loan for a business, and he charmed her right into marriage and giving him every penny Daryl had left her. He made her quit her job, so she only had him to rely on. It all happened so fast. There was nothing I could do but be here and listen."

"What happened with Hailey?" Jack asked.

"He got better at the abuse the longer he did it," she said, her eyes flashing with anger. "In the early days, I don't think he realized how delicate Nina was. She was a fragile thing. She came by the house one day, and she was helping me out front in the flower beds. When she pushed her sleeves up, I could see perfect imprints of his fingers where he'd bruised her. And then there was another time I noticed because Nina rarely wears makeup, and she had on a full face of it to hide the bruise on her cheek.

"I confronted her about it then, and she broke down. That was about the same time she and Hailey had a falling out. I guess Hailey threatened to call the police on Roy, and Nina wouldn't let her. Hailey's no pushover, and she confronted Roy about it too, and told him to never lay another hand on her mother."

Marilee paused and took a drink of tea, looking out to her backyard. It was a beautiful space. Peaceful.

"Well," she said. "As you can imagine, that didn't go over too well with Roy. He told Hailey to get out and that she wasn't welcome there anymore. And he said if he ever found out that she and Nina were communicating there'd be hell to pay. Nina didn't do anything to contradict him, and I think in that moment Hailey was just as angry with her mother as she was with Roy."

"They didn't talk after that?" I asked.

"No," she said. "Not really. Nina would send Hailey gifts for Christmas and her birthday. Hailey would sometimes do the same. But Roy found one of the boxes Hailey had sent once, and Nina paid for it. Though he got a lot better about not leaving bruises on her after those first few months. But you can just tell. The woman I'd once known was completely gone. Even after Daryl died and she had the sad, helpless look in her eyes, I could still see Nina in there, and I knew she'd be okay. She just needed time to heal and to grieve. But after she met Roy, I never saw that woman again. So no, I'm not surprised at all that Nina's gone. And there's no doubt in my mind that Roy's the one responsible."

"Did she say specifically that she was ever in fear for her life?" Jack asked.

"No," Marilee said. "This was her escape. We'd visit twice a week like clockwork. She'd come on the days Roy was on shift, so she didn't have to worry about getting home and making sure the house was ready for him. You never saw a man so prissy in the way he liked things. He was like a drill sergeant, giving orders and checking to see if there was dust on the windowsills or if a bedspread was wrinkled. He was just looking for an excuse to punish her.

"But she'd come here, and we'd talk about flowers and everything but Roy. I was careful not to bring it up because I knew it upset her. But sometimes she'd say things to let me know what was going on. Or if she got something from Hailey. She started making sure she hid those gifts better."

"You've been a big help, Marilee," Jack said. "I'm glad Nina had a friend like you."

"Me too, Sheriff," she said, dabbing at her eyes with a napkin. "Do you happen to have Hailey's number? I'd like to reach out to her if I could. I don't want her to think her mother will be forgotten."

"I'll make sure you get it," Jack promised.

"Thank you," she said.

We both stood, and Marilee moved to stand with us. "Y'all can go out back here," she said, opening the sunroom door that led into the backyard. "Just follow the path around to the side of the house." Then she looked at me and smiled. "Come see me, Dr. Graves. I might be able to help you find your green thumb."

"I'd like that," I said, shaking her hand.

I followed Jack around the side of the house thinking about flowers and Nina Walsh. And I felt lighter of heart because Jack was right. Nina hadn't been completely alone. There were at least two people who loved her and who would keep her memory alive.

11

MICHELLE HAD CALLED WHILE WE'D BEEN TALKING WITH Marilee, so Jack called her back and arrangements were made for us to pick up Doug at the police station.

The town square and municipal buildings were located at the juncture of where the four corners of each town in King George met. The courthouse was Gothic in style and was surrounded by a parks and recreation project that had come in way over budget and way under delivered.

There were trees and park benches where city workers would sometimes eat lunch if the weather was nice. There was a mishmash of statues displaying the county's history —an Algonquian Indian chief, King George I, who took the land from the Algonquians, and James Madison, because he was born in King George County. There was a grouping of cannons on the corner that faced the Potomac, signifying our part in fighting during the Civil War. The occasional tourist would stop and read the markers next to all of them, but for the most part they went unnoticed.

The municipal buildings were across the street and took up the entire block. The jail, the sheriff's office, and fire station were all connected to one another. Parking was a nightmare, and there was barely room for the two fire trucks to get in and out of their slots.

Jack's parking spot was right in front of the sheriff's office, so he pulled into the vacant slot and we headed inside to get our first look at Doug. The front of the sheriff's office had glass doors that led into a small waiting area with hard plastic chairs against the walls. I didn't recognize the officer sitting behind the plexiglass wall that protected the rest of the building from the outside world. He was a little overweight and probably in his late fifties, with a round face and a few strands of hair he still valiantly tried to comb over. He looked like he was perfectly content to be sitting behind the desk, checking people in and out.

"Hey, Sheriff," the man said.

"How's it going, Hitchcock?" Jack asked.

"Nice and slow for the most part. Got a kid waiting for you in the break room. Said he was hungry, so Ramirez ordered him a pizza."

"Good thinking," Jack said. "This is Dr. Graves. Jaye, this is Arnold Hitchcock. He just came on with the new recruits."

"Nice to meet you," I said, giving him a smile.

"I've heard all about you, Doc," he said. "Word is you've got a mean right hook."

"No point in using it if it's not mean," I said.

"Isn't that the truth," he said, nodding.

Jack typed in his code on the keypad on the door that was used by personnel, and I followed him toward his office. Betsy Clement had been secretary for every sheriff King George had elected for the last forty years, and she sat like a sentinel in front of Jack's office in a three-sided cubicle.

"Hey, Sheriff," she said, looking up briefly from whatever she was typing on her computer. "Got a visitor in the break room. I put messages on your desk, but there's nothing too pressing. An FBI agent stopped by asking a bunch of questions about the wreck out by your place, but I might have misplaced his contact information."

Jack grinned. "You're a treasure."

"I know," she said. "Don't think I'm not expecting a raise with this new windfall of tax money."

"It's at the top of my list," Jack said.

He didn't stop in his office, and we made our way down the long hall that held a couple of interrogation rooms and the break room. I could hear the hoots and hollers before we even got to the room.

"This should be good," Jack said, opening the door wide.

A myriad of expressions greeted us as a mix of cops and other staff looked up from a computer monitor. The computer was sitting in front of a teenager with a red hoodie on, despite the fact it was summer and hot as Hades outside. There were empty pizza boxes spread out across the table.

Eyes widened and everyone moved back from the kid,

taking the "every man for himself" approach, and several people took the opportunity to slip around Jack and out the door as we made our way farther into the room.

"Look, Ramirez," the kid said. "You can even do this from home. It's simple. I can fix you up for a hundred bucks. I'd do it for free, but a guy's gotta eat."

"No thanks, man," Ramirez said. "I told you I wasn't interested."

"What are you talking about?" the kid said, oblivious to his surroundings. "I thought you wanted to see if she was cheating?"

"As fascinating as this sounds," Jack said, giving Ramirez a look that had the officer flushing red with embarrassment. "We're going to have to take our visitor with us. I'm sure everyone else has work to do, considering we have an open homicide and I saw at least six cars illegally parked outside."

The kid finally looked up from his screen and locked eyes with Jack. He didn't look ashamed at all. He just gave Jack a lopsided grin. I covered my mouth with my hand to hide the smile. He looked so much like Carver it was eerie.

"You must be Sheriff Lawson," he said. "I'm Doug. Thanks for the pizza. I was starving and my mom said she wanted to get me here as fast as she could, so I didn't have time to eat before we left. Uncle Ben says you shot him. That's wicked, man."

"Thanks," Jack said, looking at me.

"I think that means you're cool," I whispered, and Jack rolled his eyes.

Doug's gaze turned toward me, and he waggled his eyebrows. "How you doin'?"

The snort of laughter snuck through before I could control it. "I'm good. I'm Dr. Graves." I pointed at Jack and said, "His wife."

"A doctor?" he said, closing his laptop and putting it away in his backpack. I noticed it looked an awful lot like Carver's computer, Miranda. "I've always had a thing for a woman with a brain. Let me buy you some ice cream. I saw a place on the way here. You got a Snapchat account?"

Jack was clearly entertained as he watched Doug work his magic. "You remind me a lot of your uncle," Jack said. "Do I want to know what you were doing for Ramirez?"

"Nothing much," Doug said. "Just a simple surveillance using satellites. Big Brother really is watching. No one has any privacy anymore. All you have to do is link up and you can see anyone, anywhere. I built a kind of safeguard, though, on my computer, so if you stick close to me no one can watch you without me knowing about it."

Doug slung his backpack over his shoulder and grabbed a couple of duffle bags from under the table. I looked at them in surprise and wondered how long Doug thought he was staying.

"Seriously, though," he said. "I saw this ice cream place not far from here on the way in. If we could drive through that would be awesome. Have you ever seen this really old movie *Gremlins*? I, like, have to eat or it's not pretty."

Jack took both of Doug's duffle bags and slung them over his shoulder, looked at me, and then headed out the door.

Doug talked the entire way, telling us everything he could about pop culture and his eating habits on the three-minute walk back to the car.

Doug paused and looked at Jack's unit with distrust as Jack opened the back door for him.

"Man, I've got bad memories about riding in the back of a police car," Doug said. "It's just too soon. You think I could sit in the front?"

"No," I said, but I smiled at him to soften my answer.

Jack tossed the bags in the back and closed the door behind Doug. When I got in, I noticed Jack looked kind of shell-shocked. One Ben Carver was enough, but to find out there were two was a little overwhelming.

"Ice cream sounds good," I said, fastening my seatbelt.

"Yes!" Doug said. "Travel makes me super hungry. So, what's this problem y'all are having? Auntie Em said Uncle Ben was trying to figure it out before he had his wreck."

"Auntie Em?" I asked, turning to look at him.

He grinned, a mischievous glint in his eye. "Yeah, she hates it. But she loves me, so she tolerates it."

Jack pulled into the drive-thru line for Lickety Splitz. Doug hung his head out the window like a dog and ordered The Trough, which was a banana split on steroids that came in a giant bucket and was covered in whipped cream, cherries, and nuts.

"I'm good with a cone of rocky road," I told Jack.

He ordered one for each of us, and then we paid and drove away with our treats.

"Is that going to make you sick?" Jack asked.

"Probably not," Doug said. "I have crazy good metabolism. I, like, have to eat all the time or I feel sick. I hardly ever throw up or anything. Well, this one time when I ate a bad batch of cookie dough, but mom said that's one of those live-and-learn lessons."

Jack turned onto Anne Boleyn since it was the main road we took to get to our house. It was wide and there were usually cars parked in front of the cute, cottage-style houses that lined each side of the street, since most didn't have a garage. Big sycamore trees were spaced evenly on each side, and the sidewalks were cracked from gnarled roots.

It was almost four o'clock in the afternoon, and there'd still been no word from Nash. Jack wasn't one to show a lot of outward emotion, but I could tell it was on his mind. We needed to find evidence if Roy Walsh really did kill his wife, otherwise he'd be getting away with the perfect crime, just like he planned all along.

We were just passing the last two houses, before Anne Boleyn turned into a narrow country road, when something exploded against my passenger side window. Something sharp struck my cheek, and I automatically leaned toward Jack, covering my head with my arms.

"What the hell," Jack said, turning the wheel hard enough to make me jerk back the other direction.

Water was shooting against the front windshield and pouring inside the broken window on my side, soaking me to the skin. My ears were ringing, and I tried to undo my buckle, but I was completely disoriented. I wasn't sure if I was hurt or not. I couldn't feel anything.

Jack pulled up a little farther, so the water was no longer hitting the car, and then he flipped on his lights and jumped out. He opened the back door for Doug, and then Jack was opening my door and reaching in to undo my buckle for me.

"Let me see where you're hurt," he said, running his fingers across my neck and face. He looked worried.

I tried to push his hands away and tell him I was fine, but his hands were covered in blood, and I stared at them a few seconds, wondering where it had come from. Then I realized it belonged to me. He put his arms beneath me and lifted me out of the car, and then set me gently in the grass of a stranger's lawn and knelt down beside me.

"I'm fine," I told him. My hearing and senses were starting to come back, and the blood was rushing loudly in my ears. "It probably looks worse than it is."

"I don't know," he said. "It looks pretty bad. That's a lot of blood."

"The head always bleeds a lot. I don't even feel anything."

"Which is a worry in itself," he said.

He went to the back of the Tahoe and grabbed my bag and then came back and knelt down beside me. He found a package of white cotton squares and pressed a couple to the side of my face.

"It's from the glass," I told him. "I'm okay."

"Yeah," he said, and pressed his forehead against mine for a bit. "Still scared me to death though. I'd prefer not to do that again."

"Man, that was crazy!" Doug said, looking at the two of us. He still had his ice cream bucket in hand and his backpack slung over his shoulder. It looked like only some of the ice cream had slopped onto his shirt during the crash. "Does that happen a lot?"

We all looked over to the fire hydrant that was spurting water straight up into the air like a geyser and flooding the street, and Jack and I both shook our heads from side to side.

"No," Jack said. "Definitely not normal."

Jack went over and picked up the cap that had blown off and hit my window. I was lucky it hadn't hit me directly in the head. If it had, we'd be dealing with a much different scenario. Bleeding would be the least of Jack's worries.

"Hey, Sheriff," a lady said, running toward us. "I called 911."

"Thanks," he said.

I noticed there were several people who'd come out of their houses to see what had happened.

"I saw the whole thing," the lady said. "The cap just shot right off the hydrant and smacked right into you. That's rotten luck."

"Yeah," Jack said, turning the projectile over in his hands. "Rotten luck."

A compact white car was heading toward us from the

country road—an older model Volvo with tinted windows. It slowed to a stop and the window rolled down.

He looked different, was all I could think. His hair was darker, and he had a goatee. But it was him.

"Looks like you guys had a heck of an accident," Malachi said.

I felt my blood run cold, and Jack dropped the hydrant cap to reach for his weapon. But just that quick he was driving away, passing the line of emergency vehicles coming toward us. I lost sight of him before he reached the end of the block.

"Son of a bitch," Jack said, kicking his front tire.

"We need to know where he's been," I said. "He came from the direction of the house. Please tell me the flash drives aren't there."

"No," he said. "Not at the moment."

I let out a sigh of relief. Maybe Malachi had unfinished business at our family home. Just because the deed belonged to someone else now didn't mean it would stop him from making himself at home if he needed something.

Jack's unit had minimal damage. The cap from the hydrant had hit my window, shattering it, and then the cap had skipped across the hood, leaving some interesting dents. Water had soaked the interior, and I watched it drip in a steady cadence from the running boards onto the pavement.

"Blasting cap," Jack said, looking closer at the hydrant. "Set on a remote time. He was probably sitting down the street the whole time waiting for us to pass by so he could hit the detonator."

"That was on purpose?" Doug asked, visibly swallowing. "Oh, man. That's not good."

A fire engine and a couple of squad cars had parked behind us, and the ambulance pulled in front of Jack's Tahoe. Two EMTs rushed out, grabbing the gurney and medical bags, and came straight toward me.

"I'm fine," I told them, holding up both hands to ward them off. There was nothing I hated more than being doctored by other people. "I promise. Just some cuts from the glass, and a ringing in my ears from impact. I just need some ibuprofen."

The male EMT looked at the female EMT for direction as she knelt down beside me, completely ignoring my protests. She took my vitals and shined a light in my eyes.

She was short and slightly plump, and her thick blond hair was pulled back into a ponytail. Her eyes were a gorgeous shade of violet.

"I'm Shelly," she said, taking the blood-soaked dressing from my face. "That's my partner, Joe."

"Hi," I said. "Thanks for coming out. But really, I'm fine."

"You will be," Shelly said. "But first we need to get the glass tweezed out of your face and someone to sew up that gash. Not too many. You probably won't even have a scar."

"Then it's probably not worth getting stitched. Just put some superglue on it and a butterfly bandage."

"Come on, Doc. You know you're going to have to put on your big-girl scrubs and come with us."

I blew out a sigh. I could've gotten Joe to let me go. I sensed weakness in him, and I narrowed my eyes at him for letting me down. But Shelly was no pushover. I was going to have to go to the hospital.

I noticed a couple of the officers were bagging the pieces of fire hydrant, and the firemen were trying to cap it off so the water would stop gushing into the street.

Jack came back over to me and looked at the side of my face again.

"Shelly says I have to go to the hospital," I said.

"You should probably listen to Shelly," Jack said, pushing my hair back behind my ear. "I think she's probably right."

"I hate hospitals," I said.

"I know, babe. I need to take Doug to the house and get things set up there. I'll send an officer to pick you up when you're done being stitched up."

"Stitched up?" I said, looking at Shelly accusingly. "I thought I just needed to have glass removed."

"It's a two-part process," Shelly said, straight faced. "I only told you the first part."

"Sneaky," I said.

"That's why they pay me the big bucks," she said.

Jack helped me to my feet, and he put his arm around me. I leaned into him because I could. Because he was there. And because I'd always been able to lean on Jack, even when we disagreed.

"I love you," he said against my temple. Then he leaned down and kissed me, and it was like being given a bottle of water after being out in the desert.

"I love you too," I said. "I'll see you in a little while. Just take care of Doug. My dad saw him. He's going to want to know who he is and why he was with us."

I kissed him one last time and got in the back of the ambulance. And on the way to the hospital, I looked out the tiny back windows expecting to see my father driving behind us, but I didn't.

But I could feel his eyes on me anyway.

12

It was just under two hours later when Officer Cheek picked me up at the hospital and took me back to the house. My face was numb from the local they'd injected to administer my four stitches. Four stitches were hardly worth a trip to the hospital, in my opinion, but whatever.

"You should take a vacation, Doc," Cheek said. "Whoever this guy is who's after you means serious business. Maybe Hawaii. Or Vegas. I always like Vegas. They've got a hotel that looks just like the Eiffel Tower. No reason to spend all that money going to Paris if you ask me."

"Good point," I said. "A vacation sounds nice."

"Yeah, when you and the sheriff were on your honeymoon, we hardly had any crime while you were gone. Maybe taking a vacation would give the rest of us a break too."

I couldn't fault his logic. He pulled into our driveway and parked behind another unit. I noticed Jack's Tahoe was nowhere in sight. I grabbed the plastic bag they'd put my wet clothes in, and got out of the car. They'd given me a spare set of scrubs to change into at the hospital.

Cheek followed me to the front door, and I used my key to unlock it. I automatically walked into the kitchen to find the ibuprofen and a glass of wine. Cheek headed toward the sound of the television. To my surprise, Jack was already in the kitchen pouring two glasses.

"I figured you'd need this," he said and then looked at me. He looked dumbfounded for a moment, and then he raised a brow and he got a certain look in his eyes that could only mean one thing.

"What?" I asked.

"I just realized I've never seen you in scrubs before. I like it. You should wear them later."

"Much later," I said, taking the glass of wine. He handed me two ibuprofen and I wanted to weep. "I really love you."

"Good," he said. "Because Doug might literally be the death of me. He's like Ben times a million. I'm exhausted."

"It's been two hours," I said.

"It feels like two years. I've ordered more pizza. He's eaten most of the good stuff already. How's your face feel?"

"Just a little throbbing where they put in the stitches. The wine will help. What's Doug doing?"

"He and the guys are having an Xbox break. I didn't want to explain what we need him to do until we've got a little privacy."

"Any news from Nash?" I asked.

"Yeah," he said. "The tissue and blood samples all came back with a positive, so they corroborated your findings. They're testing possible sources right now."

"So, we're exactly where we started," I said. "I'm going to be really pissed if Roy Walsh gets away with this."

"Slow and steady," Jack said. "Something will click eventually."

"Hey," Doug said from the doorway. "When does the pizza get here?" Then he noticed I was home. "What's up, Doc?" And then he snorted out a laugh. "The guys told me to say that."

"I can see they're being a good influence on you," I said.

"Oh, for sure. I'm thinking about being a cop. You live in this pretty sweet house with all this cool technology. Your security system sucks, but most people's do, so I'm not worried about that too much."

"I noticed you've got a computer similar to Ben's Miranda," I said. "Did Ben give it to you?"

"Kind of," Doug said, shrugging. "Hey, can I have a beer? I noticed you've got some in the fridge."

"No," Jack said. "What do you mean, kind of?"

"Uncle Ben made a prototype of Miranda. It was supposed to be the Miranda II, but she turned out way different than he expected so he named her Matilda. I think Uncle Ben felt like he was, like, cheating on Miranda or something, so he gave her to me. So, I tinkered with her a bit and took off all the restrictions Uncle Ben had put on. The FBI has a lot of rules about computers and stuff. Once I gave her an overhaul, she most definitely wasn't a Matilda anymore. I call her Trinity. Have y'all ever seen that old movie *The Matrix*?"

I found Doug highly amusing, but I could see how his level of energy might be exhausting after a while.

"We've got some flash drives that your Uncle Ben was working on for us. The drives are encrypted, and it almost destroyed Miranda before he was able to block it and shut it down. But he wasn't able to get past the encryption before the accident. This is very dangerous. Your Uncle Ben was almost killed because of those flash drives. I want you to know what you're getting into."

Doug was momentarily shocked into speechlessness.

"We don't just need you to get past the encryption," Jack said. "But we need you to do it without alerting anyone at the FBI or any other agency. The guy who made those flash drives is wanted by everyone, but not everyone can be trusted."

"Wicked," Doug said. "Who is this guy?"

"My father," I said.

"That's bad," Doug said.

"You have no idea," I told him. "No one knows about him but the three of us and your aunt and uncle. We need to keep it that way."

"Do you think you can do it?" Jack asked. "There's no shame in saying no. It's dangerous, and it's going to be difficult."

"Of course I can do it," Doug said, looking offended. "Like I said, Miranda has regulations. Trinity does not. She's a wild child. Sexy as hell."

I shook my head. "It's like *The Twilight Zone*."

"What's that?" Doug asked.

"A really old show," I said.

The doorbell rang and Doug said, "Pizza! Finally." And he headed off to the front door. But I heard Lewis intercept him before he could open it and explain about letting one of them open the door.

My phone started ringing from inside my bag, and Jack's started buzzing on the counter. That was never a good sign. I looked at my glass of wine with sorrow. "I didn't even get to drink half."

Jack sighed and answered his phone, and I dug around in my bag until I found mine, but it had already stopped ringing.

"Lawson," he said and listened to whoever was on the other end of the line. His face went stony and I had no idea what was happening. "We'll be right there," he said, and hung up.

"What's going on?" I asked.

"Dispatch took a 911 call a few minutes ago. Woman said her husband complained of a headache, took some aspirin, and then dropped dead seconds later."

"Okay," I said, not quite sure why we'd both be going out on a call like that.

"The guy drops the pills on the ground when he falls, and their little dog comes up and eats one."

"Uh-oh," I said, starting to get the gist. "Poison?"

"That's what the wife thought. They sent it straight to us because of the Walsh case."

There was no reason to change clothes. I had a spare pair of coveralls in the Suburban.

"Damn," I said. "Suburban's still at the funeral home."

"They took the Tahoe in to be repaired. Cheek can drive us into town, and we'll grab the Suburban. Crime scene is in King George."

"What about Doug?" I asked.

"Lewis is here for the night, and Chen and Durrant are working the perimeter until midnight. He'll be fine until we get back."

I nodded and grabbed my bag. "Is it wrong that I hope Roy Walsh is an acquaintance of these people?"

"No, but my gut has said from the beginning we're going to have to let Roy go. All we can do is hope karma comes back to bite him in the ass one day."

"Sometimes your gut is a pain," I said.

"I don't suppose you're going to put a quarter in the jar for earlier," Jack said.

"I have four stitches in my face and a serious lack of wine in my system," I said. "Do you really want to ask me that question right now?"

"Yep," he said. "You told me to hold you accountable no matter how grouchy you got." He grinned and dug in the drawer for a quarter, and then he dropped it in the jar. "I'll spot you this one though."

I narrowed my eyes and said, "You're a class act, Lawson."

"Anything for you, Doc."

13

THE VICTIM LIVED IN AN UPSCALE NEIGHBORHOOD IN KING George proper. It was a gated community with a guard who took the names of anyone who entered. I was driving since we were in the Suburban, and I handed the guard my credentials as we pulled up to the gate.

The guy was mid-forties and bulked up past the limit of his uniform sleeves. His head was cut in a close buzz and he had a chubby, pug-like nose that seemed out of character with the rest of him.

He looked at my credentials and then shone his flashlight into the Suburban. Jack held up his badge when the light flashed across his eyes for the second time. "Open it up," he said. "And just leave the gates open on both sides. There's going to be more personnel in and out."

"No can do, Sheriff," the guard said. "These people pay for their privacy. It's my job to make sure they get it."

"You're going to want to leave both gates open," Jack said.

His smile was razor sharp, and I just shook my head and pressed back against the seat so I was out of the way. "A homicide trumps an HOA. And I'm sure you didn't hassle my deputies or the EMTs when they came through, just like I'm sure you're not going to hassle anyone that comes in after. Right?"

They stared at each other a few seconds longer and the guard mumbled something before he shoved my credentials back through the window. He punched a button and the iron gates on both sides slid open. I pressed the gas and drove through, barely clearing the Suburban.

"He seemed nice," I said. "Maybe a potential new hire?"

Jack snorted out a laugh and said, "Take a right here."

There was a small lake with fountains and white lights that led into the addition, and there was a bridge that arced over the water and led to a golf course.

"Wow," I said. The road was smooth and winding, and every blade of grass, shrub, and flower was precisely tended to along the path.

"Lots of old Virginia money around here," Jack said. "They like to hire their own security to patrol the area instead of using the sheriff's office, so we rarely make trips out here."

"Unless someone dies," I said.

"That's pretty much it."

Red and blue flashing lights cast eerie shadow off homes and trees. There was a police unit and an ambulance parked in front of a big white house. It literally looked like a smaller version of the White House.

"That's not over the top at all," I said, pulling in behind the police unit. "I bet they've got a helipad somewhere."

"That's a sucker's bet," Jack said.

I went to the back of the Suburban and pulled on my coveralls and gloves, and then put my camera around my neck and slung my bag over my shoulder. Jack took a pair of gloves from my box and put them on, and I grabbed a couple pair of sterile booties.

The front door was open, and we waited until we got to the threshold before we put the booties on over our shoes. I didn't have to step inside to recognize a palace when I saw one. Everything from the marble floors to the chandeliers dripped with opulence.

A grand double staircase arced from each side of the foyer and met at the landing on the second floor, but it didn't end there. The arc of the staircase was the biggest aquarium I'd ever seen, and it was full of exotic-looking fish.

"Is that a shark?" I asked. "Who actually owns a shark?"

"Lifestyles of the rich and famous," Jack said, and then called out, "Hello?"

Martinez popped his head out from the kitchen door. He always had a smile on his face, and he always looked like he'd just done something that would get him in trouble. Martinez was very popular with the ladies in King George.

"Hey, Sheriff," Martinez said.

"Thanks for calling us right away," Jack said.

"Sure thing," he said. "I had ten minutes until end of shift.

Ten minutes and I would've been on my way to scoring with the finest woman I've ever laid my eyes on."

"Oh, yeah?" Jack asked. "What happened to Julia? Last week she was the finest woman you ever saw."

Martinez shrugged and his grin widened. "She had a beautiful face and a lot of bridal magazines sitting around her place. It was a little creepy. I think she was measuring me for a tuxedo while I was sleeping."

Jack snorted and then said, "Where's the vic?"

"Here in the kitchen," Martinez said. "The wife is in the master bedroom with Holly."

"Who's Holly?" I asked.

"New girl," Martinez said. "Looks like bubble gum fluff, but swears like a sailor. The wife is pretty distraught."

"Well, she watched her husband die a horrible death in front of her," I said, following them into the kitchen. "It's not for everyone."

"I think she's more distraught over the dog," Martinez said. "She kept asking the EMTs if they could revive him, or if she could give blood to help save him."

"She wanted to give blood to her dog?" I asked.

"Yeah, well," Martinez said, shrugging. "Takes all kinds."

The victim was lying on the floor not far from the sink. He was an older man, maybe in his late fifties or early sixties, but he was in good shape. He wore a pair of silk pajama pants and a white T-shirt, and it was obvious he took care of himself. He had a full head of sandy blond hair that was stylishly silver at the temples. There was a small silver tin on the floor next to him and several pills scattered about.

"Where are the EMTs?" I asked Martinez.

"Back with the wife," he said. "She was pretty hysterical, and she was going into shock."

"Any attempts to resuscitate?" I asked.

"No," Martinez said. "He was DOA when we got here. EMTs checked for a pulse and didn't find one, but since poisoning was suspected after the dog died, we all kept our distance."

"Where's the dog?" Jack asked.

"I've got him bagged up," Martinez said. "I figure you'd want samples from him too."

"Good," I said and knelt down beside the victim. "What time did the call come through?"

"7:38," Martinez said.

"Already dressed for bed," I said, more to myself than anyone else. "What's his name?"

"Warren Buchanan," Martinez said. "Age sixty-four. Wife's name is Isobel. She's thirty-seven. She's the one who called it in. The husband complained of a headache after dinner and he came into the kitchen to take something for it. They keep aspirin in the cabinet next to the sink. She said he washed the pills down with water, made a sound like he was choking, and then fell to the ground."

There was a glass sitting next to the sink with a couple of inches of water left in the bottom. Jack collected the water so we could get it sampled, and then he bagged the glass.

"The wife said Warren had his cell phone in his pajama pocket, so she used it to make the 911 call," Martinez went on. "The dog actually came in and started eating the pills that had fallen when she was on the call with 911."

I looked over at the tin in question and picked it up. Most of the pills were on the floor, but there were a few still left in the box. They were small red-and-white capsules, not normally what you'd see when taking plain aspirin. I closed the box and read the label, but I already knew where it had come from.

The Witches' Brew Apothecary was a fairly new business in the grand scheme of Bloody Mary businesses, having only been open the last ten years or so. It had a prime spot in one of the front-facing shops in the town square, and Esmerelda Owens was not only the owner, but she was also a licensed toxicologist and herbalist, and she made everything from soaps to toothpaste to aspirin.

Esmerelda's packaging and labels were very distinctive and old fashioned looking. "Please tell me one of these wasn't recovered from the Walsh home," I said.

Jack already had his phone out and was calling Nash on speaker. "

"Hey, Sheriff," Nash said.

"I've got you on speaker," Jack said. "I'm at a scene with Jaye and Martinez. Gotta DB who took some pills for a headache. The dog ate one off the floor and died too."

"We collected several pill bottles and prescriptions from the Walsh house," Nash said.

"This one is a little rectangular tin from the Witches' Brew. The pills are red-and-white capsules."

"I know what you're talking about," Nash said. "That's a match. We recovered something exactly like it."

"I need you to bother whoever you need to bother to get someone to test those pills right now," Jack said. "I'm going to have someone drive down this sample to you so we can get a match."

I felt the bottom drop out of my stomach. We were about to have a countywide panic on our hands if we weren't careful. Everyone shopped at the Witches' Brew, including us.

"You got it, boss," Nash said and hung up.

"We've got to do this very carefully," Jack said. "We're going to have to call in the CDC." Jack looked at Martinez. "I want everyone on alert and available. Check with the other funeral homes in the area and see if any heart attacks or unsuspected deaths have come in over the last few days. I want a warrant for Esmerelda Owens' home and the Witches' Brew."

"You got it," Martinez said and left the room.

Other deputies were starting to show up and I could hear Martinez briefing them in the other room.

"There's no way Esmerelda did this," I said to Jack. "She's a little nutty, but she's not a killer."

"We've got to start somewhere," Jack said. "Let's get the body transported and put on ice for the night. Resources are going to be thin between guarding the house and the warrants, so I'd like you to wait on the autopsy until morning when someone can be with you."

I wanted to argue. I wanted to get Warren Buchanan on my slab and open him up, especially now that I knew what I was looking for. But I didn't argue. I understood Jack's position, and I didn't want him to worry about me needlessly.

The EMTs and Officer Riley came into the kitchen, and I recognized Shelly and Joe from our earlier encounter.

"You're looking better, Doc," Shelly said.

"Better than you," I said, looking her up and down. "I could take a nap in the bags under your eyes."

"We got the call just before end of shift," she said. "That's usually how it happens."

I knew that to be the truth. Jack or any one of his cops could tell you on the days where there's absolutely nothing going on, something catastrophic and time consuming will happen just before shift change. It was just one of those perks of being a public servant.

"We gave the wife a little something to calm her down," Shelly said. "Hops is still in the bedroom with her, but the wife can't seem to get past the dog. She keeps talking about Schwartz like he was a person, and how heartbroken everyone is going to be to hear the news."

"Wait a second," I said, looking at Jack. "Deputy Holly Hops?"

Jack grimaced. "Like Martinez said, she looks like cotton candy fluff. The name fits her perfectly."

Riley snorted. "She might look like cotton candy fluff, but I wouldn't want to face off with her in an alley. She sometimes gets a look in her eyes that make my balls crawl right up inside my body."

"Beautiful imagery," I told Riley.

"The dog's name is Schwartz?" Jack asked Shelly.

"Short for Schwartzkopf," she said, smiling a little. "Apparently, Warren was a Stormin' Norman fan."

"Who's Stormin' Norman?" Riley asked.

"Geez, kid," Shelly said, "How old are you?"

"Twenty-three," Riley said, clearly offended.

"Riley," Jack said. "I want you to bag up any remaining pills and then drive them and the container straight down to Nash in Richmond."

"You got it," Riley said, grabbing an evidence bag. He was already wearing gloves.

Jack turned his attention to Shelly and Joe. "Do you think you guys could get the vic suited up for transport? I'd like to see if I can get anything out of the wife while it's still fresh."

"Sure thing, Sheriff," Joe said.

"Oh, now you talk," I said, giving him the side-eye.

He grinned sheepishly, and he and Shelly got to work on getting Warren Buchanan bagged up and on the gurney.

I followed Jack out of the kitchen and toward the back of the house. The fish tank was the first thing you saw when you entered the house because it was on the inside of the enormous staircase, but what you couldn't see from the front was that the fish tank continued along the wall and ceiling, creating a tunnel that led into the master bedroom.

"That's kind of creepy," I said, looking up. It felt like the shark was following us. "What happens if there's an earthquake, or if the glass cracks?"

"Fortunately, that's not our problem," Jack said.

Jack and I were very fortunate. We lived in the kind of house most people never got the opportunity to experience. With that being said, the Buchanan's house made ours look like a log hut.

The master bedroom was almost as big as our entire first floor. The east wall was floor to ceiling windows, and it gave a perfect view of the pool that glowed blue from the underwater lights.

The bedroom had its own living area, and everything was white. *Everything.* The carpet, the furniture, the bedspread, and the walls. It was the whitest room I'd ever been in. Even the woman lying on the bed was wearing white silk pajamas and covered with a white throw. Her hair was white-blond, and her nails were French tipped. She had a cool pack over her eyes, and she was breathing evenly.

The detective sitting in the chair at the side of the bed did remind me of cotton candy fluff. She was cute as a button and looked like she belonged on the high school cheer squad instead of sitting there in her uniform and a weapon strapped to her side. Her skin was peaches and cream, and she had freckles across the bridge of her nose, and her hair was pulled into a tousled ponytail. I wanted to ask her how she did it.

"Is she asleep?" Jack asked.

Holly gave him a megawatt smile that was so bright it almost hurt. "No, sir. She's just resting."

I almost tripped over my own two feet the second words came out of Holly's mouth. She sounded like a two-pack-a-day off-road trucker.

"Mrs. Buchanan," Jack said. "We're about to transport your husband. Is there anyone we can call for you so you're not alone?"

Isobel Buchanan removed the eye pads and scooted up on the bed, so she was propped up on her pillows. She had the refined, delicate bones of royalty, and the lips of an excellent plastic surgeon. Even though her eyes were slightly swollen from crying, her skin was flawless, and she looked pretty close to perfect. She also had the spaced gaze of someone who's been given a nice dose of Valium.

"My mother is coming," she said, holding up her phone. "I texted her earlier. What about Schwartz? What's going to happen to him?"

"He's being transported with your husband so samples can be taken," Jack said. "We believe your husband was poisoned."

Jack moved closer to the bed, and Holly got up out of the chair so he could sit down. I stayed out of Isobel's line of sight, and Holly came to stand next to me. Women tended to want to talk to Jack once they got a good look at him. Jack had that alpha presence that made anyone around him pay attention.

Almost like clockwork, Isobel's eyes widened, and she changed her posture on the bed so her very excellent body was displayed better, and her pajamas slipped off her shoulder, showing the delicate skin.

"I'm sorry," she said. "I didn't catch your name."

"I'm Sheriff Lawson," Jack said.

"Oh," she gasped. "Imagine the sheriff himself coming to check on me. I do appreciate your service."

Holly and I looked at each other and rolled our eyes. I felt a kindred spirit in Holly.

"I know you've been through a traumatic event, losing your husband like you did," Jack said, emphasizing the word *husband* since Isobel had apparently forgotten that she'd been a married woman up until about an hour ago. "But I'd really appreciate it if you could walk me through what happened. Whoever did this to your husband and Schwartz needs to pay."

Tears sparkled in her eyes at the mention of Schwartz. "My poor baby," she said. "Do you think he suffered?"

"No," Jack lied. "I think he went very quickly."

"Thank you for that," she said, dabbing at her eyes with an actual handkerchief.

"You said your husband was complaining of a headache?" Jack asked.

"Yes, we had dinner with the Carmichaels tonight," she said. "They've been dear friends for years. Oh, my." She brought her hand to her chest dramatically. "I'm going to have to let Lorraine and Tommy know what happened. They're going to be devastated. Tommy and Warren had a lot of business dealings together."

"You left to go have dinner?" Jack asked, prompting her to finish.

"We went for drinks about five o'clock, and there were serving dinner at six. They live on the other side of the golf course, so we just rode over in the golf cart. Sometimes Warren gets these migraines when he's stressed, but he said he was fine, so we went to dinner anyway. But he was only halfway through his sherry when the headache got worse, and he said he wanted to come home. It was bad enough that he let me drive us back."

"I noticed that Warren was in his pajamas," Jack said. "As are you."

"Sure," she said. "It's not like I was going to get to go out again. As soon as I walked in the door I came and got changed."

"What did Warren do?" Jack asked.

"He went straight into the bathroom. I figure he was sick because he was in there a while. I went to the kitchen to open a bottle of wine and get something to eat, and he came in about twenty minutes later wearing his pajamas. He was really pale and kind of clammy, and he asked where the aspirin was. He likes the stuff we get from the Witches' Brew. He said it works better than any of the big brands."

"When did he buy it?"

"I bought it a few days ago. We ran out, so I picked up more after I got my hair done."

"Was the packaging already off or did he have to take it off?" he asked.

Isobel looked confused.

"Was the tin of aspirin sealed?"

"Oh," she said. "Yes, it was. Warren got it out of the cabinet, and his hands were a little shaky, so I peeled off the plastic and opened it up for him. I gave him two of the pills and then set the tin down on the counter so I could get him a glass of water. After that…" Her breath hitched in her chest and she seemed to pale, reliving her husband's death.

I was wondering if her focus on the dog was her coping mechanism for not thinking about her husband's death.

"It didn't take very long," she said softly. "There was nothing I could do. He'd barely swallowed the pills and he was gone. When he fell, he knocked the rest of the pills onto the floor. I called 911, but that's when Schwartz came in." Big tears were rolling down her cheeks now, and it was the first time I felt like she wasn't trying to put on an act.

"Do you or your husband happen to be acquainted with Roy and Nina Walsh?" Jack asked.

Her movements were lethargic from the drug, so it took a second for the question to penetrate.

"No," she said. "I don't think so. Are they new to the club?"

"I appreciate your talking to me, Mrs. Buchanan," Jack said. "We'll let you know when you can claim Warren's and Schwartz's bodies for burial."

She slunk back down on the bed and covered her eyes again.

14

WE TOOK WARREN AND SCHWARTZ TO THE FUNERAL HOME, and I had time to get them logged in and put into the cooler before the warrants came through for Esmerelda Owens and her shop.

"They're bringing Esmerelda into the station," Jack said. "Martinez and Walters went to pick her up. Martinez said she seemed concerned and was very cooperative."

"I'd be concerned too," I said. "This is going to kill her business. If she's innocent in this, then she's a victim too. I love that shop. She's got the best body scrub."

"Is that the stuff that makes your skin so smooth?" Jack asked.

"That's the stuff."

"I love that shop too," he said. "Come on. Time is working against us. The more information we have the better to stop it."

We got back in the Suburban and headed for the station. The square was almost empty of civilian cars since most of the businesses closed at six, and Jack pulled into his parking spot. The front doors were locked, and Jack used his key to open the doors, and then hurriedly typed in his code to let us through to the back.

"You made good time," Martinez said from behind his desk. He was catching up on paperwork. "She gave us the keys for the shop, so the guys headed over to do a search."

"Thanks, Martinez," Jack said. "That paperwork will wait until tomorrow. I know you're way past shift. Go home and get some sleep."

"I'll just finish it up if it's all the same to you," he said. "Getting behind is worse than having to do it at all. Suspect is in Interrogation A. I got her some coffee. She was about to go to bed when we picked her up."

"Impressions?" Jack asked.

"Nice lady," he said. "She's got this really great cream that makes your hands and elbows really soft."

Jack raised a brow.

"Sometimes I get dry skin," Martinez clarified. "She's worried about the victims and her shop, and she's been nothing but cooperative."

"Thanks," he said, and we walked down the same hallway we had earlier in the day to Interrogation A.

Esmerelda Owens could have been twenty-five or sixty-five, it was impossible to tell, but she was probably somewhere in the middle. Her eyes held a wisdom that people in their twenties didn't have. Her skin was impossibly smooth —a good testament to her products—and her hair was raven black and waved down her back.

She typically wore brightly colored caftans, and lots of chakra necklaces and bracelets around her neck and wrists so she jangled every time she moved, and she didn't disappoint now. She smiled when she saw us, but her dark eyes were tired and worried.

"Dr. Graves," she said. "I'm so glad to see you. It's nice to see a friendly face." Her gaze moved to Jack. She had a way of studying people that could sometimes be unnerving.

"This is my husband," I told her. "I don't think the two of you have met before."

"No," she said. "I haven't had the pleasure. Though I've always wanted to after hearing you speak about him."

"I'm sorry we had to meet under these circumstances," Jack said. "Two people are dead."

"Yes, that nice officer told me," she said, gripping one of her necklaces in her hand. "He said there's poison in my products, and that's what killed them, but I just don't see how that can be. I've never even gotten one complaint of people getting sick from using my products. I'm very careful."

"That's what we're trying to find out," Jack said.

The room wasn't big—maybe eight by ten—and the walls were covered in blue fabric. There was a mirror so people in the observation room could see, and there was a camera in the corner of the ceiling, so everything was documented. We took the two chairs across from her. It looked like her coffee had gone untouched as the little Styrofoam cup was still full.

"We know for certain the second victim died after taking your Witch Doctor brand of aspirin. He complained of a headache, took two pills, and died instantly. Which could have been a coincidence, but their dog ate one of the pills and died too."

"No," she said, shaking her head. "That's definitely not a coincidence. You're not sure on the other victim?"

"An identical tin was found in her bathroom. They're testing it now to see if it contains cyanide. You make everything you sell? No other hands touch it?"

"No," she said. "And I know that doesn't help me any, but I'm very careful. I don't use poisons of any kind at all. I don't understand how cyanide would be in those pills. I'm a naturalist. All of my medicines are plant based."

"We're going to have a chemist at the lab break down the pills," he said. "What do you use in them?"

"Feverfew is the main ingredient," she said, looking at me. I guessed she thought I would be more knowledgeable about herbal supplements, but those classes weren't offered in med school.

"What's that?" Jack asked.

"It's a plant that does exactly what it sounds like," she said. "I also used plant-based magnesium, some peppermint, ginger, turmeric, and cloves. It's a fairly lengthy process. I've got to dry all of the plants and roots, and then I crush them in my mortar and pestle until they form a powder. Once I have the powder at the right consistency it goes into the press."

"What do you do about packaging?" Jack asked.

"I buy those tins in bulk from my supplier, use a little precut wax paper to fit inside of it, and then each box gets exactly twenty-four pills. I close the lid, stick my label on top, and then I have one of those plastic wrap and seal things like you see on the infomercials. Usually easiest is best."

"You do all that yourself?" I asked, amazed.

She smiled and said, "If it's worth doing, it's worth doing right. It's also why a tin of twenty-four pills costs forty-eight dollars. On the upside, I'm able to make a fairly large batch at a time, so once I get going it's easy to restock."

"When did you make this last batch?" Jack asked.

"Oh," she said, thinking. "The whole process takes three to four weeks, but most of that is to make sure the plants are dried good. I finished this last batch a couple of weeks ago and restocked the shelf. I was down to my last two tins, and I don't like to let my supply get down that low."

Something had caught my attention when she'd been talking about the process of making the pills. "What do you mean when you say you put the pills in a press? What about the capsules?"

"What capsules?" she asked, clearly confused.

Jack reached in his pocket and took out a baggie with a

couple of the pills we'd taken from the Buchanan's house. "These capsules."

She stared at the red-and-white pills. "I don't understand. I thought you said these came from my tin?"

"The victim had just taken the wrapping off the tin, and this is what was inside," Jack said.

"I'm telling you that's impossible," she said. "You can check my inventory. I don't use capsules. They're not natural. My pills are tablets."

"Do you have surveillance cameras in your shop?" he asked.

"No," she said, shaking her head. "But I do keep a customer log of who makes purchases. Would that help?"

"More than you know," he said. "I appreciate your help, Ms. Owens."

"Call me Esmerelda," she said. "I hope you catch whoever did this."

"Believe me," Jack said. "We will."

———

HALF AN HOUR later we were back home, and once again I was too tired to even pour a glass of wine, much less drink it. It was after ten o'clock, and Lewis and Doug were still in front of the TV playing a game that made me dizzy to watch, and where a lot of people were getting shot in the face. Doug had a headset on, and you would have thought he was landing an actual aircraft in a life-or-death situation instead of rotting his brain on a fantasy.

"What?" Jack asked, staring at me. We were in the sitting room off the den so we could at least hear each other talk.

"What do you mean, what?" I asked.

"You sighed," he said. "What are you thinking about?"

"I just realized I'm officially old," I said. "What are we going to do about this? We've got nothing but two dead bodies and a dead dog. Our suspect list could be endless."

"We need to sleep on it," Jack said. "We're both exhausted. What we do know is someone tampered with those packages. Walters opened every one of the aspirin packages they confiscated from the shop. Except for two of them, all the rest looked exactly as how Esmerelda described. So, someone was able to get hold of the tin and her label and put their own capsules inside. She uses a plastic shrink-wrap machine from the infomercial aisle. Anyone could copy that."

"Like I said, the suspect list could be endless."

"Esmerelda said she'd email her customer logs over by tomorrow morning," Jack said. "In the meantime, the chemist at the lab is going to break down the ingredients for us. Maybe there's something unusual about the capsules that'll give us a place to look. They'll start making announcements about the recall on the morning news, and the paper is going to put a warning on the front page. We've got a hotline and help center all set up."

"I've still got to dig in to Warren Buchanan," I said.

Jack grimaced. "That's an unfortunate choice of words."

"Yet accurate," I said. "We can't keep delaying the

inevitable. No matter how many bodies show up. We've got to get those flash drives in Doug's hands. I'm more than happy to pretend Malachi doesn't exist while we deal with this case, but that doesn't mean he's going to go away."

Jack blew out a breath. "Are we still fighting?"

I felt my body go rigid. At some point we'd just fallen back into our natural pattern of things. It was easy for work to become a buffer between us. It bridged a gap when nothing else would.

"I don't know," I said. "You hurt me. And I don't even know why. Maybe it doesn't matter. But if you think I'd purposely try to sabotage our happiness then we have bigger problems than a madman on the loose. So yeah, I guess we are still fighting. And I am still mad."

"I'm sorry," Jack said. "I'm sorry I hurt you. I don't know what normal is supposed to feel like with us because we haven't had normal yet. And I'd be lying if I said it wasn't frustrating."

"None of this is a surprise, Jack. My father was alive and making our lives hell before we got married. Maybe it's your expectations that aren't meeting the standard. Because I've always known what we're dealing with. I don't know what normal is. I don't know what a normal marriage is. But I know we won't have it until he's out of our lives. And pretending things are normal isn't going to help the problem. If you weren't up for this, then you shouldn't have been in such a hurry to get married. Maybe all your frustration is really just regret."

"No," he said, denying it emphatically. "I could never

regret it. And maybe you're right. Maybe this is on me and my expectations."

"Once you figure out what they are make sure you let me know," I said. "I've got to go to bed. I've got to be up early."

He didn't stop me as I left the room.

15

I'D MANAGED TO DO SOMETHING I NEVER HAD BEFORE. I woke up before Jack, snuck into the shower like a thief in the night, and I was downstairs pouring a to-go cup of coffee just as the sun was starting to turn the sky gray.

I felt guilty for leaving like I was, so I snuck back upstairs and left a cup of coffee on the nightstand for Jack, and then I crept back down and grabbed my bag off the hook. Chen was waiting for me.

"I didn't realize you stayed the night," I told her, surprised.

"I was supposed to be off at midnight, but with all hands-on deck we were short a couple of people. It's not like it's a hardship to sleep in your house. That couch is a hell of a lot more comfortable than my mattress. I take it you're heading to the funeral home?"

"I've got the Warren Buchanan autopsy," I told her. "I need him to give me some answers."

"Good luck with that," she said, unlocking the door and going outside first.

The patrol car parked in the driveway flashed its lights so we'd know they were there. It was still too dark for me to see who'd been on babysitting duty outside.

"It's Durrant and Smith," Chen said. "They came on at midnight."

Jack had explained that he put two men in the car so they could relieve each other with short catnaps. It couldn't be easy keeping a vigilant eye on things with nothing but total darkness and the sound of rushing water from the Potomac and the tree limbs blowing in the wind.

They'd take turns patrolling the perimeter of the house and looking for signs that someone had been trespassing. They'd also take the occasional trip up and down the street to make sure there were no cars hidden off the road.

Durrant rolled down his window and said, "Morning. Been a quiet night. We did a pass-through about half an hour ago."

"We're heading to the funeral home," Chen told him. "Boss and the kid are still inside."

I unlocked the Suburban and Chen went around to the passenger side to get in. I tossed my bag in the back like usual, but when I moved to get in the front seat something caught my eye.

There in the middle of the seat was my mother's ring. Again. Popping up like a bad penny when I least expected it.

"What's that?" Chen asked, eyeing the ring.

"I'd put it in my pocket yesterday," I said. "It must have fallen out."

I picked it up and put it back in my pocket. With everything that had happened I'd completely forgotten to tell Jack about the ring. I got in without saying anything else and drove to the funeral home.

It was Tuesday, but still well before any of the staff was due to show up. I unlocked the side door, and we went in through the kitchen.

"I'll make the coffee," Chen said, heading over to the pot. "I don't suppose you have any breakfast here?"

"It depends on what kind of breakfast you're looking for," I said. "Jack's idea of breakfast is oatmeal or one of those protein bars that taste like sawdust. But if you'd like something that has actual taste there's donuts and Captain Crunch in the pantry. And there's soft drinks in the fridge. Help yourself."

"You can lock yourself into the lab downstairs, right?" Chen asked.

"Sure," I said.

"And you've got video surveillance monitors?"

"Of course." I was confused as to what she was getting at.

"What about a couch? Do you have a couch down there?"

"A small one. It's not really a place I like to take a lot of thinking naps, but it's shoved into the corner just in case."

"Perfect," she said. She opened the pantry, grabbed the bag of donuts, and then took a Coke from the fridge. "I'm ready when you are."

"You're going down with me?" I asked, floored.

"Sure," she said. "I'll be in the way up here, and I'd much rather watch you with you in my sight instead of hoping there's not some crazy secret passageway for someone to steal you on my watch."

"Weirdly enough," I said. "I've wondered the same thing. The autopsy won't bother you? I've yet to get a cop to make it through a full autopsy with me."

"That's because they're soft," she said. "I'm from Atlanta. I can watch your autopsy and eat my donuts. No problem."

"Alrighty," I said. "It'll be nice to have the company. Company that's still breathing, I mean."

She snorted out a laugh while I unlocked the metal door that led down to the basement. The bright lights came on automatically, and I pulled the door closed behind us and listened for the click that signified it had relocked.

We took the stairs, and I pointed Chen to the couch and showed her how to turn on the monitors so she could see everything that was happening around the rest of the funeral home. Once she was settled, I opened the cooler and rolled Warren Buchanan to the autopsy table. I unzipped him and cut off his pajamas while he was still on the gurney, and because he was a good-sized man and a lot heavier than he looked because of his muscle mass, Chen came and helped me get him onto the autopsy table.

"Today feels like it's going to be a weird day for me," she said, going to the sink to wash her hands.

"Look on the bright side," I told her. "You could be where Warren is right now."

"Good point," she said.

I turned the overhead lights and the ventilator on, and then I turned on my recorder, documenting anything I could see with the naked eye. For a man in his sixties, he was in excellent shape. But considering he had a wife twenty-five years younger, I could understand why.

He had a scar about three inches long on the right side of his abdomen, consistent with an appendectomy, but I'd be able to confirm once I opened him up. I took blood samples, and I swabbed the inside of his mouth carefully.

I was able to move very quickly with victim number two. I had my tissue samples and Mr. Buchanan was all put back together in just over three hours. I used the ChemSee test strips I had in the drawer just like I had for Nina Walsh, and the results came back positive.

"Cyanide," I said. "It's a match."

Chen looked startled at the sound of my voice. I'd been silent for hours while I was working. I'd forgotten she was even there.

"Jack said they recovered two more tins with the poisonous capsules during the search of the shop," I said. "It'd be helpful to know how many tins the killer replaced."

"That would make things too easy," Chen said. "The first

news alert went out a couple of hours ago. When I checked in at the station the guys said they were flooded with calls from panicked people, and everyone was bringing anything they'd ever purchased from the Witches' Brew and demanding it be tested."

I grimaced. "This will ruin Esmerelda. It doesn't matter if she's exonerated. She'll always be guilty in the eyes of the people."

"Or maybe she really is the killer, and she's throwing us all off track," Chen said. "Never let your guard down. Sometimes it's the most unsuspected who can do the most damage."

"And what if she's innocent?" I asked.

"Then you're right," Chen said. "She's through. She'll have to move out of state if she ever wants to open another shop. The one thing I've learned about the people in this area is that they have long memories and they're not exactly forgiving. The sheriff said Esmerelda is already getting death threats. He had to assign a man to protect her."

"Eventually Jack is going to run out of men," I said. "We've been thrown into chaos from all sides. Everyone has more than one job to do. That can only sustain so long."

"He's already run out of men," Chen said. "He's called in reinforcements from Stafford County. He sent out a memo a little while ago."

I'd been so preoccupied with the autopsy I hadn't stopped to check my phone. I took off my gloves and lab coat, and picked my phone up off my desk. I had six missed calls and a dozen texts, most of them from Jack.

Thanks for the coffee.

And then a few minutes later he texted again.

I'm assuming you've already started "digging in" to our victim. Let me know once you have preliminary test results.

His next text was about an hour later.

Be glad you're underground. The news alert went out and people have lost their minds. Esmerelda getting death threats. Someone set her car on fire.

"Yikes," I said to myself.

Forgot to mention I brought Doug into work. Figured it was safest place for him to work. He wasn't happy to get up early, but I gave him a dozen donuts and a bottle of Mountain Dew, so I'm hoping he's coherent enough to get started.

It was another hour before he texted again.

I'm going to assume you're still wrist deep in body cavities and not ignoring me. Nash said pills were identical. The chemist is analyzing ingredients in the poisonous pills, but it could be a couple of days for results. All other items clear.

"Martinez texted and says the vic's wife is asking for her dog," Chen said. "She wants to know when she can claim the body."

"I just need to collect some samples to send with the human tissue to the lab," I said. "Then she can take both the dog and her husband. We can have him sent wherever she'd like for him to be interred."

Chen relayed the message to Martinez, while I was still looking down at my phone, trying to decide what to say to Jack.

Just finished. Prelim results came back positive. Will send samples to lab.

I read it again after I hit send, and wondered if I could make it any less impersonal. I sounded like I was talking to my assistant instead of my husband.

Sorry about Esmerelda. People suck.

I put the phone back on the desk and went to get the dog so I could take his samples as well, though it was pretty conclusive that cause of death would be the same as his owner. What would be great is if we had a suspect.

"What's wrong?" Chen said as I put the dog back and cleaned up my work space.

"I'm worried this is one of those cases that might never get solved," I said. "It makes no sense. We've got two victims who didn't know each other and couldn't be more opposite in every way. What if there was no motive behind the killings? What if whoever it was just wanted to kill, and it didn't matter who the victims were?"

A thought crossed my mind that had my heart beating harder in my chest. What if the killer just wanted to create chaos? Or run Jack's resources and attention into the ground so no one was paying attention as much as they should've been? I needed to talk to Jack.

"I'm finished here," I told Chen. "Just let me check in with the staff and make sure they don't need me for anything, and we can head to the station."

I grabbed the samples, and Chen and I went back upstairs to the funeral home.

When we walked out of the basement and into the kitchen, we both took a breath of fresh air.

"Do we smell weird?" Chen asked, sniffing her arm.

"Nah," I said. "Maybe don't hug anyone today. It's the embalming you have to watch out for."

I went to the kitchen sink and washed my hands and then grabbed a Coke from the fridge. I'd drink anything as long as it had caffeine in it.

"Help yourself to anything in the kitchen," I told Chen. "I'm going to check in with Emmy Lu and make sure everything is okay."

Emmy Lu Stout had been working for me the last few months, and there were many times I wondered how I'd ever gotten along without her. She was somewhere in her middle forties, and she was a Bloody Mary native. She'd been pregnant with her first son when she'd walked the stage at graduation, and she married the baby's father the day after graduation. She gave birth to four more boys before she turned twenty-five, and she'd been a stay at home mom until her last son had graduated from high school and her no-good husband left her for a younger model. She'd been left flat broke without any real job experience, and I hired her on the spot.

"Sounds like it was a busy weekend," Emmy Lu said when I walked into her office.

Emmy Lu was what I imagined a middle-aged Gidget who was thirty pounds overweight would look like. She was cute as a button, and she wore a pair of readers on the tip of her nose.

"It wasn't one of my most relaxing," I said, taking a stack of messages she handed me.

"Maybe you should go on vacation," she said. "Have you noticed things slow down around here when y'all are gone?"

"It's recently come to my attention," I said. "A woman might be in later to make arrangements. I've got her husband and dog down in the lab."

"Are you doing pet embalmings now?" she asked, her eyes going wide.

"Weirdly enough, having a dog in my autopsy space brought me more anxiety than I expected. I'm not a fan."

"Maybe you're just not a dog person," she said.

"I think that it's just I'm not a dead animal person," I said. "Is Sheldon here?"

"He's coming in for an eleven o'clock meeting with a potential client," she said. "They're looking at caskets. And I need you to sign these purchase orders. Make sure you send me a list if there's anything you're running low on in the lab."

I grabbed a pen from her holder and scribbled my signature across each form. "I'm going to be in and out all week. Unless I'm needed specifically for something, Sheldon can take care of it. We're swamped with this case."

"I saw the news this morning," she said, clucking her

tongue. "It's just awful. I love that store. I've taken those same pills for headaches. Esmerelda's work better than any name brand. You think I need to throw away my box? I mean, I've had it for months. Isn't it just the new ones that are contaminated?"

I raised my brows in surprise. Emmy Lu was hanging pretty fast and loose with her life. "Wow, those must be pretty good pills."

She nodded solemnly. "Sometimes it's worth taking the chance. You know she'll never be in business around here again. Do you remember when Blue Bell ice cream had that listeria outbreak a few years ago?"

"One of the saddest days of my life," I told her.

"I had three half gallons in the freezer, but there was no way I was throwing those things in the garbage. Some things are worth dying for."

"Usually it's people you love," I told her. "Not herbal remedies and dairy products."

She shrugged and tilted her head. "I love both of those things more than I love a lot of people."

"Can't argue with that," I said. "Are the ones in your box red-and-white capsules or tablets?"

"Tablets," she said. "I'm assuming I'd be dead already if they were poisoned. During my divorce I popped those things like candy. Though I wouldn't necessarily mind my ex getting a hold of one of these new batches, if you know what I mean."

"We should probably keep that just between us though."

"Right," she said.

I looked through my messages, but there wasn't anything pressing, so I dropped them on my desk and went to find Chen. She was in the bathroom, so I yelled through the door that I'd meet her in the car.

I refilled my bag with extra medical supplies and grabbed my keys off the hook. I saw my reflection in the mudroom mirror and grimaced. My hair was haphazardly pulled up into a knot on my head, and I was paler than usual. Or maybe the dark smudges under my eyes made me look paler than usual.

I left through the side door that led to the carport. It was still early enough that the sun wasn't oppressive, and there was a nice breeze in the air.

"Hey, Doc," Morris Biggs called out as he jogged by. Morris was one of those guys who was addicted to jogging. I didn't know if he actually worked for a living; there were times I passed him around town two or three times a day, always in his black jogging shorts and a white sweatband around his head.

"Hey, Morris. Make sure you stay hydrated," I yelled back.

He gave me a thumbs-up and turned the corner onto Catherine of Aragon. The strip mall across the street was hopping, and cars were pulling in and out outside the new deli. Which reminded me that it was lunchtime and I was starving.

A group of moms walked by with strollers, lost in conversation, and I really stopped to look at what was going on around me. I'd had tunnel vision for the past week, moving from one victim to the next, including Ben. I'd not had one moment to sit and think or let my mind rest. I hadn't gone for a walk or gotten fresh air. If I kept going like I was, I'd look up and it would be October, and I'd be wondering where the sunshine and pretty trees were.

I went to the back of the Suburban and opened the hatch, and then I put my bag on top of the gurney. A sharp pinch hit my thigh, and I yelled, "Ouch," even as I brought my hand down to rub at the spot. But an unfamiliar hand caught mine before I could touch it.

"I wouldn't do that," my father said.

My head snapped up so we were eye to eye, and then I looked down to see the syringe sticking out of my thigh.

"I wouldn't want you to accidentally hit the plunger," he said. "I'm afraid that wouldn't end well for you. I'm way past the point of patience, Jaye. If you keep getting in my way, I will take you out."

I jerked against him, but he was too strong. "I never doubted that for a second," I said between gritted teeth.

He'd changed his appearance once more. His hair was mostly silver and he was clean shaven, though his jowls were more pronounced and the lines in his face were deeper. Even his posture was different, so he was slightly hunched and rounded at the shoulders. If it weren't for his eyes, I wouldn't have recognized him at all.

"You're being stupid," I said, looking him in the eye again. "If you keep popping up like this it's only a matter of time before someone takes you down."

"Oh, yeah?" he said, smiling, showing slightly crooked and yellowed teeth. "Who's going to do that? Your friend in the hospital? Or maybe Jack? The last I checked he was a little busy."

My heartbeat was pounding in my throat, and I wanted to fight him, to call out, but I knew he wasn't bluffing. Whatever was in that syringe would kill me. I didn't doubt that. "Was it you?" I asked. "Was it you who poisoned those people?"

"It's a very interesting case," he said, not answering the question. "The perfect crime."

"There's no such thing," I said.

"Wanna bet?" he said, and smiled again. "Let me tell you how this is going to end. I want those flash drives. And I'll do anything and go through anyone I have to to get them. I'd sure hate for that kid to get hurt. I've enjoyed watching him play his video games. Seems like a bright kid. He must've come with a security upgrade because I've been in a blackout ever since he walked through your door. I've had to go back to the old-fashioned way of doing things. But it's just like riding a bike. Young people today wouldn't know how to survive without technology."

"Maybe you should write a handbook."

His eyes crinkled at the corners. "Ha. Maybe that's not such a bad idea. It'll give me something to do when I finally get to retire. I'm looking forward to the Golden Years. I hope you can understand my position."

"I understand that you're a monster and completely insane," I said defiantly.

"To some I'm a hero," he said.

"Not to me. Never to me."

"The flash drives aren't in your house. I looked yesterday before you had your little accident. I've searched your lab and the funeral home with the same results. Which means you and Jack are either keeping them with you at all times or he's put them in a safety deposit box. Maybe he even locked them up in the evidence room at the station. But you're going to bring me all five of them by midnight, or I'm coming to get them. Do you understand what that means?"

"It means if I have a clear shot I'm going to take it," I said with much more bravado than I felt.

"As long as we're clear." He jerked the syringe out of my thigh and put it in his pocket. "It really is an interesting case," he said again. I hadn't even noticed that he was carrying a cane until he walked off around the carport.

I felt so helpless—powerless—and it made me angry. I couldn't call out for help. I couldn't tell people that my dead father was haunting me. Not unless I wanted to put everyone at risk. Ben had already paid a price, and I knew if we didn't come up with a plan soon then Jack would be next on the list.

My legs were jelly, and I was leaning against the back of the Suburban, propping myself up as best I could. The side door to the funeral home opened, and my head snapped up as Chen came out.

"What's wrong?" she said, immediately looking around for trouble. It was no use. Malachi was long gone.

"I hit my knee on the bumper," I lied.

"I hate that," she said and went around to the passenger side. "You ready?"

I closed the hatch and made my way back to the driver's side. "As I'll ever be," I said, but I didn't really believe it.

16

JACK HAD BEEN RIGHT WHEN HE'D SAID I WAS LUCKY I GOT to stay underground. The town square was a nightmare of people and cars, and there were picketers marching in front of The Witches' Brew. I beeped my horn for people to get out of the streets, but no one was budging.

"Just park in the alley at the backside of the station," Chen said.

"I don't think I can get there."

There were cars parked in the street, and I could see uniformed officers setting up barricades, trying to get things under control. The officers must've been from Stafford County because I didn't recognize anyone. They were moving the barricades right in front of us and waving for us to back up, but Chen rolled down her window and stuck out her badge.

They managed to push the people back long enough for me to slip through, and then they set up the barricades behind us. There was an unfamiliar car parked in Jack's spot, so I pulled up close behind it and blocked it in since there were no other spaces available.

I saw Floyd Parker before I got out of the vehicle. He was standing with a photographer and a cameraman, and he was interviewing a woman who was in hysterics and pointing wildly toward The Witches' Brew.

Floyd's gaze locked on mine, and I couldn't help but smile. His nose was still red and swollen, and his left eye showed the colorful shadows of a black eye. Technically, he'd been impeding an investigation by blocking my transport of a body, so I'd taken the liberty of moving him out of the way. I had the authority to do so as the coroner, but it was a little bit of a gray area as far as how much force I was allowed to use. I figured I'd be hearing from his attorney at some point, but for now, I felt immense satisfaction looking at his fat nose on his fat face.

"Man, if looks could kill," Chen said, following me inside the sheriff's office. "I'd watch your back with that guy."

"He's a weasel and a coward," I said. "He likes to use his size to intimidate. But he's tenacious. I'll give him that."

The lobby was full of people, and Hitchcock was signing people in and giving them a waiting number. The door on the right side of the lobby led to common rooms where reports could be taken, and I assumed they had everything set up to collect any medicines or products that had been dispensed by The Witches' Brew.

Chen keyed in her passcode to the door on the left, and we quickly walked through and shut the door behind us. I handed her the tissue samples so someone could get them to Richmond, and she headed off in the opposite direction. I saw Jack in his office and went straight for him. Malachi was still fresh on my mind, and if I was being honest, I was still shaky from my run-in with him.

Betsy didn't even look up from her computer screen as I walked around her desk and into Jack's office. He was on the phone, so I closed the door behind me. His office was in the middle of the west wall and there were three sides of windows so he could see the station from every angle.

He had a big L-shaped desk, and there was an old conference table on one side of the office, and on the other side was a battered leather couch and two matching chairs with a round coffee table between them. Behind his desk was a door that led back to a private bathroom, and a room no bigger than a closet where he had a cot set up so he could crash if he had to work crazy hours. There was a gunmetal-gray gun safe next to the door.

Jack liked to keep weapons close. I knew he probably had a backup in his desk drawer, and he always wore his ankle holster. I found guns in random places all around the house —dish towel drawers, under a sofa cushion, and in the tank behind the toilet.

I paced around the office and felt my anxiety increasing, and I realized it was because of what Malachi had said about watching us. I'd felt his eyes on us. It was impossible not to. He'd conditioned me, ever since he'd come back from the dead, to look over my shoulder. I was surprised I didn't have ulcers.

I went around to each of the windows and closed the blinds. We couldn't see out, and no one could see in. Jack raised his brows in question, but I just shook my head. We needed to be more careful. If Malachi had set up these poison murders to distract us, then we were playing right into his hands. And now there were unprecedented crowds in the streets, and he could move in and out of spaces easily.

"Listen, Ernie," Jack said, leaning back in his chair. "I'm not sure what more you think can be done. It almost sounds like you're blaming me for not preventing a crazy person from killing people. But last time I checked, neither you nor I can tell the future. We've contained this very quickly, and we'll continue to investigate every lead and talk to every person until we find out who's responsible. The crime lab in Richmond is working around the clock, and the CDC was called in after the second victim showed up. The best thing you can do right now is stop griping in my ear and let me get back to my job."

Jack listened for a few more seconds. "I don't care if it costs me an election. No offense, but I'm not particularly worried about how much your opinion influences the people when everyone in town knows you've been messing around on your wife for the last six months with Margaret Miller. Worry about your own election."

"Dang," I whispered. Everyone in Bloody Mary suspected something was going on between Ernie and Margaret, but Ernie's wife was so sweet no one wanted to cause her any problems by speaking up.

Jack pulled the phone away from his ear and looked at the screen. "I guess he hung up," he said. "What's going on? What's wrong?"

I took the ring out of my pocket and then my body crumpled onto the chair in front of his desk. I tossed the ring so it landed on the pile of papers sitting in front of him.

"Where'd this come from?" he asked, not picking it up.

I couldn't blame him. It was a bad omen.

"I found it on my desk yesterday," I said. "After I finished Nina Walsh's autopsy. Nash had staked out, keeping watch the whole time I was down there except for when I brought him down to tell him about the poisoning. We came back up and I showered, and when I came out it was just there."

"When you put it in the safe," Jack said. "You never took it out again?

"I haven't thought about it since I put it in there," I said. "After I saw it on the desk, I shoved it in my pocket, and then we got busy with Doug coming into town and Warren Buchanan's murder, so I forgot to tell you about it."

"We know your dad likes to play these games," Jack said. "He likes to keep you off guard, constantly looking over your shoulder. It's psychological warfare. And he's good at it."

"Believe me," I said. "When Chen and I left the house this morning the ring was sitting in my seat in the Suburban. I never took it out of my pocket from the other day. I'd forgotten about it. I just tossed all my clothes in the dirty clothes hamper in the bathroom. Malachi knew exactly where I put it, and exactly where to look for it."

Jack stared at the ring, and I could tell he was trying to get a rein on his temper. The news wasn't going to get any better, so I pressed on.

"There's more," I said. "He stopped me outside the funeral home today."

Jack's head snapped up. "What?"

I nodded. "Broad daylight. There were people and cars everywhere. He has no fear of getting caught. He'd changed his looks again. An old man this time. If I'd seen him from a distance, I would've pegged him as late seventies or eighties, and I wouldn't have recognized him at all. He walked with a cane. But his eyes were the same. He can't hide his eyes."

"What did he say?" Jack asked. "Where was Chen?"

"Bathroom," I answered. "I went out and put my bag and the samples in the trunk, and he came up behind me. He stabbed me in the leg with a hypodermic needle, and then told me if he pressed the plunger that I'd be dead before I hit the ground."

The scar over Jack's eyebrow turned white, and he pushed back from his chair so he could walk around. He paced like a caged lion, and violence simmered just below the surface.

"Are you okay?" he asked.

He finally dropped down into the seat next to mine and took my hand.

"I have no idea," I said. "I'm not dead, so in that regard I guess I'm fine. But I've got an idea that I want to float by you. And I'm hoping you'll tell me I'm crazy."

"What is it?" he asked.

"I don't know," I said, pulling my hand back and rubbing

my hands over my face. "Maybe I'm crazy. But is it outside the realm of possibility that Malachi's the one behind these poison murders?"

Jack opened his mouth to say something, but then he paused and sat up straight in his chair. "No," he said. "It's definitely a possibility. And I don't think you're crazy. Unless we both are and are just suffering from acute paranoia."

"Good to know," I said. "But think about it. Think of the chaos this has caused. You've got personnel doing double duty, us included. Our attention is splintered, and we're not taking the care we should be. He can move freely through the crowds and no one would think twice about it or notice. He's got us running all over the place. He's been in our house. I asked him if it was him who had killed those two victims."

"What did he say?" Jack asked.

"He said it was an interesting case, and that it seemed like the perfect crime."

Jack blew out a breath. "There's no such thing," he said, his eyes hardening with a steely determination I wasn't feeling at the moment.

"That's what I said," I told him. "Malachi disagreed with me. He's curious about the kid, so it'll only be a matter of time before he's got the intel he needs on him. He's been watching us, and I've felt his eyes on me for days. He knows there's something up with Doug. He mentioned how odd it was that the minute Doug stepped into the house all outside interference was shut down."

"He's getting desperate for the flash drives," Jack said.

"Yeah, he mentioned that," I said. "For whatever reason, he's ramped up the timeline. He said he hadn't found them in the house or the funeral home, and he mentioned something about you maybe having them locked up at the station or in a safety deposit box."

"Desperation leads to mistakes."

"Jack," I said, pleadingly. "He's done playing. He gave us until midnight tonight to hand them over, or he said he's going to come and get them."

"Then we need to be ready for him," Jack said. "Let's go see what kind of progress Doug is making."

"Hey, Sheriff," Betsy Clement said as we came out of the office. "That FBI guy called again. I told him you were a little busy with murders at the moment, but I'd be happy to send him the initial police report on Carver's crash. I told him I'd fax it to him."

Jack's lips twitched. "Did the fax machine get fixed when I wasn't looking?"

"Oh," she said, putting the tips of her fingers to her mouth. "I'm always getting the technology stuff confused. I'm old, you know."

Jack nodded solemnly, and then knuckle-bumped her on the way by. There was a narrow hallway over by the bathrooms, and because I care about my personal safety, there were two things I wouldn't touch at the station—the coffee and the bathrooms.

There was a door at the end of the narrow hallway with a rectangular window, and crooked blinds on it.

"What room is this?" I asked.

"Screening room," Jack said. "Kind of. It's dark and it has a TV, so it's the easiest place to watch surveillance tapes. Doug said he does his best work in a dark room and with pizza."

Jack opened the door and I felt like I was walking into a college dorm room. I crinkled my nose in disgust involuntarily, and my lips peeled back from my teeth.

"Eww," I said.

"It's on the list for upgrades," Jack said.

"You should probably just burn it to the ground and start over. Did you raid the elementary school from 1988? That looks just like the TV cart they brought in on movie day."

"Those were my best memories of school," Jack said. "I wanted to preserve them."

"I thought most of your best memories from school happened under the bleachers," I said.

"I can't even bring those memories up, they were so meaningless," he said.

"Nice save."

"What are y'all talking about?" Doug said. "Close the door. The light is causing a glare."

Doug looked a little worse for wear. Jack must have rolled him out of bed and put him in the car without a chance to change clothes. His hair looked like he'd combed it with an eggbeater, and he had the squinty-eye, glazed look of someone who'd been sitting in the dark for too long.

Besides the TV cart, there was a modern projector hanging from the ceiling and a wall screen. Doug was sitting at the table with his computer open in front of him, an empty pizza box next to him, and *Bob's Burgers* was playing on the screen, though there was no sound.

"This is crazy messed up, man," Doug said. "I mean, like, I've never seen an encryption cadence like this. Whoever made this is crazy skilled."

"Does that mean you can't do it?" Jack asked.

"*Pssh*," Doug said. "Not to worry. I've totally got it. But usually stuff like this takes me an hour or two. It only took me seven minutes to hack into the Pentagon. This has been, like, hours. But now that I've got it figured out, I should be able to transfer all the data to a separate server and make backup files."

Jack looked at his watch. "It's two o'clock. We've got until midnight to make our deadline. How long will it take to transfer everything?"

"Trinity is doing everything she can," Doug said. He turned the computer screen so we could see a series of numbers and screens were flashing in rapid succession. "It's going to take time. Especially if the other five are as complicated as this one."

"Other five?" I asked, looking at Jack.

"Yeah," he said. "I've got the others in a safe place. I

figured it would be harder for him to break into the police station than the house or anywhere else."

"My dad said there were only five total," I said, gripping Jack's arm. "He specifically said he wanted all five back by midnight."

"Maybe he didn't realize what we had," he said. "We took those flash drives out of a box from the bunker where all his stuff was. Maybe he just forgot how many were in there."

"Maybe," I said. But my dad wasn't one to get the details wrong.

"We need to get home," Jack said. "You're right about the chaos. If your dad is the one responsible for the murders of Nina Walsh and Warren Buchanan, then we're playing right into his hands. And we'll probably have more victims. If he's not the killer, then there's nothing we can do until we hear back from the lab in Richmond. Nash can take point on that."

"Can we see some of the things that are on the flash drive?" I asked Doug.

With a few strokes on the keyboard the rapid jargon changed into something else. There were scanned documents dating back more than twenty years, but also electronic files that had dates of just over two years ago. There was a Super Top Secret Clearance stamp at the top of each form.

"Looks like authorization forms," Jack said, scanning quickly. "Malachi was working for the CIA. We already knew that. But he was triple dipping. He was brokering arms deals and gathering intel for his boss. And at the same time, he was selling the names and locations of the deals to foreign governments, setting up two drops so the CIA was happy getting their target, and then Malachi was siphoning off the rest of the shipment and money for a side deal.

"The CIA knew they had a mole, so they set up a team of agents to track everything back to the source. It looks like Malachi sold those agents' names to competing agencies and every one of them was picked off."

"This could be bad," Doug said, sweat starting to form on his upper lip. "I'm already kind of in trouble with the government. It would be really not good if they found out I hacked into this stuff. Do you know how much it sucks to wear an ankle bracelet and be on house arrest? Do you know how many social issues I have?"

"You're going to be fine," Jack told him. "And we'll work on your social issues when this is all over. Maybe toss a ball around or something."

"I don't have good depth perception," Doug said. "I used to get hit in the face with balls quite a bit when I went to public school."

"Then we'll try the arcade," Jack said. "My point is we're in the middle of this now, and there's no going back. We can only go forward. These people have been using the government as their personal piggybank, with no account-ability for decades. They'll kill us all if they find out we've seen any of this."

"That's not making me feel better," Doug said.

Jack clapped his hand on Doug's shoulder. "Your Uncle

Ben is my best friend. And he believes in you. Just like I do. I think you can run circles around anyone sitting in some office and throwing out orders. I know it's a lot of pressure on you. But we need you to keep a shield around us. We don't want anyone to be able to listen or watch by electronic means. Can you do that?"

"Yeah," Doug said, wiping his upper lip. "I can do that. There's no way they're getting through Trinity. She provides a one-mile shield for satellite imagery and listening devices. The government doesn't have anything that comes close to that."

"There you go," Jack said. "I'm going to go get the rest of the flash drives. Why don't you pack up and we'll head back to the house? I want to get us away from these crowds."

"Okay," Doug said. "But you're out of food at your house."

"We'll find something," Jack said. "And kid, good work. Your Uncle Ben would be proud."

Doug flushed a little and shrugged. "Thanks. It's easier not to follow the rules. Of course, that gets you in bigger trouble if you get caught."

"How'd you get caught the first time?" Jack asked.

Doug grinned. "Uncle Ben. He said it was an important lesson I needed to learn, and that if God gave me this much talent then I needed to do something with it that could change the world. Not just something for myself."

"Yep, that sounds like Ben," Jack said. "Can Trinity run interference when she's closed?"

"No," Doug said. "I could technically route everything through my cell, and then ping it off different locations, but there's always the chance someone could piggyback off my signal and get in. Trinity is the safest way to go."

"Then wait until right before we walk out the door before you shut her down," Jack said. "We need to keep all our cards as close to the vest as we can. Which means I don't want a word from anyone the entire way back home."

Doug and I shared a look, and then I followed Jack out of the room.

He stopped in the middle of the squad room and put his hands on his hips. "Listen up," Jack said. "Martinez, Cole, Lewis, Colburn, Smith, and Walters. I want you all to suit up and work a protective detail. We've had some new developments that are life threatening, so you're on a need-to-know basis right now. I'll give you a full briefing once we get back to my house. Push anything to do with the poison murders and The Witches' Brew over to Nash, Riley, Cheek, and Chen.

"Everyone else," he said. "Nash is in charge of the poison murders. Keep working it. Keep talking to people and collecting products. Everything has to be tested. Knock on doors if you have to and make sure people know what's going on. Put out PSAs for people to check on elderly neighbors, or anyone who doesn't show up for work.

"Work with the guys from Stafford, and let's start getting the people outside dispersed. It's turned into a street party, and I'm not sure half the people out there know what's going on. Risky's Bar was doing a nice business, so make sure people are driving safely and responsibly, and make sure they stay inside the bar if they're still drinking. I saw Harley Jacobson tossing out six-packs from his lawn chair.

"I want all available units out and visible. Let's get people off the street and back into their homes, and if someone looks out of place or like they're up to no good I want you to stop and talk to them. The important thing is to keep the community calm, and keep crime to a minimal. Be friendly and helpful, but don't tolerate any bullshit."

Nash came into the squad room looking harried, and he stopped where he was when he realized Jack was talking.

"Let's go," Jack said to his officers. And then he looked at Nash and nodded to his office. "Nash, catch me up."

Jack motioned for me to come too, and I remembered my mother's ring was still on Jack's desk. I went over and picked it up, shoving it back into my pocket, before Nash could see.

"Anything new on The Witches' Brew homicides?" Jack asked.

"Just collecting and compiling data at this point," Nash said. "I've typed up all the statements, and reviewed the autopsy reports. I've gone through and cross-referenced people and places, anything to give us a lead. There's not one person Nina Walsh and Warren Buchanan have in common. At least not that I can find. They don't shop at the same grocery stores, share any business interests, or use the same bank. The only thing they have in common is that they bought headache medicine from The Witches' Brew."

"What does Esmerelda have to say?" Jack asked.

"She remembered both by name, and she said they're

regular customers. She said Warren Buchanan gets chronic headaches, and he swears by her herbal remedy. He keeps it stocked in his private plane, and their various homes around the world. Isobel Buchanan told Esmerelda that Warren hated to be without it, and always made sure she carried some in her purse and had an extra in his travel bag."

"Sounds obsessive," I said.

Nash shrugged. "I guess the headaches were pretty bad."

"What about the financial aspect of it?" Jack asked. "Anything jump out at you there?"

"Nina Walsh's policy was for a hundred K," Nash said. "In the grand scheme of things, it's not that much considering Roy's third of the moving company is a million dollars. Roy and the daughter are equal beneficiaries, so they'll each only get fifty thousand. The daughter was pretty upset, and you could tell she felt guilty about the estrangement. She's got nothing good to say about Roy."

"Can't blame her on that one," I said.

"What about the Buchanan's?" Jack asked.

"Rich, rich, rich," Nash said. "Isobel is Warren's third wife, and they've been married just over ten years. Their relationship started before the second marriage ended, and wife number two got a nice settlement in the divorce.

"Warren owns Buchanan Gems and Minerals. Basically, all the high-end retailers like DeBeers and Cartier buy their gems from him. He owns diamond, gold, and platinum mines all over the world, and he's got interests in others."

Jack whistled. "And who does that go to?"

"Warren has a son from his first marriage. Tate Buchanan. A couple of years older than wife number three. He's set to take over the company. Everything dealing with the company goes to him. Isobel gets the house, personal jewelry, and whatever is in their shared personal checking account, but that's about it. From what I understand, Warren kept most of his liquid cash in his business accounts, which now belong to the son. I called and talked to the estate attorney."

"What about life insurance policies?" Jack asked.

"He's got a million-dollar policy," Nash said. "But it doubles if Warren has an accidental death."

"That's interesting," I said. "And a pretty unusual policy."

"When I talked to the wife again, she said it was because Warren sometimes liked to visit the mines and get his hands dirty," Nash said. "Those mines can be dangerous, and the insurance was in case something happened to him on one of those trips. Isobel said he took her to a diamond mine in Africa and let her search for a diamond for her engagement ring. That's how he proposed to her."

"That house is worth a few million at least, plus two million for the life insurance. Then jewels and a bank account. That's not too shabby of a haul for her."

"In theory," Nash said. "But when you add in the fact that Warren makes around fifty million a year, it's chump change. They had a prenup, but he's definitely worth more to her alive than dead."

"Good work," Jack said. "I assigned Riley, Cheek, and

Chen at your disposal. Just keep me updated on any progress."

"You got it, boss," Nash said.

"You've got the flash drives?" I asked after Nash had left.

"In a manner of speaking," he said.

He went to the gun safe behind his desk and used the keypad to open it. There was an assortment of handguns, several high-powered rifles, and a shotgun. He took the shotgun and racked the chamber, ejecting a shell. He caught it before it hit the ground and then he tossed it to me.

"Umm," I said, holding the shell casing. "What am I supposed to do with this?"

"Open it," he said.

Jack ejected a second shell, and kept repeating the process until the shotgun was empty.

I grabbed a pair of scissors from the desk and stuck it in the end of the shell, folding back the crimped plastic until I could see inside. I turned it upside down and a flash drive fell out into my hand. Jack brought over the other four shells and I continued to open them.

"Six flash drives total," he said. "Not five."

"An inconsistency that makes me very uneasy," I said. "We've got to make sure Doug is protected. He's just a kid."

"If any agency gets a whiff that Malachi is alive before we can alert the attorney general and blast this to the public, none of us will make it out of here alive. They'll drop a bomb on King George County and walk away smiling. There are too many people in too many powerful positions. And we haven't even scratched the surface to see what else those flash drives hold."

It was just starting to dawn on me how big this could get. *Would* get. How did a sheriff and a coroner from small town Virginia end up in what was sure to be a national scandal? We would be lucky to make it out alive. People died for political reasons all the time. Because they knew too much or were a potential problem. It wasn't uncommon for those *problems* to be found dead in a freak accident or by suspected suicide. Washington D.C. had been taking care of problems like that for a lot longer than Jack or I had been alive.

"Jaye," Jack said, stopping me from opening the door to his office.

I stopped to look at him and felt the lump in my throat.

"I'm sorry I hurt you," he said. "It's not something I ever intentionally want to do. I love you. I hope you know how much. But maybe this time I did mean to hurt you. I think…" He stopped to gather his thoughts, and he looked down momentarily. "I think I said that about you sabotaging our happiness because I was starting to resent everything we've been through the last year or so. It was just a moment of temporary weakness, and I was feeling sorry for myself. I kept wondering why. And how.

"The things that have happened to us aren't normal. And I want normal. The things that have happened to us since this started don't happen to most people in a lifetime. No one would believe it if we wrote it as fiction. Most couples probably wouldn't make it through with their relationship intact, but we're stronger because of it.

"I feel the pressure to keep you safe. To keep everyone safe. And I feel your father breathing more and more down my neck with every passing day. All I can say is I'm sorry. I know we'll get through this. I know that this is just a small slice of our lives together."

"It feels like a pretty big slice," I said, trying to smile, but I don't think I accomplished it.

"Yeah, it does," he said, dropping his head to rest his forehead against mine. "But we're doing it together. And twenty years from now we'll look back and this will be a fun story we can tell our kids. It'll barely be a blip on our radar."

"I'm sorry too," I said. "He's getting to me. I had a brief moment today with that syringe sticking out of my leg where I wanted to call his bluff." Jack squeezed my hands tight in his. "I thought, very selfishly I might add, that if he just pressed the plunger it wouldn't be my problem anymore."

"I'm glad it was only a brief moment you had the thought," he said.

"Very brief," I assured him. "Because my anger took over pretty quickly after that. I might have been sarcastic."

"Then it makes perfect sense why he gave us the deadline," he said with a short laugh.

I put my hand on his face and kissed him softly. "I wouldn't leave you," I said. "Not if it was in my control. And I won't let Malachi Graves separate us. He underestimates us because we're stronger together. He wants our attention splintered. He wants us to fight. He knows the only way he can win is if he separates us."

Jack nodded. "You're right. I think it's time we smoke him out of hiding."

17

JACK TOLD DOUG TO GET INTO THE BACK OF THE SUBURBAN and lie down for the ride to the house. He didn't want to take a chance of any more projectiles coming through the window and injuring the one person who could make sense of the flash drives.

It was a long, silent twenty-minute drive. I felt bad for Doug. Despite the advanced understanding of his brain, he was still just a fifteen-year-old kid.

Martinez and Smith were in the unit in front of us, and Colburn and Lewis were in front of them. That left Walters and Cole in the unit behind us. It felt like my head was on a swivel the entire drive. I looked for every tree limb blowing in the breeze and in every car as it passed us by. Jack reached over and grabbed my hand, but he didn't speak.

There were still a few hours of daylight left, and the last mile on Heresy Road felt like the longest stretch. We slowed as we reached the turn to our driveway, and Jack put his weapon in his lap, keeping his hand on it in case he had to use it quickly.

We parked in our usual place, and Martinez and Smith got out of their unit and came up to Jack's window. Jack rolled it down.

"We'll go in and check it out," Martinez told Jack, and Jack handed him the keys to the house.

I could tell Martinez had questions. A need-to-know basis wasn't easy, but everyone Jack had chosen trusted him, and Jack trusted them.

Colburn and Lewis checked the outside perimeter, and Walters and Cole stayed close to us for added protection. Martinez stuck his head out the front door and gave us the all clear, so we quickly gathered our things from the Suburban and headed inside, keeping Doug sheltered between us.

Walters and Cole stayed outside to keep watch, but Colburn and Lewis followed us inside. Jack locked the door and then directed us into his office. He pointed for Doug to get Trinity up and running so we were protected from outside intruders, and stuck his hand up to keep anyone from asking questions. Jack took a remote that was sitting on his desk and closed all the blinds. Then he pointed it at the far wall and several screens came down.

"We're good to go," Doug said. "Man, I'm starving."

"What the hell is going on?" Colburn asked. "This doesn't feel like a standard stalker situation. It feels like some serious shit is about to go down."

"That's why you're here," Jack said. "Because I trust you

with my life. And with Jaye's and Doug's. We've got a situation that's been brewing the past year or so. You all remember what happened with Jaye's parents?"

Four sets of eyes turned to me, and I fought the urge to squirm. It was second nature after living through the hell and ridicule I'd gone through after their "deaths." Memories were long in Bloody Mary.

"Sure," Martinez said. "Don't worry, Doc. We know you're a good seed. You're not guilty just because your parents were."

"I appreciate that, Martinez," I said. "Really, you have no idea how much. My father is alive."

You could've heard a pin drop in the room, and Lewis sat down onto the couch as if his legs had given out.

"Wow," Martinez said. "I wasn't expecting that one."

"Believe me," I said. "Me neither." I filled them in as quickly as I could and brought them up to speed on why Doug was there and what Malachi had said to me when he'd cornered me outside the funeral home.

"You should have told us sooner," Colburn said, looking at Jack. "We could've been looking for him."

"I couldn't take the risk that something might happen to one of you," Jack said. "Look what he did to Carver."

"He's been watching us," I said. "He's better than any of us could possibly imagine. He's slipped in and out of this house and the funeral home while y'all were watching. He's the one who caused that fire hydrant to explode. And we think there's a possibility…" I hated to even say it. To admit that the man who'd raised me might have killed two innocent people just to get what he wanted. "A possibility that he might be responsible for the two poisoning murders."

No one said anything for a few minutes, and then Colburn nodded his head. "Makes sense," he said. "Throw everything into disorder. Split resources and attention."

"I still want Nash and the team to work it like a regular homicide, just in case," Jack said. "But the priority is drawing out Malachi. And that's what Doug was brought in for. He was able to get through the encryptions of the flash drives."

"Is this a bad time to tell you that I can feel my blood sugar dropping?" Doug asked.

"It's not a great time, no," Jack said. "But I'm sure we've got something you haven't eaten yet in the freezer."

While we'd been filling everyone in, Doug had been setting Trinity up next to Jack's laptop, and connecting them so the wall screens were filled with the information that had been downloaded so far. I didn't even want to know how he'd gotten into Jack's computer so easily.

"This is the information from the first flash drive," Doug said, rubbing his stomach when it rumbled.

"Well," Lewis said. "That's not good. What's the plan?"

"I've been thinking about it," Jack said. "And I think the best thing—the safest thing—we can do is to download all the information, give Malachi wiped versions of the flash drives, and then upload everything to the internet. The only way this is going to be put in the right people's hands is for it to be public knowledge. The Department of Justice can decide what to do from there."

"I can do that easy," Doug said. "And I can make sure the information can't get buried. I can send it in a personal email to the president even. Sometimes I like to send him emails with my thoughts. They can never figure out where the emails are coming from. It's hilarious."

Colburn shook his head. "Geez, kid."

"What?" Doug asked. "I've got to have a little fun. Besides, I'm telling him important stuff. I've alerted him to potential military catastrophes twice. I built this really cool program, so it's basically like playing a real-life version of Risk."

Doug and Martinez started talking video games at that point, and Colburn went outside to update Walters and Cole. I followed Jack into the kitchen and helped him hunt for anything that Doug hadn't already eaten.

"Wheat Thins," I said, holding up a box from the pantry. "I think we've still got some cheese and grapes."

"That's good," Jack said, and then he opened the fridge and dug around until he'd found enough to put on a platter. He also grabbed some steaks and chicken he'd put in the drawer to thaw out.

I raised my brows. "Seems like an odd time to have a cookout."

"We're going to have a cook in," Jack said. "We're stuck here for the moment, and the kid needs something normal, or as much as we can give him."

I narrowed my eyes at Jack, and cocked my head to the

side. Something was brewing in that brain of his. "We can't keep him, Jack," I said, and realized I'd hit the nail right on the head. "He has a mom and a family."

"He's not a stray puppy," Jack said. "Of course we can't keep him. But he needs people in his life, especially men. And Ben is going to be out of commission for a while, and Michelle has her hands full between Ben and the kids. From what I've gathered, his mom works a lot. It'd be good for him to have a place to go."

"I see your point," I said, moving across the kitchen to kiss him. "You're a good man, Jack Lawson."

"Not according to Ernie Rodgers," Jack said.

"Ernie Rodgers is a horse's ass," I said, and Jack pointed to the jar. I didn't have any quarters left so I went to my purse and found a dollar. "There, now I'm paid up for three more times."

"Probably not the best way to look at it," Jack said.

———

OVER THE NEXT FEW HOURS, the guys rotated from outside to inside and back again. We ate, we talked, and we watched a continuous amount of information come across the screen. Names of agents who'd been compromised, and illegal deals that had been sanctioned by the head of the FBI. After the attorney general cleaned house, there was going to be no one living there anymore.

Doug had wiped each flash drive after he'd made sure the information was securely downloaded and stored. He'd also eaten the biggest steak, the rest of the Wheat Thins, a jar of olives from the back of the fridge, and a box of Grape Nuts that I knew had been in the pantry at least two years when our friend Vaughn had left them after he'd stayed the weekend.

I was helping Jack clean up the kitchen when I heard a woman's voice coming from the office. I dropped the pan into the sink and suds splashed everywhere, and I ran into the office, my heart in my throat.

I hadn't heard my mother's voice since before her death. At least the fake one. Malachi had told me things had been too dangerous and she hadn't made it. But he'd never given me the details.

And now, here she was on the screen, and I wanted to throw something at the wall. Her face looked the same. My mother had those timeless bones and good skin that never seemed to age. Her hair had always been dark like mine— I'd always thought that was the one thing I'd gotten from her before I found out she wasn't my biological mother. Her eyes were dark and serious, and her lips hypnotic as she spoke matter-of-factly into the camera.

"Look at the date," Jack said, pointing to the top corner of the screen. "That's only months ago."

I gasped and put my hand over my mouth.

"My name is Angela Davis Graves. Agent number 20014. I've been sanctioned by the CIA to bring in my husband, Malachi Graves. In exchange, I'll be given leniency for crimes I committed after he recruited and trained me.

Malachi is a threat and a danger to anyone he comes in

contact with. He has no conscience. No fear. And he has his own agenda, which makes him dangerous.

I felt Jack's hand on my shoulder, and everyone in the room was silent. It took me a moment to process what she was saying.

Malachi has in his possession several flash drives with sensitive information. His need for power far surpassed his need for money. He liked being the man who stood in the background. The man those in power relied on, but who was strategically calling all the shots. He's a master chess player, and there's only one way to beat him at his own game.

If you break through the encryption on the flash drives, you'll discover names and bank accounts where he's keeping large amounts of money that are funding terrorist organizations all over the world. There are names of agents, past and present, who've been compromised and have prices on their heads. There are names of world leaders who have sold nuclear weapons to countries who would use them against their own people.

Malachi can pull the strings because he has information on everyone. Information is his greatest commodity. He can sell it, or he can use it. He's desperate for the flash drives because I destroyed his entire network with a well-placed bomb. This information is his lifeline. It's his access to his money, to his contacts, and it has the formula for the disease he's getting ready to spread across Europe and cause a global panic. And he's got the keys to the antidote he can sell to the highest pharmaceutical bidder. He'll do whatever it takes…"

"Whoa," Doug said, rolling his chair over to Trinity. His fingers typed furiously across the keyboard, and he was swearing under his breath.

"What's going on?" Jack said.

"Someone is overriding Trinity," Doug said. "This is impossible."

I watched the screens go blank, and the information that we'd been reading disappeared, image by image. And then in its place was a satellite image, blurry at first and then it came into focus.

"That's the house," Jack said, "And they've got infrared."

My brain was slow to process the red images on the screen, but then Jack moved to the desk to get an extra weapon and I watched him do it in real time on the screen.

"Shut it down," Jack ordered Doug.

"I'm trying," Doug said. "The only computer that has the capabilities to do this is Miranda. She's out there somewhere."

"Jack," I said, pointing to the two heat signatures lying prone outside.

Martinez was gathering extra ammo from Jack's gun cabinet, and Lewis and Colburn each took a rifle. Smith drew his weapon and waited for instructions.

"Jaye, take the kid and Trinity upstairs," Jack said. "I guess Malachi couldn't wait until midnight."

He handed me a revolver, and I grabbed Doug by the shirt-sleeve to pull him up and get him moving. He was still trying to block entry to the intruder.

"Let's go, Doug," I said, tugging harder. "You can do that upstairs."

We filed out of the office with Martinez and Lewis in front of us, and Jack, Colburn, and Smith behind us. I was hoping Cole and Walters were only incapacitated instead of dead.

We were past the kitchen and Doug and I were about to split off to head toward the stairs when I heard a terrible whistling noise. The windows at the back of the house exploded simultaneously, and all I could do was tackle Doug, forcing him to the ground.

I landed weirdly on my arm and felt my shoulder pop out of socket, and I cried out in pain. Doug's pale face was inches from mine, his eyes rolling from side to side. I pushed him as best I could toward the stairs, to tuck us into the little wedge that might give us some protection.

My ears were ringing, and smoke and dust filled the air, making it almost impossible to see. I kept scanning the room for Jack, but I didn't see anything but Martinez's and Lewis's prone bodies on the ground, covered in blood. They'd taken the brunt of the blast.

The house became a warzone, and gunfire erupted all around us. I couldn't tell the direction it was coming from because it felt like it was coming from everywhere. I saw a man walk through the smoke, and I knew it was my father, and he had his weapon pointed right at Jack.

"No!" I cried out, and I saw the evil in his smile as his finger pressed down on the trigger.

The shot cracked loudly, and my body jerked on top of Doug, almost as if I'd felt the impact of the bullet. I was already crawling on my hands and knees. I didn't care if I became the target.

But as I pulled myself along the floor with one working arm, the glass cutting my hands and pricking into my knees, I swore I heard my name. I jerked my head up and watched my father fall to his knees, his chest a bloom of red and a trickle of blood dripping from the corner of his mouth.

He turned his head and looked straight at me, even as the life faded from his eyes.

"I want all weapons on the ground," a voice called out. "I'd hate for anyone else to have to die tonight."

"Hello, Angela," Jack said.

A sob escaped my throat at the sound of Jack's voice. He was alive.

"Congratulations on the marriage," my mother said. "Put down your weapon. This isn't your fight anymore."

"Honestly," Jack said. "I don't know whose fight it is. What I do know is that there are a lot of people who need to pay for what's on those flash drives. You shouldn't have killed Malachi. Death is too easy for him."

"Hell is never easy on anyone," she said. "My mission was to take out Malachi and collect the flash drives. I'm also supposed to dispose of anyone who's seen the information.

There's not an agency in the world who doesn't have something to hide in there. So, I'm going to do one good deed in my life and tell you to hit that button, so all that information is spread to every corner of the earth. And do it soon. If the cleanup team gets here before you do it, they'll finish the job for me."

My mother looked at me, and I realized I'd never known who she was. Not even a little bit. She might as well have been a stranger to me.

"You'll need to get that arm seen to," she said. And then she disappeared into the chasm between what had once been our house and the night.

18

Jack and I stood over Martinez's hospital bed the next morning. He had a big family, and they'd all trickled into the waiting room sometime during the night. It was nice to watch them together—to watch them pray for their son, brother, and uncle—to watch them shed tears for the loss of Lewis.

That's what a family was supposed to do. What they were supposed to be.

Lewis's family hadn't been as big and boisterous as Martinez's, but they were just as much a unit. And for this moment in time, it was that unity that was holding the broken pieces of their lives together.

Jack had spoken with them at length. He'd held Lewis's mother as she'd cried over the loss of her only son, and he'd assured Lewis's shell-shocked widow that her unborn child would know his father. That her son would always have a family.

Our losses were great, but they could've been much greater.

And all I could think was, *It's over*. Malachi was dead, and my mother had disappeared back into the custody of the CIA. We'd followed her instructions and all of the information that had been on the flash drives had gone public. Doug had even sent personal emails with attachments to the president and the attorney general. We were hoping it was the best way for the cleanup crew to not follow through on killing us. I was too tired to care at the moment.

We'd hastily packed bags and called in the troops. I didn't know my mother. Didn't trust her. And there were no secrets anymore. The more traffic and publicity there was, the safer we'd be.

Cole and Walters had been shot with tranquilizers, so they were sleeping off the hangover in a hospital room. Doug had been taken to his mother at the hotel she and Michelle were sharing, and immediately given her a hug.

The EMTs had brought Lewis, Martinez, and Malachi to the hospital, but Lewis and my father had been DOA, so they'd been taken straight to the morgue. Martinez was lucky to be alive. That's all there was to it.

Carver's wife, Michelle, had been right. I'd watched the entirety of my mother's video. She hadn't started as an agent with deception in her mind. She'd been young and in love, and my father had been a manipulative bastard who'd molded her into exactly what he'd needed. My mother hadn't been innocent through the years, but she'd recognized that there were wrongs that had to be righted, and that Malachi had to be stopped.

She'd been planting the seeds of faking their own deaths for years before Malachi had eventually felt the heat of his activities catching up with him. And then once they'd escaped their death together, she'd had to do it again and make him believe she was really dead so she could lure him in.

"You ready?" Jack asked.

We'd both been patched up, and my shoulder had been slipped back into socket. They'd put my arm in a sling for good measure, and I was grateful for it because any movement hurt. We'd gotten a room at a hotel for the night, and we'd at least been able to shower and change clothes.

Jack was good about thinking of the future and different scenarios, so he'd told me to dress nice, and he'd helped me with my hair since I couldn't brush it myself. I'd gone with simple black leggings and a black sleeveless tunic that had been the least amount of trouble to put on. Jack had chosen gray dress slacks and a light blue shirt. And he'd brought his sports coat for good measure.

There'd been an army of reporters waiting outside the doors at the hospital when we'd come back to check on Martinez and to talk to Lewis's family. Not just Floyd Parker either, but reporters from all over the country.

"Yeah," I said. "I'm ready. I guess we're going to need to remodel the living room."

"I'm not sure explosions and bullet holes are the décor we're looking for," Jack said. "But we can go for a Valentine's Day Massacre look if you'd prefer."

"Hilarious," I said. "When do you think we can go home?"

"I don't know," he said. "We'll take it day by day. Staying alive is the first priority."

"Do you really think they'll leave us alone?" I asked.

"Yeah," he said. "I do. They've got too many problems to deal with us. The best thing they can do is leave us alone and let us go about our lives. Malachi is gone, and they have a leash on your mother."

We left Martinez's room and headed out of the hospital to the Suburban. Jack's unit wouldn't be ready for another week. The sun was bright in a cloudless sky, and I searched for my sunglasses, annoyed that it was my right arm that was constrained.

"When do you think they'll want to do Lewis's funeral?" I asked, taking a little longer to haul myself into the passenger side.

"The family wants to do it Sunday with the viewing on Saturday," Jack said. "They'll be in to see you later this afternoon or tomorrow morning. I gave them your cell number. I didn't think you'd mind. They asked for you specifically."

"No," I said, the words barely audible. "I don't mind. I'll be available for them."

"He's the first line of duty death in King George County in thirty-five years," Jack said.

"You can't blame yourself," I told him. "You'll drive yourself crazy with what-ifs. This sucks. There's no doubt about it, but you know better than anyone it's the risk of the job. It could just as easily have been you or me, or one of the other guys.

"When you went on that raid where you got shot, were you

thinking about how it might be the last time you'd ever see your friends or leave your house?"

"No," he said, his grip tightening on the wheel.

"It's because it's the job. The thought is there in the back of your mind, but you can't dwell on it every time you leave the house. Lewis and all the other guys weren't thinking about it either. They came because it was the job. Lewis died protecting us. I'll never forget that."

Jack let out a slow breath. "I know," he said. "Martinez is going to have a rough time getting through this. He and Lewis were like brothers. Martinez is going to be Lewis's kid's godfather."

"That's good," I told him. "They'll need each other."

"I've been getting nonstop calls from reporters," he said. "I'm going to give a press conference this afternoon. Maybe that will slow them down some. They know about your father and that he was the one responsible, but because there are so many people on those flash drives who are alive and in serious hot water, I don't think they'll spend too much time on you. But I'm sure you'll get calls."

"I turned my phone off," I said. "I'm thinking about getting a new one with a new number."

"They'll find that too," he said. "They're relentless." Jack's phone started to ring and he said, "See? Relentless."

But it was Nash's name that came up on the screen on the dashboard. Jack hit the answer button and said, "What've you got, Nash?"

"I just wanted to tell you I'm sorry to hear about Lewis.

Hitchcock is taking up donations for Sherry," he said, referring to Lewis's wife. "And a bunch of the guys are headed to the hospital. They're going to rotate sitting with Martinez and his family."

"That's good," Jack said. "Let's see if we can get local businesses to get involved in the donations for Sherry. I don't want her to have to worry about anything financial right now."

"Will do," Nash said. "I also called to update you on the case. I just got off the phone with the lab guys in Richmond. They finished the analysis of the poison in the capsules, and I think you're going to find this interesting."

"After the night we've had," he said. "I don't know if I can handle interesting."

"Ha," Nash said. "The powder inside the capsule was pure sodium cyanide. Specifically, it's the exact formula found in a certain brand produced back in 2006. Gold and gem miners use it because it'll eat away at the rock without damaging the gem."

"Oh," Jack said, perking up. "You're right. I do find that interesting."

"But here's the kicker," Nash said. "They also found these tiny green flecks in the powder that were only visible under the microscope. The green flecks are consistent in all the capsules from the poisoned tins. They didn't know what the green stuff was, but it was mostly copper sulfate and something called..." We could hear Nash flipping through papers until he found what he was looking for. "It's called diuron. Anyway, it took them a bit to figure it out, but those two things together are what's found in algaecide."

"Algaecide?" I asked, confused.

"Yeah, for saltwater fish tanks and pools," Nash said. "There's a store in Fredericksburg and a store in Richmond that sells that specific brand, so I called and asked the store managers about the stuff and how it was used. They both said that it comes in a tablet form and that it works best if you grind it up first before you put it in the tank."

I looked at Jack and raised my eyebrows in surprise. "Ohh-hh," I said as the lightbulb went off.

"That is very helpful information," Jack said. "Excellent work. Where are you now?"

"I'm heading to Fredericksburg. Both places said they'd send over a client list, but the store in Fredericksburg isn't computerized. How do you feel about serving a warrant and making a possible arrest this morning?"

Jack looked at me. We both lived the mantra that it was always better to do something than nothing. And going back to the station or to the hotel left too much room to do nothing but think about what we'd lost.

"We're in," I said.

"That's what I thought you'd say," Nash said. "I've already got you a warrant for the Buchanan house. I'll bet dollars to donuts you find the poison and the algaecide right there on the premises."

"I definitely think it's worth having another conversation with Mrs. Buchanan," Jack said.

"I think you're probably right," Nash said, and they disconnected.

Jack immediately made another call to the station, and Betsy Clement answered the phone.

"Who's on today?" Jack asked her.

"Pretty much everyone after what happened to Lewis and Martinez," she said. "The sheriff in Stafford said to keep his guys as long as you need them. Colburn's the LT on duty right now, so he's got everyone where he wants them to be. He refused to go home and miss his shift after last night. I know he was right there in the thick of things. Colburn's got a head as hard as a rock." She paused for a few seconds and then asked, "How are you doing, Sheriff?"

Betsy Clement rarely got personal. It was why she'd been a good secretary for so many years.

"I've had better days," Jack said, the surprise on his face evident. "It's going to be hard on everyone for a while.

"I remember the last time it happened," she said sadly. "Sergeant Smith's father. He was just a little thing at the time. Not even a year old. He's taking it real hard. He felt like he should've been able to do more last night. He and Colburn both. Survivor's guilt."

I could feel the weight of the world in Jack's sigh. "Can you patch me through to Colburn?"

"Sure thing," she said.

"Oh, and Betsy," he said. "Take the time off if you need it. It's hard on all of us. I know you love every person who puts on a uniform."

"Well," she said, her sniffle audible. "Never had kids of my own, and I've been married to this job. Being here is the best thing for me. I'm patching you through to Colburn," and then she was gone.

"Lieutenant Colburn," said a gruff voice into the phone.

"It's Jack. What the hell are you doing at work?"

"I'm fine," Colburn said. "I barely have a scratch on me, which isn't the case with Martinez, Cole and Walters. I need to work. And you need me to work. We're shorthanded."

Jack cut his eyes to me, and I mouthed the word, "Stubborn."

"Who do you have available to serve a warrant?" Jack asked him.

"Take your pick," Colburn said. "Everyone wants to be here, and things are slow."

"Send me Smith, Durrant, Riley, and Hops," Jack said. "Nash sent a copy of the signed warrant to email. Have them print it and bring it with them to Isobel Buchanan's house."

They said goodbye, and I held onto the door as Jack took the roundabout that merged onto the highway faster than the speed limit.

"That's good of you to have him send Smith," I told Jack. "I didn't know that about his father. It was before my time."

"Mine too," he said. "But my parents were friendly with his, and it was my dad that gave Martha the loan so she could open up the diner after her husband died. Widow's benefits were a fraction of what they are now, and she had three babies at home. My mother always said she got married to her second husband just because it was so hard being on her own with those three boys. Of course, then she ended up with three more boys and her husband left her soon after. But she's a tough old bird. She supported all of them."

The drive to the exclusive gated community was different in the daylight hours. The golf course could be seen from the highway, and the rolling hills and white golf carts looked like they belonged on a postcard. The manmade lakes were impossibly blue, and you could see the enormity of each of the houses that had a view of the course.

Our same friend was at the guard shack, and he automatically opened the gate for us as we pulled up. His scowl was the same as it had been the first time we'd met.

"Don't announce our visit," Jack told him, and the guy put down the phone, obviously about to do just that.

We turned near the fountain and the bridge that led to the golf course, and made our way down the winding road. There were several people out in golf carts, and they all stared long and hard as we passed by. They'd probably never seen a Suburban before.

I hadn't realized on our first visit how much space was between each of the houses, but the Buchanan's mini-White House finally came into view at the end of the street after what seemed like an eternity. There was a white panel van parked in the circular drive in the front, and it had a ladder on the roof. There was a bright blue Bentley convertible parked behind it.

Jack pulled in close behind the Bentley, and we walked to

the door. I stood off to the side so she'd see Jack first. But it wasn't Isobel who opened the door.

A man stared eye to eye with Jack, and I had to admit, even I was taken a little by surprise. There weren't very many men who were as big as Jack in height and muscle, but this guy ran a close second. Jack was in good shape. Better than good shape. But this guy made Jason Momoa look like a couch potato.

His hair was shoulder length and had that messy, tousled look, and he had it pulled back at the sides and clipped at the back of his head. His eyes were crystalline blue, his face perfectly stubbled, and his lips full and sensual. He was wearing old jeans and a plain white T-shirt and no shoes.

"Come on in," he said. "You're a little early, but feel free to look around. Isobel said she'd be down in a minute."

"We appreciate that," Jack said, and we followed him inside. "I'm Jack, by the way."

"Carter Long," the guy said.

"We're very sorry to hear about the loss of Isobel's husband," Jack said.

I could tell Jack was feeling his way, trying to figure out who Carter was before Isobel came down and ruined it. I figured it was best to just stand back and be an observer. Between the stitches and bruising on my face from the accident and my arm in a sling, I looked like I'd been through the wringer.

"It was just one of those things," Carter said, not looking

like he cared overly much about the loss of Warren Buchanan. "You look really familiar."

"My face is around quite a bit," Jack said vaguely.

"Yeah, I guess so," Carter said. "You guys feel free to do what you need to do. I'm just checking one of the pumps on the tank. I think something is caught in it."

"The upkeep on them must be a beast," Jack said. "But they're stunning. A great statement for the house."

"It's not too bad," he said. "I come twice a week just to make sure everything is working properly. Some days I'll come more if I've got something to add to the tank. Just added the shark last week. He's doing well."

The shark made an appearance on the inside curve of the staircase and then quickly disappeared again.

"How do you keep algae and stuff like that from growing?" Jack asked. "It's such a big space, and there's so much light. You'd think it'd grow like crazy."

"Dealing with the algae is easy. You just drop algaecide in the tank and move on. It's doing the deep cleans on this thing that are a pain. I've got to put on full dive gear and it usually takes a solid week."

Jack whistled appreciatively. "It must make a lot of extra work for you to have to haul all that stuff around for one house. I can't imagine there are too many tanks like this one."

Carter shrugged and started up the stairs, but he stopped on the third step up. "You'd be surprised. Exotic fish are one of those rich people things. I do houses all over D.C., but this is my biggest. Since I'm here twice a week I keep my equipment off the kitchen. I've got to head upstairs so I can look at the pump. Go ahead and get a good feel of the place. I know Isobel is anxious to get it listed."

He headed the rest of the way upstairs and disappeared toward the back of the landing.

"You heard the guy," Jack said, smiling. "Let's get a good feel of the place. If you can manage to roll your tongue back into your mouth."

I felt my face flush with heat. "All I'm saying is I think it's pretty weird for the fish tank guy to look like Aquaman. I also think he's coming here a lot more than twice a week. Did you see that smirk on his face?"

"Oh, you noticed his face, did you?" Jack asked, grinning.

"Shut up."

We went into the kitchen, and it seemed surreal that we'd been standing there just two nights before.

"I'm guessing Isobel is anxious to get the house on the market," Jack said. "I'm betting she and fish boy have plans."

There was a closed door in the back corner of the kitchen, and Jack opened it, revealing a laundry room that had three full-sized washers and dryers, an ironing station, and one of those folding machines. It led to a mudroom, and there was a glass door that led into a garage full of cars on the right, but on the left was an open arch that was almost an extension of the mudroom that had floor-to-ceiling shelves, paddles, and long poles with different attachments.

And right there on the shelf was a large bag of algaecide and a mortar and pestle. I'd stuck latex gloves inside my sling since I didn't want to carry my bag around, and I handed Jack a pair. He put them on and then picked up the bag and the mortar and pestle and took them back to the kitchen.

I heard the sound of footsteps coming down the stairs, and Jack and I both stared at the door as Isobel Buchanan made her entrance. She didn't look like a woman who'd lost her husband two days before. Her white pants were like liquid against her tanned skin, and her cobalt-blue halter top showed off the benefits of having a home gym. Her white hair was slicked back off her face, showing arresting features that weren't swollen from crying. She and Aquaman would've made some beautiful babies. If they weren't killers.

"Oh," she said, coming to a fast stop. "Carter said the real…" She smiled and tried to put her mourning face back on, but it didn't do a lot of good. "I didn't realize you were stopping by. The guard usually tells us when we have guests. I would've been downstairs to greet you."

Her eyes glanced down at the bag of algaecide and the mortar and pestle, and I saw the slightest flicker of worry.

"It's no trouble," Jack said easily. "We were able to occupy ourselves."

"I'm afraid I don't have time to talk right now," she said. "I have some appointments."

"Realtors?" Jack asked. "Thinking of selling the house?"

"I just can't…" She put a shaking hand to her heart. "I just can't live in a house where something so horrible happened. Every time I come into this room I see his body on the floor."

"I can see where that would be troublesome," I said.

"Who are you?" she asked, as if she just noticed I was standing there.

Maybe she *had* just noticed.

"Dr. Graves," I said. "I'm the coroner for the county. I did the autopsy on your husband."

She paled a little.

"I thought I might have heard from you about claiming Warren's and Schwartz's bodies. I'm sure you want to plan the burial as soon as possible."

"Yes," she said. "Actually, his son said that he would take care of all the planning, so I don't have to. I think it would just be too traumatic to pick out a casket and flowers."

"Warren's son," Jack said. "That would be Tate, right? He's inherited the company?"

A flash of something glanced across her face and then it was quickly gone. "He's been Warren's number two for years now. I don't want the hassle of running a company I know nothing about."

"That's smart," Jack said. "A lot of people would be greedy, especially since as his wife of ten years, you think you'd be entitled to some amount of cash or assets other than the house. But he just left you what's in your personal account. And of course, his life insurance policy. Crazy thing about the life insurance policy, though. It's just a million dollars if Warren dies of natural causes. But if he has an accidental death that rises to five million."

"I don't know what you're saying," she said briskly. "I haven't had time to think of such things."

"You've had time to hire realtors to get the house on the market," I said. "I'm surprised you haven't asked what I found during the autopsy. You think you'd want to know exactly how your husband died."

"I know how he died," she said. "I've been watching the news. They said some terrorist poisoned random people to distract law enforcement. My husband was an innocent victim."

"That's true," I said. "He was. Unfortunately, killers are never quite as smart as they think they are. Take the poison that killed your husband. It was sodium cyanide, by the way. Did you know that chemists can tell exactly what kind of poison was used, even down to the brand and the year it was made? There are such tight regulations on things like that. This particular brand of cyanide is from 2006.

"It's not easy to purchase bottles of the stuff, but it's a common tool of the trade for gem miners. Did you know that? Apparently, it doesn't do damage to the gold or gems, but it separates it from the rock. Incredible, isn't it?"

She didn't say anything, but her eyes narrowed slightly.

"Quite a coincidence that the particular brand that killed your husband is used for gems and such, especially with him owning a gem-mining company."

Isobel shrugged. "So what? I don't know what that has to

do with me. I told you I've got appointments, so I really do need to ask you to leave."

"Sorry about that," Jack said. "We're going to have to pass. We've actually got a warrant to search the premises. Carter was kind enough to let us in, so we went ahead and got started." Jack pointed to the algaecide and the mortar and pestle.

"That's ridiculous," Isobel said. "I'm calling my attorney. I want you both out of here right now."

There was a knock at the door, and I could see the police cars out front. "That'd be the cavalry," I said. "You should probably open the door for them."

"Carter!" Isobel yelled. Red streaks of fury had appeared on her neck.

"What, babe?" He came running down the stairs, but the knocks at the door were more insistent, and he stopped to open it.

Officers filed in and started spreading throughout the house. Stewart Smith had the printed copies of the warrants and handed them to Isobel, but she didn't even read them.

"Start in the pool house and the garage," Jack told him.

"You got it, Sheriff," Smith said.

Isobel's mouth was opening and closing like a fish, and Carter was standing back, looking back and forth between Isobel and all the cops.

"I didn't tell you the funny thing about the poison that was in those capsules," Jack said. "The chemist found these little green flecks in all of the pills they analyzed. It took them a bit to realize what it was, but it turns out it was algaecide. Whoever ground up all of that cyanide used a tool that had been previously used to grind up algaecide tablets. Specifically, this kind of algaecide. Science is pretty amazing, isn't it?"

"I want a deal," Carter said out of the blue. "I'll tell you everything, but I want a deal."

"Shut up, Carter!" Isobel yelled.

He ignored her. "It was all her idea," Carter said. "Every part of it. Warren could be a vindictive ass, and he found out about us, so he moved a bunch of money into his business accounts and changed some of the wording in his will. The attorney just told her about the changes yesterday. She's basically got this house and a few thousand dollars in cash. He even donated all the cars, so she can't sell them."

"I said shut up, Carter," Isobel said, and she launched herself at Carter, but Hops came out of nowhere and clotheslined her so Isobel went down on her ass. Hops had her rolled over and in handcuffs before anyone could blink. And then she just left her face down on the ground.

Detective Cole was putting cuffs on Carter. "Do I get a deal?" Carter asked. "I don't want to go to jail."

"Oh, you're going to go to jail," Jack said. "But you won't go for as long as her. You don't happen to know where the bottle of cyanide is, do you?

"There's a bunch of it," Carter said. "There's the trap door in the garage where Warren kept stuff like that. She used a couple of bottles to fill all those capsules."

"How many tins were made all together? We found the two

from victims' houses, and then there were two more we found still on the shelf. And then there was a woman who turned in an unopened pack."

"There were just the five," he said. "She thought if other people died randomly then no one would look at her for Warren's murder."

"Things rarely turn out how we plan," I said.

Carter laughed, but there was no humor in it. "Isn't that the truth."

———

AN HOUR LATER, we'd confiscated the poison and had Isobel and Carter in lockup. Nash had met us at the front entry of the station, and Jack had handed Isobel and Carter off to him so he could officially make the arrest. Jack and I followed behind as Nash led them through the station and into holding. Cops everywhere broke out into applause.

Jack waited until the applause had quieted and said, "It's been a rough twenty-four hours." Everyone got very quiet and stared intently at Jack. "We've lost a brother and we've got one more in the hospital. But I've never been more proud to be a cop than in these last twenty-four hours when things went to hell. You guys stood your ground, you fought, you helped, you worked overtime…you did whatever had to be done, because that's the job. I'm thankful to be your sheriff. And this community is thankful for you too."

I saw Betsy dab at her eyes.

"It's hard to lose a friend," Jack said. "Stay close to each other. Lean on each other. Stay here and work if you need to work, or go home to your wives and children and enjoy the time with them. It's time you won't ever take for granted again. I promise. And if you need me, I don't care if it's in the middle of the night, call me. We're a unit, and we'll heal as a unit. Be safe out there."

There were enthusiastic cheers and applause, and Jack moved back toward me and took my hand.

"What are we doing?" I asked.

"I'm taking some personal time to spend with my wife," he said, smiling. "We're going to go to the hotel and pretend there's not a hole in our living room. We're going to lock ourselves in and make love until we fall asleep."

"Man, you're full of good speeches today," I said, following him outside and to the Suburban. "I especially like the part about sleeping. Maybe we could do that first."

Jack sighed and tried to look disappointed, but he failed. "Yeah, I regretted it as soon as I said it. Between your arm and my exhaustion, I'm afraid we'd hurt ourselves. That'd be an embarrassing 911 call to make."

"It's the thought that counts," I said. "Who knows what can happen after a couple of hours of sleep."

Jack grabbed my hand and squeezed it. I could feel the desperation in him, and it made me love him even more. "I love you," he said. "Yesterday, today, and tomorrow."

I leaned into him, and he was careful not to jar my arm. "I love you, too," I said. "We have a lot of tomorrows ahead of us. This is the start of the rest of our lives."

WHISKEY AND GUNPOWDER EXCERPT

Enjoy an excerpt of WHISKEY AND GUNPOWDER, from Liliana Hart's bestselling Addison Holmes Series. Now available at all retailers and brick and mortar bookstores.

My mother liked to say that the Lord worked in mysterious ways, and I'd have to agree with her on that one. In fact, I was pretty sure the Lord was working overtime in the mysterious department where I was concerned. There was no other way to explain why Pastor Charles Whidbey was sitting in my office at the McClean Detective Agency.

"I need your help," he said. He sat stiffly in the straight-backed chair in front of my desk, his hands clamped together tightly in his lap and his back ramrod straight.

Pastor Charles was probably in his mid-fifties, and he'd been the pastor at the First United Methodist Church in Whiskey Bayou for the last ten years. He was dressed casually—khaki slacks, black turtleneck, and a shabby sport coat with patches on the sleeves. He wore round, wire-rimmed glasses and had piercing blue eyes. His hair was dark, but there was a hint of silver at the temples. He was also ripped as hell. I was guessing when he wasn't praising the Lord he was spending the rest of his time at the gym.

Pastor Charles looked like he might be of some Hispanic descent, but no one really knew much about him. He'd come from another church somewhere in Kansas or Nebraska, and he'd come alone. No wife or kids to speak of, and no relatives that ever came to visit. He'd occasionally share meals in various homes when invited, but for the most part he stayed to himself. He never dated, and the only cause he created for gossip was the lack of a reason for gossip.

"I don't understand," I said. "You need to hire the agency?"

I felt sorry for him. I wondered if in all the time he'd lived in Whiskey Bayou he'd ever grown close to anyone.

"Not exactly," he said, and embarrassment colored his cheeks. "I was hoping we could work out some sort of trade. I don't have the kind of money it takes to hire an agency like this one. But what I do have is an available church on Friday night. I hear you're getting married?"

After the past couple of years had given me some hard knocks, I'd mostly given up on being a religious person. But this was a miracle. Plain and simple. There was no other explanation for it.

"You're saying Nick and I can use the church to get married on Friday, and have the reception there, in exchange for helping you?"

"Yes, that's right," he said, nodding.

"You would marry us?"

"Of course," he said. "Your mother is still a member and attends faithfully. And I was going to perform your last wedding if you remember."

"It's hard to forget," I said, rolling my eyes.

"All things happen for a reason," he said. "Just like the church becoming available at the last minute. Maybe it happened because this was the wedding you were supposed to have all along."

"Oh," I said. I had the overwhelming urge to burst into tears and felt them welling up in my eyes. I blinked rapidly to try and cut them off at the pass.

"Wedding hormones," I said. "It's been a crazy week."

"So I've heard," he said. "You've been making quite a few headlines in the Savannah papers the last month or so."

I grimaced. I'd stopped reading the papers whenever I solved a high-profile case. Especially if I was naked when I cracked a case. My last two cases had ended up with me naked. I was trying to end that streak.

"I imagine with as fast as everything is happening you need as much help as you can get. I saw the open invitation in the Gazette this morning. You might have a couple hundred people show up."

"There was an open invitation in the paper?" I asked, wide-eyed.

"Oh," he said. "I'm sorry. I thought you'd placed it there."

"No," I said. "It was probably my mother."

"Or someone who hopes your wedding causes another spectacle."

That sounded ominous, but I guess it wasn't out of the question.

"Don't worry about it," he said. "It'll be a wonderful celebration. John and Edna Korbel were supposed to have their sixtieth anniversary party that night, but they decided to go to Jamaica instead, just the two of them. They said they had too few years left to try and please everyone but themselves, so they'd go celebrate alone."

I blew out a breath, envious of the Korbels' moxie. But they didn't have Phyllis Holmes and Nina Dempsey to deal with.

"Can we serve alcohol at the reception?" I asked.

"We're not Baptists," he said, smiling a little. "A wedding is a celebration. Enjoy it."

"You've got a deal," I said.

Technically, what I'd just done was completely against agency policy. I wasn't supposed to take on private cases, but since this one wasn't for actual money, I was pretty sure I could convince Kate that the loophole would stand up in court. Or she could just fire me, but she was my maid of honor, so I figured the chances were slim. Though Kate was a stickler for the rules.

I'd deal with it later. I took out a legal pad from my desk drawer and grabbed a pen. "What can I help you with?" I asked.

"I've been receiving threats," he said calmly.

This was not what I'd been expecting at all. "Threats," I said. "Why wouldn't you go to the police?"

He reached inside his sport coat and took out an envelope. "I'd prefer to keep this quiet. You know there are no secrets in Whiskey Bayou. It could be a prank, but it could also be something more serious. There's no need to draw attention to it unless absolutely necessary. That could be what they want."

I took the envelope from him. It was a standard size white envelope and inside were several photographs. I looked through them one by one. Obviously, someone had been following Pastor Charles and taking pictures of him without his knowledge.

"Where did they leave the pictures?" I asked.

"Here and there," he said. "A couple in the front seat of my car. Some in my office at the church. And the last one I found on my nightstand this morning."

I looked at the last photograph. It was a picture of Pastor Charles sleeping in his bed.

"Scary," I said.

"To say the least," he agreed.

"When did they leave the first pictures?" I asked.

"A couple of weeks ago. And then I would get more every three or four days."

"Whoever's been watching you has been doing it for a while," I said, turning one of the photographs around. "There's still leaves on the trees at the park, and there are people out and about, so the weather wasn't too cold. So we're looking at least at late fall."

"I see," he said, nodding slowly, and the color seemed to drain from his face. "I missed that. So they've been watching me for months. And now they've decided to play with me."

"Are you sure the police isn't the better option here? At least until you know if you're in any real danger."

"No." He shook his head rather adamantly. "I'm sure about that. I don't want the police involved. I support law enforcement, of course, but they have much more important matters to deal with."

"Have you received anything else?"

"A couple of phone calls where no one was on the other line. And a note stuck to my car window."

"What did it say?" I asked.

"Remember."

"Remember what?"

"That, I don't know," he said. "I'm fifty-eight years old. I've got a lot of life behind me. It could be anything."

"Have you ever had any disagreements or complaints within the church?" I asked. "Unhappy congregation?"

"Nothing out of the ordinary," he said. "Of course, people will come and go from the church. They might disagree with my teaching, or there might be a squabble or so inside the congregation. I've had couples angry because I refused to marry them if I felt they weren't ready. But nothing egregious or that stands out in my mind."

"What about personnel? Anyone let go or hired recently?"

"Pastor Elaine is our newest hire, and she's been with the church for five years now. My secretary and the custodial staff have been there since long before I came to Whiskey Bayou."

"What about your previous church? I was told you came here from the Midwest?" I was straddling a line between professional and personal curiosity.

His lips pressed together and he nodded. "Yes, from a small town outside of Omaha. But I'm afraid my life just hasn't been that exciting."

"Do you have a card?" I asked. "With your cell number? I might have some more questions once I start investigating. When I find out who's doing this, what do you want me to do?"

"Just give me the identity," he said. "Maybe they'll listen to reason if I speak to them face to face."

Or you could get your head bashed in. But I decided not to say that out loud.

Pastor Charles took his wallet from his back pocket and opened it, revealing a thin stack of business cards with the church's logo on it. He handed me one and I paper-clipped it to the pad I'd been writing on.

"I'm sure I don't need to tell you to be careful," I said. "But I'm going to anyway. Don't take any unnecessary chances.

Make sure you lock your doors and windows at night. Be vigilant when you go out. Let me know immediately if you think someone is following you, or if you recognize anyone."

"It seems quite foolish for anyone to try and attack me," he said. "Everyone knows me, and I'm out in the community all the time."

"Speaking of, do you have a day-to-day routine? Do you go to the same places or take the same routes every day?"

"Ahh," he said, nodding his head. "I see. Yes, I do for the most part. Unless someone is sick or I need to make a hospital visit or bury someone."

"Could you text me your schedule?" I asked. "It's more than likely that whoever is doing this knows your schedule as well as you do."

"Sure, I'll send it over as soon as I get back to my office. Today is my off-day," he said, and then smiled and pointed up to the ceiling. "There's never really an off day doing His work."

I smiled, but it was forced. I was really worried about Pastor Charles. If someone had taken a picture of me sleeping and left it on my nightstand, I would've been inconsolable.

"Please be careful, Pastor Charles," I said and shook his hand.

He squeezed my hand and placed his other hand on top of mine. And then he looked me in the eyes, and I realized there was a lot more depth to Pastor Charles than I'd ever realized.

"I have faith," he said. "Do you?"

He released my hand and then he was gone, leaving me alone in my tiny office. I sat back behind my desk and made a new file for Pastor Charles, putting my notes and his pictures inside, along with his business card. I lingered over it a little longer than normal because it kept my mind off of the wedding.

The minute I started thinking about it again the pressure returned to my chest and I had trouble breathing. I tried to stick my head between my knees, but there wasn't enough room to maneuver between my desk and the wall.

I pounded on my chest and realized I was more than likely having a panic attack. Or maybe a heart attack. The pressure in my chest had reached epic proportions, and the Costco-sized bottle of Tums I'd bought a couple of days ago sat empty on my desk.

I scooted off my chair and crawled to the front of my desk where there was a little more room, and I laid flat on my back and sucked in deep breaths. I found it only slightly ironic that Pastor Charles had asked if I had faith less than fifteen minutes ago, and here I was about to meet my maker.

The really ironic thing was that I was about to die just like my dad. Of course, I wasn't screaming at the television during a Falcons game, but I did have a pile of open cases on my desk, a boatload of stress, and a half-eaten éclair within arm's reach, so it was mostly the same.

The only difference was I was going to die in my little office at the McClean Detective Agency. Alone. In a space that had been a janitor's closet until I'd taken the initiative to clean it out and claim it as my own. No one would ever find me. At least, not until the smell of decomposition overpowered the scent of the fresh baked goodies that were constantly being delivered from the bakery down the street. I'd gained four pounds since I'd passed the physical fitness portion of the private investigator's test.

A whimper escaped my mouth, and a tear trickled out of the corner of my eye. I was feeling downright sorry for myself now that the chest pains were subsiding.

What I needed to do was focus on work and not on the fact that I was getting married in five days. It wasn't even the idea of marriage that was giving me heart palpitations. I loved Nick and I was ready to take the next step in our lives.

No, the problem was that I was tethered by Southern etiquette and a bunch of crazy women I was supposedly related to. I haven't run a DNA test yet, so there's still hope I'm adopted.

It had been three days since I'd agreed to become Nick's wife. He'd been very patient over the last month while he waited for my decision on whether or not I was going to marry him. So I couldn't really blame him for my newfound arrhythmia.

He'd given me the choice of eloping or having a week to plan a wedding so our family and friends could be involved. Then he'd gotten called out to a triple homicide in the middle of the night and I hadn't seen him since. The lucky duck.

Nick was a good man, and he really did love me. But I'd needed the time to decide if he was the right man for me.

He was a cop. And I was the daughter of a cop. But I knew from watching my parents' marriage that there was a whole lot of extra baggage that went with being a cop's wife. My parents had survived their marriage, but that's the best thing I could say about it. I didn't want to end up like that.

I'd made my decision to get married, and I wasn't turning back. I'd been all for the elopement option, but the thing about Southern etiquette was it also included Southern guilt. My mother would never let me hear the end of it if we ran off to some island paradise and exchanged vows without her and half of Whiskey Bayou present. So I'd decided the right thing to do was put together a smallish wedding for close friends and family. Only I must have been in denial because the days were ticking away and I hadn't done one blessed thing to plan for it except ask Kate to be my maid of honor.

Except now it wasn't a smallish wedding at all because Pastor Charles had seen an open invitation in the Whiskey Bayou Gazette. Though I did have a venue for the ceremony and reception, so that was a check in the plus column.

I figured the best thing to do was deal with the rest later. I'd have either died from the heart attack by then or thought of a way to get everything done for the wedding and clear all my cases.

I rolled to my hands and knees and boosted myself up, and then I gathered the case files on my desk. The faster I started working, the sooner I'd clear them. I shoved them into my oversized Kate Spade travel bag. It was hot-pink, and the splash of color broke up the gloom surrounding me. I wore jeans, a fitted black sweater, and black Yves Saint

Laurent galoshes that came almost to my knees. They were quilted on the inside and worth every penny.

I'd gotten a reward a couple of weeks ago for catching the Romeo Bandit, and it had fattened my bank account quite nicely. I'd bought the boots, the bag, and a giant custom van that was perfect for stakeouts and quickies. I knew both of these things from experience. It even had a bathroom and tiny kitchenette.

My bank account was back to empty again after my extravagant purchases, which meant I had to get back to solving the cases I'd been assigned. Nick was rich. His whole family was rich. But I wasn't marrying Nick for his limitless bank account, though I did enjoy the little BMW convertible he'd bought me as a surprise. I had principles, but I wasn't stupid.

My mother always said to never look a gift horse in the mouth. When I was a kid I'd thought the saying was never lick a gift horse in the mouth. As an adult, both sayings make about as much sense as the other to me. I still don't know what a gift horse is or why I'd want to look at it or lick it.

I grabbed my holster from the hook on the back of my door and strapped it around my waist, and then went through the process of putting on my pink-and-black plaid scarf. I hated winter. Everyone in the South hated winter. And we were in the midst of record-breaking temperatures. Southerners weren't meant for single-digit temperatures and snow. No one knew how to dress or drive, and at the first mention of the word snow, people flooded the grocery stores and bought out all the toilet paper and condoms.

I took my black puffy coat from the hook and was just about to put it on when there was a knock at the door. I thought about not opening it and pretending I wasn't there.

"It's me," Kate said. "I can hear you breathing."

I opened the door and came face to face with Kate McClean. She'd been my best friend for as long as I could remember, and we were about as opposite as two people could get, but it seemed to work for us. She was a couple of inches over five feet and cute as a button. She looked a little like Meg Ryan before Meg had made so many poor plastic surgery choices, and her blonde hair came just below her chin and was slightly tousled.

Kate was one of the most no-nonsense people I'd ever known. She said what she meant and meant what she said, and you could always count on her for loyalty and the truth. It's how she'd made such a success out of the agency after she'd quit being a cop after a couple of years.

"Could you really hear me breathing?" I asked.

"No, but your van is still parked out front, and there's fresh cinnamon rolls in the break room. I know you can't smell them from in here, so I figured you were in here hiding."

"That's good detective work."

"That's why they pay me the big bucks."

As soon as I stepped into the hallway the smell of freshly baked cinnamon rolls assaulted my senses and my mouth began to water.

"That's just cruel," I said. "I'm supposed to get married on Friday. They're going to have to roll me down the aisle."

Kate arched her brow and didn't say anything.

"I'm still going to have one," I clarified. "I just want you to know it's cruel."

"Duly noted," she said. "Cute bag. You off to do wedding stuff?"

"Sure," I lied. "I'm also hoping to catch Matt Martin and his nooner. It's not always easy to find parking for the van, so I want to give myself plenty of time."

"Good thinking," Kate said, but she seemed distracted.

I followed her down the hallway to the conference room and had an out-of-body experience the second I could see who was waiting for me. Even though my brain hadn't quite registered what I was seeing, my body kept moving until I was inside the room and it was too late to escape.

"What fresh hell is this?" I hissed at Kate.

"This is what's called a necessary evil. And as your maid of honor, it's my job to make sure things get done. No arguments. We're going to kick this wedding's ass."

"You're fired," I said, panic starting to take hold of me. I felt the pressure in my chest again and was sure this time my heart was really about to explode.

"You can't fire me," she said, entirely too smug. "But this needs to be done. You have work and I'm stuck testifying in court most of the week. Everyone else is working overtime so you can take the next two weeks for your honeymoon, so suck it up. What you're about to witness here is my genius, so sit down in that chair and let's get this over with."

I shook my head slowly. "Do you even realize what you've done? None of us might escape here alive."

"Don't worry," she said, giving me a shove toward the giant conference table. "I've got my taser if things go downhill."

"You think a taser is going to stop them?"

"What's all that whispering about?" Aunt Scarlet yelled from her place at the head of the table. "I don't have all day. The police are on my tail and I could die at any moment. I'm an old lady."

"Demons never die," my mother said under her breath.

This was my own personal hell. My family managed to coexist by never being in the same room at the same time. It had worked that way for generations. The Holmeses were avoiders. If there was a conflict or disagreement, we were pros at burying it deep inside so we could gripe about it to someone who didn't share blood at a later time.

"I'm not going to lie," Kate whispered. "I've never experienced this kind of terror."

"That's very helpful. And this is all your fault. God's going to punish you."

"You don't think standing in this room is punishment enough? I'm not even related."

"Good point," I said.

The conference room was where we had our weekly case briefings, and also where we brought clients we didn't feel a hundred percent comfortable with. It was hooked up with cameras and audio. Just in case.

There was a marble fireplace against one wall, and a fire crackled soothingly in the hearth. The cinnamon rolls sat untouched in the middle of the huge rectangular conference table. Twelve plush chairs sat around it. Three of the chairs were occupied by my family—my mother, sister, and Aunt Scarlet.

Scarlet sat at the head of the table like a general. I personally liked Aunt Scarlet, but she was best had in small doses. I'd shut down a black market organ harvesting ring the week before, and Aunt Scarlet had helped in a big way. I was also almost positive that she'd murdered the man who'd masterminded the whole thing. Ugly Mo had been a crime boss for more than two decades in Savannah, and even the police hadn't been able to touch him. But I was proud to say that with my training and a whole lot of dumb luck, we'd cracked the case.

It didn't change the fact that the police wanted to talk to Scarlet since she was a person of interest. But the last I'd heard, she'd skipped town and was heading back to the cruise ship she lived on for a good part of the year. I was pretty surprised to see her.

She'd changed her hair over the weekend. Gone was the white helmet of curls that had sat so rigidly on her scalp. She'd at least had the appearance of looking like anyone's eccentric grandma with that hair. But now her hair was a cross between Blac Chyna and Bette Davis in Watcher in the Woods.

She had it pulled up into an artful ponytail that trailed halfway down her back. Little wisps of hair framed her wizened face, and the white seemed brighter than normal.

The bulk of it was almost half the size she was. I didn't know how she was holding up her head.

My mother sat to Scarlet's right. I was pretty much the spitting image of my mother, which was good news for me because my mom was aging well. Her hair was dark like mine and pulled into a messy bun on top of her head. Her eyes were dark and the only signs of aging were the small lines around her eyes.

Mom was in her mid-fifties and starting a new life. She'd recently gotten married to my dad's old partner, Vince Walker, and they seemed very happy. She'd also started to come into her own a little. I hadn't realized how repressed she'd been during her marriage to my dad. It was nice to see her blooming, but also terrifying at times. My mom no longer had a filter. I hoped Kate had her taser on high stun.

Mom had started going to pottery classes and naked yoga, and she'd set a bonfire in the backyard to burn all her pantyhose and suits from her days as a CPA. She mostly did people's taxes now in yoga pants or overalls. I was still getting used to it.

A fourth chair was occupied by Rosemarie Valentine. She was my other bridesmaid and had a giant binder sitting in front of her. She looked terrified and was pale as a piece of paper.

"I guess the newspaper article is true," Scarlet said, looking me up and down and then zeroing in on my middle. "I guess we're getting another seven-month baby in this family."

I sucked in my stomach and narrowed my eyes. "I'm not pregnant. It's winter. Layers make everyone look heavier."

Scarlet hmmphed and shook her head. "That's the problem with people nowadays. Their scandals are boring. Nobody cares about seven-month babies. Your great-great-uncle sired half the babies in Whiskey Bayou back in his day, but it was his wife that made headlines." Her eyes were animated and she clicked her tongue in approval. "Maudine had enough of his tomcattin' around and cut his doo-dad right off. Stuck it in a jar of vinegar on her windowsill like some lumpy potato. I saw it for myself when I was a kid. She watched him bleed out while she ironed the rest of his shirts, bless her soul. Of course, she was a Holmes too, and Holmes women don't handle being cuckolded well. Just look at you and how you ran over that fiancé of yours. I was real proud of you. I read about it in the newspaper on my cruise ship."

I opened my mouth to deny any wrongdoing. It's not like I ran over him on purpose. But my sister Phoebe's gasp drew everyone's attention.

"Wait a second," she said. "How could our great-great-uncle's wife be a Holmes too? Are you saying they were related?"

Everyone scrunched up their noses in disgust, and Rosemarie took the opportunity to reach for a cinnamon roll.

I hadn't seen Phoebe in a few months. She was an artist, so she tended to not put down roots in any one place for very long. She was a few inches shorter than me, had long blonde hair with turquoise streaks, and a diamond stud in her nose. She was wearing a black skinsuit that looked like it was made of rubber and a pair of biker boots that came up to her knees.

"Third cousins, so it hardly counts," Scarlet said. "And they didn't have any children. Probably for the best since they were both batshit crazy. The population was a lot smaller then, and men weren't easy to come by. Fortunately, they also didn't live as long so no one had to suffer for too long."

"Sweet Jesus," my mother said. She had a to-go cup of something in front of her, and I was guessing it wasn't hot coffee, because she took a long drink and looked a lot more relaxed when she put the cup down. She glanced at Rosemarie's half-eaten cinnamon roll and reached for her own.

"I'm not pregnant," I repeated to get things back on track. "Nick is just tired of waiting. We want to get this done as quick as possible with as little hassle."

"Hmmph," Scarlet said. "That's just what your mother said before she and your father got married."

My mom rolled her eyes. "How many times do I have to tell you that I got pregnant on our honeymoon. We didn't have to get married. Phoebe just came two months early."

"So you said at the hospital when you were trying to explain to anyone who would listen how a seven-month baby could weigh nine pounds."

"Damn," Kate whispered. "Burn."

"You changed your hair," I said to Scarlet, mostly because I couldn't think of anything else to diffuse the tension between her and my mother.

"I got extensions," she said. "Costs a fortune and they're heavy as hell. But Chermaine told me long hair is back in style, and you know how I'm always on top of the trends."

Chermaine was Scarlet's very expensive stylist. She was…unique.

"Can you believe women half my age are dyeing their hair white on purpose? People are idiots."

My mother snorted. "The women half your age still have white hair naturally," my mother said. "You're older than dirt."

"The musket ball in my hip may slow me down some, but my hearing's as good as ever, Phyllis. If you weren't family I'd have ripped out that forked tongue of yours decades ago."

I knew things were escalating fast and that I should probably step in before punches were thrown, but I was still stuck on what Aunt Scarlet said about long hair being in style.

"Wait a second," I said, touching the fringe of my new pixie cut. "A week ago you told me I needed a change and Chermaine said short hair was all the rage. I had long hair. Why would you do that to me?"

I wasn't an irrational person. I didn't overreact. Well, maybe sometimes I did, but only when there was a good reason. But I could feel my blood pressure spike and my eyes bulge out of my head. It was wedding stress. It had to be. I was turning into Bridezilla.

Scarlet shrugged. "I can't help it. I'm programmed to eliminate the competition. I thought I had a shot with that hottie, and I could tell he was into you."

"Of course he's into me," I yelled. "We're getting married." I marched over to the table and grabbed a cinnamon roll. To hell with wedding diets.

"Not that one," Scarlet said, waving her hand dismissively. "The other one. With all the muscles and the cute butt. Looks dumber than he is. I was always a sucker for a jock with a brain. How's his package?"

I shoved the cinnamon roll in my mouth so I didn't have to answer.

Phoebe laughed and knuckle-bumped Aunt Scarlet. "You've got good taste. That man is hot. I thought about giving him a spin myself, but I don't poach. And I don't think he was interested. I can always tell when a man is interested."

"Maybe he's gay," Scarlet said. "Or maybe he has one of those micro-penises and he's too embarrassed to get naked. I read all about micro-penises in Cosmo. Apparently, it's much more common now because of all the hormones that get pumped into our foods."

"Kill me now," my mother said.

Rosemarie hadn't said a word, but she was eyeing a third cinnamon roll like it was the Holy Grail and she was the last Templar knight.

Scarlet reached down and plopped her giant Louis Vuitton handbag on the table. She dug around inside and pulled out her checkbook.

"That settles it," Scarlet said. "I'm hiring this agency. Addison, it's your duty to find out if he has a micro-penis. It's dishonest for him to present himself as an eligible bachelor if he can't perform in the bedroom."

"Available to whom?" my mother asked. "You think your fake hair is going to make you look sixty years younger? One look at you naked would probably turn him off sex forever."

"You've always been jealous, Phyllis," Scarlet said, shaking her head. "I've got the best body money can buy. Addison and Rosemarie can attest to that. We spent all week at that nudist colony. I was fighting men off like flies. Hell, Addison and I are practically twins. She's the spitting image of me."

"I want to die," I said, and Kate patted me on the back soothingly.

"I'm so sorry," she whispered.

My mother shot me a look that somehow managed to look horrified and disappointed in my life choices at the same time.

"It was for a case," I said, defending myself.

Between the nudist colony and being kidnapped and almost having my organs harvested, I figured it was best to keep things on the down-low until life got back to normal. Mom tended to worry. I had no idea why.

"Aunt Scarlet's been here two weeks and look at what an influence she's had on you," my mother said, her voice getting higher as she spoke. "You're not Mata Hari, Addison Holmes. For all we know, all those stories about being a spy and dead husbands and musket balls are complete hogwash. There's no proof of anything other than the fact that she got shipped off to France for being a whore."

We all gasped and I nudged Kate in the side. "Do something. This is your fault. Get out your taser."

"I might have underestimated the outcome of this meeting."

"I'll take the case," I blurted out, hoping it would distract everyone and prevent an all-out brawl. "I'll find out if he has a micro-penis and put in a good word for you if he's... healthy," I said for lack of a better word.

I already knew Savage didn't have a micro-penis. We'd kissed a time or two when Nick and I were in our off-again stage, but that's as far as it had gone. The thing about kissing is it does things to a man's body that's hard to miss, and I could say with certainty that Savage most definitely did not have a micro-penis.

Someone knocked, but the door was open, so it was only for formality. Everyone at the table got unusually still and Rosemarie choked on her cinnamon roll to the point my mother had to slap her on the back a few times.

"Is this a bad time?" Savage asked.

I closed my eyes and wished I could sink into the floor. There was no way he hadn't heard part of that conversation.

"Speak of the devil," Scarlet said, giving him a wink.

Savage moved in next to me and squeezed my shoulder, but

I couldn't bring myself to look at him. I was so tense I was surprised I didn't snap in two.

"What are you doing here?" I asked.

"I came about a case, but figured I'd stay for the sideshow."

"Get your money's worth?"

I could practically feel his grin.

"More than," he said. "And it's not even noon yet."

"We're having a meeting about the wedding," Scarlet told him. "She's getting married Friday. Do you have a date?"

"I always go to weddings alone," Savage said. "I like to keep my options open."

"Good thinking," Scarlet said. "Options are important. I've always said that just because you get married doesn't mean you're dead. Lordy, I've been through five husbands. You've always got to be on the lookout for the next one because husbands have a tendency to die or get shot or pushed off balconies. They're very fragile."

I snuck a look at Savage and his grin grew wider. My mom took another drink from her to-go cup, and Rosemarie took another cinnamon roll. We all dealt with stress in different ways.

"Speaking of the wedding," Savage said. "The NAD Squad would like to know where to send their gift."

I sucked in my cheeks. Before I moved in with Nick I was the owner of a cute little white house on an older street in Savannah. It turned out that Savage was my across the street neighbor, which he'd failed to mention to me when he'd suggested I buy it.

My neighbors had been an eclectic mix of races and ages, and they could give Whiskey Bayou a run for its money in the nosey department. They'd also formed a neighborhood watch group called the NAD Squad. I'd been confused at first until they'd told me NAD stood for Neighbors Against Delinquency.

I couldn't even imagine what a gift from the NAD Squad might be, so I said, "Tell them no gifts, but they're all welcome to attend."

His eyebrows raised at that. "Lesser of two evils, huh?"

"Something like that," I said. "What are you drinking, Mom?"

"Orange juice," she said primly.

Phoebe snorted. "I watched her put a teaspoon of orange juice into that vodka this morning."

"Narc," my mother said, and I raised my brows. I felt nothing but sympathy for my mother. For the first time in my entire life she seemed happy, then she finds out Aunt Scarlet is back in town and her daughter is getting married all in the same weekend.

"I hate to chat and run, but I've got work to do," I said, taking a step backward.

"But what about the wedding?" my mother asked. "Where is it going to be? What about your dress? The catering and reception? It's going to take an army to put this together on such short notice."

Her spelling things out like that weren't exactly helping my heart issues. All I cared about was being Mrs. Nick Dempsey.

"Maybe we should elope," I said, and then immediately regretted it when everyone gasped. I had to admit, this was a lot of drama for a Monday morning. Even for me.

"I don't think so," my mother said, looking much too sober for my liking. "There's already been too much publicity. They put out a special edition Sunday Gazette yesterday. It's not every day someone from Whiskey Bayou marries a senator's grandson."

"Yes, that's exactly how I describe Nick when I tell people about him. Not that he's out working a triple homicide right now and trying to make the streets safer."

Savage whistled. "He must've caught the Hayward case. You'll be lucky to see him three weeks from now, much less Friday. From everything I've read, that's a messy one."

"Then get out there and help him," I said, smacking Savage on the shoulder. "Because I'm getting married Friday. I don't care who's there or if there are hors d'oeuvres and champagne or Keystone and cake pops. Oh, and by the way, I've secured the Methodist church for the ceremony, and Pastor Charles said we can have the reception there too."

"Is that why he was here this morning?" Kate asked, zeroing in on me. "I was wondering."

It's like Kate had these super mind powers when it came to the agency, and I could practically feel her compelling me to tell her that I'd taken a side job for Pastor Charles.

"Yep," I said, a little too cheerfully. "He said he saw an open invitation in the newspaper this morning, and that the Korbels had cancelled their sixtieth anniversary party to go to Jamaica, so the church was free."

Technically, I hadn't lied. I just left out the part about the threats.

"Their poor family," my mother said, clucking her tongue. "Their family has been looking forward to that party for months, and then they go off on their own and don't let everyone be a part of the celebration. Those people wouldn't even be there if the Korbels hadn't gotten horizontal back in the day. Maybe they should've thought about that." She gave a soft hiccup and picked at the rest of her cinnamon roll.

"Gross," Phoebe said. "Nobody wants to think about that."

"Are you having an open bar?" Scarlet asked. "Because I don't go to weddings that don't have an open bar. That's just rude. Bad enough I've got to buy you a gift when you'll probably end up getting divorced or one of you dying soon."

Rosemarie came to her feet and slammed her giant binder on the table. She looked scared to death, and while I admired her guts, she had every right to be scared. She was putting herself in the middle of a Holmes family feud. People had died for less.

"Listen up, people," she said. "I took off school today to be here, and I don't want to hear another word about whores, seven-month babies, or micro-penises. We have five days to put on the most spectacular wedding you've ever seen. As friends and family of the bride, it's our job to make sure it goes off without a hitch. And that's exactly what we're going to do.

"I've got everything itemized in this binder, along with a full itinerary. God didn't make Nick rich for no reason, so we're going to use his resources and pull this off. Addison, you've got cases to solve. Go solve them. Savage, you make sure the groom is at the church on time. Whatever you have to do. We've got this."

"Umm," I said.

I'd never seen Rosemarie like this, but she'd just given me my escape and I'd be stupid not to take it.

"Sorry, Kate," I said. "Looks like I've got to run. Have fun."

"I feel like I deserve this somehow," she said.

"Karma's a bitch."

ABOUT THE AUTHOR

Liliana Hart is a *New York Times*, *USA Today*, and Publisher's Weekly bestselling author of more than sixty titles. After starting her first novel her freshman year of college, she immediately became addicted to writing and knew she'd found what she was meant to do with her life. She has no idea why she majored in music.

Since publishing in June 2011, Liliana has sold more than six-million books. All three of her series have made multiple appearances on the *New York Times* list.

Liliana can almost always be found at her computer writing, hauling five kids to various activities, or spending time with her husband. She calls Texas home.

If you enjoyed reading this, I would appreciate it if you would help others enjoy this book, too.

Recommend it. Please help other readers find this book by recommending it to friends, readers' groups and discussion boards.

Review it. Please tell other readers why you liked this book by reviewing.

Connect with me online:
www.lilianahart.com

facebook.com/LilianaHart

twitter.com/Liliana_Hart

instagram.com/LilianaHart

bookbub.com/authors/liliana-hart

ALSO BY LILIANA HART

JJ Graves Mystery Series

Dirty Little Secrets

A Dirty Shame

Dirty Rotten Scoundrel

Down and Dirty

Dirty Deeds

Dirty Laundry

Dirty Money

A Dirty Job

The MacKenzies of Montana

Dane's Return

Thomas's Vow

Riley's Sanctuary

Cooper's Promise

Grant's Christmas Wish

The MacKenzies Boxset

MacKenzie Security Series

Seduction and Sapphires

Shadows and Silk

Secrets and Satin

Sins and Scarlet Lace

Sizzle

Crave

Scorch

MacKenzie Security Omnibus 1

MacKenzie Security Omnibus 2

Lawmen of Surrender (MacKenzies-1001 Dark Nights)

1001 Dark Nights: Captured in Surrender

1001 Dark Nights: The Promise of Surrender

1001 Dark Nights: Sweet Surrender

1001 Dark Nights: Dawn of Surrender

The MacKenzie World (read in any order)

Trouble Maker

Bullet Proof

Deep Trouble

Delta Rescue

Desire and Ice

Rush

Spies and Stilettos

Wicked Hot

Hot Witness

Avenged

Never Surrender

Addison Holmes Mystery Series

Whiskey Rebellion

Whiskey Sour

Whiskey For Breakfast

Whiskey, You're The Devil

Whiskey on the Rocks

Whiskey Tango Foxtrot

Whiskey and Gunpowder

The Gravediggers

The Darkest Corner

Gone to Dust

Say No More

Stand Alone Titles

Breath of Fire

Kill Shot

Catch Me If You Can

All About Eve

Paradise Disguised

Island Home

The Witching Hour

Books by Liliana Hart and Scott Silverii

The Harley and Davidson Mystery Series

The Farmer's Slaughter

A Tisket a Casket

I Saw Mommy Killing Santa Claus

Get Your Murder Running

Deceased and Desist

Malice In Wonderland

Tequila Mockingbird

Gone With the Sin